"WHY D

He leaned around

she froze and looked

legs poised in the front floorboard of the driver's seat. "Why did you say yes and give Emmy false hope like that?" He shook his head. "I've been nothing but honest with you, and you can see the state of the place for yourself. Why join a project you know will fail? Take a job I told you right off would be a dead end?"

A muscle in her jaw ticked. "Why is it guaranteed to be a dead end? Because you say so?" One blond brow rose. "Your word is gospel—is that it?"

"No." He scoffed, glancing up at the ceaseless stretch of blue above. "We've got enough gospel out here. I'm just stating facts. Sensible, practical truths."

"Is that why you're taking the kids from her? Because it's the sensible thing to do regardless of how it'll affect Emmy or the children?"

"You just met them. You don't know enough about any of us to pass judgment—"

"You're right. It's not my place to judge and that's not my intention." Her tone softened. "But I know what it feels like to lose something precious. I wouldn't wish it on anyone."

Don't miss any of Janet Dailey's bestsellers

The New Americana Series
Sunrise Canyon
Refuge Cove
Letters from Peaceful Lane

The Tylers of Texas
Texas Forever
Texas Free
Texas Fierce
Texas Tall
Texas Tough
Texas True

Bannon Brothers: Triumph
Bannon Brothers: Honor
Bannon Brothers: Trust
Calder Storm
Green Calder Grass
Lone Calder Star
Calder Promise
Shifting Calder Wind
American Destiny
American Dreams
Masquerade
Tangled Vines
Heiress
Rivals

JANET DAILEY

HART'S HOLLOW FARM

ZEBRA BOOKS
KENSINGTON PUBLISHING CORP.
www.kensingtonbooks.com

ZEBRA BOOKS are published by

Kensington Publishing Corp.
119 West 40th Street
New York, NY 10018

First Kensington Books Hardcover Printing: October 2019
First Zebra Books Mass-Market Paperback Printing: February 2020
ISBN-13: 978-1-4201-4873-2
ISBN-10: 1-4201-4873-7

ISBN-13: 978-1-4201-4874-9 (eBook)
ISBN-10: 1-4201-4874-5 (eBook)

10 9 8 7 6 5 4 3 2 1

Printed in the United States of America

CHAPTER 1

Kristen Daniels stood at the mouth of a red dirt road. The long path in front of her sloped eastward, weaving its way through sprawling fields to meet dark, low-lying clouds on the horizon. Warm late afternoon sunshine peeked between the gathering masses and dappled the flat landscape. The spring breeze, a gentle whisper for the past hour, intensified. It kicked up a cloud of dust that drifted across the road, sparkling briefly in the sunlight before a massive thunderhead rolled in and covered the sun completely.

Stomach dipping, Kristen glanced over her shoulder at the isolated stretch of Georgia highway she'd been traveling for hours. The paved road was unlined, the white and yellow markings having faded long ago, and the worn edges were either buried beneath weedy overgrowth or cracked beyond repair. With no cell service, landmarks, or street signs, it was impossible to tell if she'd made it to the right place—if there even was such a thing.

At this point, one road would serve just as well as

the other. So long as she kept moving in the opposite direction from the life she'd had three years ago, when she was twenty-six and optimistic. When she'd been sure, without a modicum of doubt, that life had more to offer if she just believed and prayed and hoped. Even when the devastating truth had literally stared her in the face.

All the way up until the day she'd had to bury her five-year-old daughter.

The straight line of ragged pavement warped into the distance, making the earth feel as though it tilted beneath her feet. Her stance faltered, and she strained to hold on to the empty numbness she'd clung to for more miles than she'd ever be able to count.

"You break down?"

Kristen started, the shout and the slow crunch of gravel beneath tires jerking her to alertness. A rusty truck idled nearby, the male driver leaning out the window, studying her.

The wind blew harder. It swirled her long hair around her neck and spit grit in her face, stinging her eyes.

"No." Teeth clenching, she blinked hard and dragged her forearm over her dry cheeks. "Just trying to figure out where I am, is all." She gestured toward her beat-up Toyota parked at the edge of the dirt road. "Do you know the name of this road?"

The older man laughed and scrubbed the heel of his hand over his stubble-lined jaw. "It ain't got a name. It's just one long driveway."

"To where?"

"Hart's Hollow." He shook his head, his salt-and-pepper hair falling over his creased brow. "Doubt that's the direction you wanna go. There's nothing out there."

Kristen fumbled in her jeans pocket and retrieved a crumpled piece of paper. She pressed it flat against her thigh, then smoothed the edges that flapped in the wind.

Help wanted: Jane-of-all-trades. Hard work.
Decent pay and board.
Hart's Hollow Farm. 762 Hart Rd.,
Stellaville, Georgia. See Emmy Hart, owner.

"Hart's Hollow Farm?" she asked. "Could you please tell me if I can find Emmy Hart there?"

"Yep, that's the place." He cocked his head to the side, a slow grin appearing. "And Emmy's there, all right."

Kristen nodded, stuffed the paper back in her pocket, then headed toward her car. "Thank you."

"Might want to make it a quick visit." Squeaky gears shifted; then the truck rolled forward as the man tipped his chin toward the overcast sky. "If those clouds open up, that clay's gonna turn to sludge, and that low car of yours won't make it out. You don't want to be stuck in a storm with Emmy Hart."

Her steps slowed. "Why?"

"She's ornery enough to make a saint cuss. My own mama—good Christian woman—says she's the damn devil." He laughed again and revved the engine.

The big truck moved swiftly down the center of the worn highway.

Kristen returned to her car and, after staring at the red dirt road through the dusty windshield for a few minutes, decided a lot of nothing—even if it was owned and run by an ornery devil—was preferable to sleeping in the backseat and going hungry for the second day in a row. She didn't do charity and needed a job. The last farm, where she'd worked for a year, had gone belly up due to drought and financial woes, and this position was the only promising one she'd come across that offered the silent, wide-open space she'd grown to crave.

It was, at the very least, worth checking out. Especially since she'd spent the last of her emergency stash on a full tank of gas to make the drive.

She cranked the engine and drove slowly down the driveway. The deep ruts in the dirt rattled the bottled water in the cup holder and bounced her around in the driver's seat. The bottom of the car thumped over a pothole, metal scraping the firm ground.

Wincing, she slowed the car even more and continued to creep along. A tall pole stood near a bend in the road. She leaned closer to the window, squinting up at the makeshift birdhouse. Several battered gourds hung from the top rack, but one dangled loosely at half-mast, and the thick shell clanked against the pole with each gust of wind. There were no passerines, not even purple martins, perched on the rack. And just two buzzards circled high above the stripped field, then swooped low in tandem with the air current.

After reaching the final leg of the circular driveway, she eased around a sharp curve, then stopped the car abruptly at the edge of lush grass. Large oaks towered toward the stormy sky, framing an aging two-story farmhouse with a wide front porch and large windows. Tall red chimneys were aligned on each side of the white structure, and Gothic trim along the porch roof added an elegant air.

Kristen whistled low as she climbed out of the car. "Nothing out here, huh?"

That wasn't altogether accurate. She strolled across the expansive lot, her tennis shoes squashing the soft grass and thunder rumbling overhead. The magnificent oaks swayed with the approaching storm, their leaves ruffling. Ducking beneath the lower branch of one, she reached up and trailed her palm across its rough bark as she passed.

Tall and sturdy. Broad, thick trunk. Long, sprawling branches.

"You've been around awhile, haven't you, beauty?" Kristen whispered.

She looked at the house, its details clearer from this vantage point. Time and the elements had chipped the white paint of the house and faded the deep red tones of the chimneys. The wooden front door had lost its luster, and a hole was punched through the flimsy screen door covering it. An orange cat weaved in and out of the exquisite—but rotted—porch balusters.

Rather than strengthening with age like the old oaks, the structure presented a tired, resigned veneer. One at odds with the sweet aura of home beckoning from the wide, welcoming steps. One that clearly said the glory days of this house had passed.

Her fingertips jerked at her sides as she imagined breathing it back to life on canvas—a dab of yellow ocher here and there to re-create the shingles, long sweeps of ivory to define the walls, several pushes and drags of crimson to erect the chimneys. The structure was so reminiscent of the house she'd dreamed of as a child, when she'd lived in shelters and longed for a home—and a family—of her own.

Kristen shook her head, a heavy ache pulling at her chest. Oh, but it'd be impossible for anyone to deny this place must have once been majestic.

"Emmy!"

The screen door slammed and a man stumbled out onto the porch, clutching a briefcase to his chest, and fumbled his way backward to the front steps. A second slam, then a wiry woman stomped out after him, leaning heavily on a cane.

Kristen eased back beneath the cover of the tree's branches, watching.

"Now, Emmy," the man sputtered as he reached the grassy lawn. "There's no need to get upset—"

"Mrs. Hart." The woman—owner Emmy Hart, Kristen supposed—clomped down the stairs, her cane clacking along the way. "My sweet Joe, God rest his soul, may have died over thirty years ago, but I'm still his wife, and if he were here right now, he'd toss you out on your butt for making such an insulting offer. Joe wouldn't stand for it. He gave his life to this place, raised it from ruin. This land was in his blood."

"I didn't come out here to cause trouble, Mrs. Hart. I came to help."

"No, you didn't. I agreed to humor you on account of thinking you were a decent man, but you suits are all the same." Emmy stopped on the bottom step, gripped the thin handrail, then sagged against it. Her chest lifted beneath her worn T-shirt on heavy breaths. "You came to take my land. To tear down my home." Blue eyes flashing, she stabbed a gnarled finger at him. "To steal from me."

The suit held up a placating hand. "Now, that's not true at all. I'm offering you a more than fair price for this . . ." He waved careless fingers toward the second floor of the house. "Establishment." He grimaced. "Believe me when I say you won't find a better offer. No one else is willing to pay what I am for this place, and if it weren't for Mitch, I wouldn't even be out here."

The man's cheeks reddened. He drew his head back and clamped his mouth shut.

"My Mitch?" Emmy's mouth opened, then closed silently, the gusty wind blowing her short gray hair against her wrinkled cheeks. "What's he got to do with this?"

He sighed. "Mitch is a friend of mine. He's the one who asked me to come out here and make you an offer. I was surprised he wasn't here when I arrived. Said he was flying down today himself and wanted us all to sit down and talk it over. He knows it's just a matter of time before—"

"He wouldn't do that to me." A wounded light entered her eyes.

Kristen cringed and shrank back, feeling like an interloper. Sporadic raindrops smacked against the leaves overhead, shaking them.

"I'm sorry, Mrs. Hart," the man continued. "I know this is hard for you, but Mitch is just doing what any decent grandson would. He's trying to get you something to live on, for a short time at least." He blinked and jerked his head as rain hit his face. "This place is done, and you're the only one who won't admit it."

"No." Expression contorting, Emmy straightened and stepped toward him. "You're just like all them others. You came to steal from me. And you're lying about Mitch."

He hissed out a breath, mumbled something involving the word *ridiculous,* then frowned up at the black cluster of clouds. "This is my final offer. You'd do well to take it."

She poked her cane at his chest, shoving him back. "Get off my land."

"Please reconsider." His tone softened. "For Mitch's sake, if not your own. He deserves the chance to put this place behind hi—"

"Go!" Her voice broke. "You don't know nothing about Mitch—or me. This is my home. My family still lives here. You probably never worked a day in your life. Don't have a clue what real work is." She continued stabbing her cane at him, backing him up until he fell into the gleaming bumper of a sedan. "You're a thief. And a liar. Nothing but a damned lying th—"

"This place is dead and buried." He slapped her cane away, voice curt. "Mitch is trying to help you, though hell if I know why he even bothers anymore. He won't tell you like it is, so I'll do it for him. Dead and buried, Mrs. Hart."

Emmy faced off with the man. Her chin trembled, and the solid line of her shoulders, which had stood so proud before, slumped.

It was a look Kristen knew well. Her face heated, and a familiar nausea roiled in her gut. She should walk away, get back in her car and keep driving. This wasn't her business or her fight, and the last thing she needed was to get tangled up in a stranger's troubles. But even so . . .

"Excuse me." Kristen sucked in a strong breath, the sharp scent of rain filling her nostrils, then ducked beneath the branches and stepped forward. Fat raindrops plopped onto her cheek and bare shoulder, cooling her skin. "I'm looking for Mrs. Emmy Hart."

They turned toward her. Stared.

She moved closer to Emmy. "Are you Mrs. Hart? Owner of Hart's Hollow Farm?"

Emmy nodded. The haunted look in her eyes deepened. Her focus strayed beyond Kristen to the darkening sky above, her whispered words barely discernible. "What'd you bring, girl?"

Kristen hesitated as she searched Emmy's expression. "I'm sorry. I'm not sure what you mean."

Emmy remained silent.

Kristen glanced at the man, who shook his head and looked down. "I-I'm looking for work. I brought two overnight bags," she continued, gesturing behind her. "And I parked my car over there, behind the trees."

Emmy blinked, then refocused on Kristen.

Thunder boomed again, shaking the windows of the farmhouse and the ground beneath Kristen's feet. She flinched, then tugged the wrinkled ad from her pocket. "I'd like to speak to you about a job, if I might?"

"That my ad you got there?" Emmy asked.

"Yes. The one with decent pay and board. I was interested in—"

"There won't be any board, ma'am." The suit shoved off the car to a standing position and straightened his tie. "At least not for long. In six months the county will give the green light to pave a bypass on this land." He pointed behind her. "Across those fields and right over this house. Something Mrs. Hart's grandson thinks is important she understand."

"Forgive me," Kristen said softly, "but I wasn't speaking to you. I was speaking to the owner, who's already asked you to leave."

He frowned, his measuring gaze raking over her from head to toe. "And you are . . . ?"

A has-been artist. Rootless stranger. Alone. Kristen

swallowed the thick lump in her throat and squared her shoulders. "No one. Just a hard worker looking for a job and a place to stay."

"You gonna steal from me?" Emmy scrutinized her through narrowed eyes.

Kristen shook her head. "No, ma'am."

"Lie to me?"

"No, ma'am."

"Murder me in my bed?"

Kristen's lips twitched despite the awkward situation. "Definitely not."

A slow smile spread across Emmy's face. "Then I'll show you around and we'll talk. Which makes you my guest." She poked her cane at the man's chest again. "And you're not. So take your tail on out."

He muttered something under his breath, got in his car and left. Clouds of red dust rose behind his tires, then dissipated as the rain fell more heavily, cutting through the dirt particles and pummeling the red clay.

Emmy clucked her tongue. "You ever come across a man as arrogant and stubborn as that?"

Kristen nodded. "Unfortunately."

"Come on, let's get out of this." Emmy walked up the front steps, cane tapping as she went.

Kristen followed, then stood by Emmy's side as she leaned on the porch rail and stared at the front lawn. Trees bowed in the wind, leaves scattered across the front steps and rain splashed into rapidly forming mudholes in the driveway. The orange cat that had been circling the porch balusters trotted over and snuggled against Kristen's leg.

"You from around here?" Emmy asked. "I know any of your people?"

"No." Kristen focused on the ad in her hand, folding it over several times. It was damp from the rain, and the soggy corners clung to her shaky fingertips. "My name's Kristen Daniels. I drove up from Adel. The farm where I was working went out of business, and no one local was hiring. Then I saw your ad. I was going to call but . . ." She looked up. "May I ask why you didn't include a phone number?"

Emmy waved a hand. "I'm the only one working this land. Ain't in the house except when I'm eating, cleaning, or sleeping, and I don't much want to be bothered then. Rest of the time, I'm outside, and I don't care for cell phones. Service is spotty out here. Besides, you can tell a whole lot more about a person face-to-face." She studied Kristen's face, eyes warming. "Thank you."

"For what?"

"For helping me run that fool off." Emmy glanced at the driveway. "I won't lie to you. I'm struggling, and a lot of people want to get ahold of this land. They think 'cuz I'm seventy-three, I got no more use for it, and they want to pave it over. Even my grandson's been trying to talk me into selling, though today's the first time Mitch has sent someone out here to bulldoze me. I know he means well but . . ." She sighed. "I got a plan, but I need help. Lots of it. That ad's been out for two months, and you're the first person to answer it." Her voice rose above the steady pounding of the rain. "I got crops to plant by the end of this month, or the first week of May at the latest. My garden needs attention, and my house could use"—her nose wrinkled—"a bit of everything."

Heavy sheets of rain pummeled the land, obscuring the empty fields.

Emmy grew quiet, then said, "That ground hasn't

felt a drop of rain in weeks. Usually, if the good Lord doesn't see fit to send us any, my sweet Joe does it for Him. But I don't think it's either one of them this time." She stretched out her arm, leathery palm upward, and watched the rain bounce off her hand. "Can't tell yet if it'll help for planting. Too little and the soil will harden. Too much and it'll weaken."

The front door squeaked open. "Nana?"

Kristen stiffened at the sound of the young female voice. Heart skipping, she turned slowly in the direction whence it had come.

A little girl stood behind the screen door, her brown curls and blue eyes framed in the torn gap. "Can we have ice cream for supper?"

"Course we can, honey. Long as you and your brother eat all your greens first." Emmy left the railing and opened the screen door. "Say hello to Ms. Kristen, Sadie. She's gonna help us get this place back on its feet."

Cheeks flushing, the girl glanced up at Kristen, then hid behind Emmy's leg.

Curiosity shined in the girl's wide eyes, but a wariness shadowed her expression. She had the same height, build, and shy disposition as . . . Anna.

When I get better, we can go back home, can't we, Mama?

A sharp pain tore through Kristen's chest, stealing her breath, the memory cutting deeper than ever. She couldn't speak but forced herself to nod in greeting.

"That's another reason I need help," Emmy said as Sadie darted back inside. "I have two great-grandkids I need a hand with."

Kristen clenched her fists, the paper crinkling in her grasp. "There was no mention of taking care of children in your ad."

"Well, I'm mentioning it now. Sadie's five, and her brother, Dylan, is ten." Emmy shoved the door open wider. "Come on in. I'm expecting Mitch soon and was about to cook supper. Figure if his mouth is busy chewing, he won't be able to gab all night about why he thinks I should sell. We can discuss particulars while I fry up some chicken."

Kristen turned away and watched the rain form red rivers in the clay driveway, stomach growling at the mention of food. Clearly, Emmy was juggling more than she could handle, and ordinarily, Kristen wouldn't hesitate to take the job, to make ends meet and keep her mind off painful memories. But that was before she knew kids were part of the bargain. Especially, a five-year-old girl so reminiscent of—

"I'm sorry, Mrs. Hart." Kristen struggled to keep her words steady. "I don't think I'm who you're looking for."

"You're the only one I've found," Emmy said. "I'm offering a free meal and bed for the night in exchange for a little shop talk. It'd be rude to turn me down without hearing me out first." She scowled. "You're not trying to be rude to me in my own house, are you?"

"No, ma'am, but—"

"Good. Then call me Emmy and come on in. You can't leave now anyway. That clay's too slick to drive on, and it's your own fault."

Kristen frowned, glancing back at her. "Why?"

Emmy smiled. A big one that creased her cheeks and brightened her cloudy eyes. "Because you brought the rain."

* * *

"She's superstitious. Always has been." Mitch Hart pressed a button on the steering wheel, increasing the volume of the call, and raised his voice above the rain pounding the rental car's hood. "Don't take anything Emmy said personally. Hope she didn't give you too much trouble."

"Trouble?" Brad Swint, a friend and coworker at Harrison Architects, issued a sound of grumbled amusement. His voice cut in and out as the car descended a hill, the headlights casting long shadows over the pine trees lining the highway. "Said I had shifty eyes. Stabbed me with her cane . . . refused to listen to reason and called me a thief."

Mitch's neck tingled with embarrassed heat. "Sorry, man. My flight was delayed. Otherwise I'd have been there to meet you. Emmy hasn't been herself for a while now, and it gets worse every year."

She'd been worse than ever when he'd seen her at his sister's funeral two months ago. Could've been grief. Or anger. Lord knows, he'd struggled to come to terms with his own rage at Carrie's selfishness.

His sister had been an addict—his head understood and accepted that. What his heart couldn't accept or understand was why Carrie had consistently prioritized getting high above taking care of her kids. Enough so that she'd dumped them at Emmy's, then taken off for a monthlong stint, which had culminated in a deadly heroin overdose.

Mitch gripped the steering wheel tighter, his knuckles turning white. He and Carrie had both grown up watching their alcoholic father drink himself senseless and had spent almost every night of their childhood protecting each other from either the cut of his tongue or the bruising force of his fist. Yet Carrie had followed right in his footsteps, and

Emmy had broken her back trying to save her. Just as she had with their father—at the expense of everything and *everyone* else.

"Look, I hate that I put you in that position," Mitch said. "But I had to give it a shot, and I seriously doubt it would've gone any better with me there. Emmy and I have never seen eye to eye."

A silence crossed the line; then Brad asked, "Why don't you come back to New York tomorrow? My plane doesn't take off until three. You could visit Emmy tonight, say your good-byes, then leave that place for good first thing in the morning. Get a head start on the Emerson project and put all this behind you."

Mitch rubbed his temples, an ache throbbing behind his eyes. "I wish I could."

And he would, except for the fact that he had a niece and nephew to consider. Not only had Carrie's death exacerbated the long-standing rift between him and Emmy, but it had also left Sadie and Dylan in Emmy's care. A scenario that was far less than ideal.

"There's no way I'm leaving those kids on a dead-end farm in the middle of nowhere," Mitch bit out. "You saw the place. Not to mention once the county takes over that land, they'll all be homeless. They deserve better, and it'll take me at least the weekend to convince Emmy of that."

"I agree with you, but Emmy's already digging in her heels. She insists she's planting new crops this month. As a matter of fact, she was in the middle of hiring someone when I left."

Hell, that sounded like Emmy. She never went down without throwing the last punch.

"Who?" Mitch scoffed. "One of Judd Harvey's laid-off factory boys?"

"No. Some wo—"

The speakers crackled and then went silent. "Brad? You still there?"

Nothing.

Mitch stifled a curse, flipped the windshield wipers on high and peered through the deluge of rain for the turnoff. It'd been a while since he'd come out here, but he had to be close. No place was as dark or as dead as Hart's Hollow.

Granted, it was past seven o'clock, and spring hadn't sprung enough for the sun to stay up that late yet. Night had fallen, and the wild beat of the storm didn't help matters.

The wind gusted, rocking the small sedan; then a dingy flash of red appeared in the glow of the headlights. Mitch slowed the car and carefully maneuvered the left turn. Mud slushed beneath the tires, slapping the underside of the car in chunks.

"Figures," Mitch muttered, struggling to keep the car moving in a straight line on the slick surface.

Every time he set foot on this land, something went wrong. Which was exactly why he'd hauled ass at eighteen. After his father had died of heart failure, Mitch had worked the farm with Emmy for two years. Every month, he'd grown more eager to kick the clay off his feet, scrape the dirt out from under his nails and set off to achieve a better life. He'd been determined to shed the filth of his father from his genes and reinvent himself into something more than an ignorant backwoods kid. New York, Cornell University, and an architectural career had fit the bill for fourteen years.

But here he was—thirty-two and back again. It was

as if this damned place had a hook in him, yanking him back at its whim.

The steering wheel jerked beneath his hands as the car slid to the left. He lifted his foot off the gas pedal and wrestled with the mud's pull to regain control, but the tires spun uselessly across the wet clay until they jerked to a stop in a deep muddy rut.

Groaning, Mitch cut the engine and dropped his head back against the headrest. Rain continued pummeling the hood, and deep booms of thunder rattled the car's interior. He waited for the worst to pass, and soon the onslaught slowed to a steady rhythm, and the once sharp stabs of lightning dulled to distant sporadic flashes.

Stuck, with no decent hope of rocking the car out of the clay's vicious grip, he yanked off his tie and suit jacket, shoved open his door and got out. Rain soaked his hair and clothes, seeping into his skin and sending a chill through him.

He stood still for a moment and stared at the dark barren fields. Their stark outlines appeared with each pulse of lightning. The storm renewed its fury, battering his face with wind and rain. The sting against his flesh was a painful reminder of the back of his father's hand. He could still taste the tang of dirt on his tongue from the hundreds of times he'd been knocked down over the years.

"Yeah." His lip curled. "I'm back, you bastard."

After wrenching his feet free of the sucking mud, Mitch retrieved his overnight bag from the trunk and trekked toward the house. He stumbled upon a car parked at the edge of the circular driveway. Pausing, he bent, cupped a hand over his brow to block the rain, and read the license plate.

Wasn't Emmy's car. Probably belonged to the new hire. Some desperate guy from out of town, with no clue how dismal the outlook was for this place. Who else would take a job on rotten land with no prospects for recovery?

Mitch shook his head and trudged on. The massive oak trees bent and groaned beneath the slash of rain. Gnarled branches clacked together in a rhythm eerily similar to the one his father's belt had made as it smacked against his palm when he'd stood on the front porch, shouting at Mitch drunkenly.

Where are you, boy? Ain't no place to hide. Might as well come on out.

Mitch swallowed against the bile rising in his throat. Man, he hated it here. Dreaded what lay ahead even more. It soured his gut and spread a sick, unsettling feeling through his veins.

The best thing to do would be to get this over with fast. He would talk Emmy into selling, would prove it'd be in the kids' best interest to be placed in a good, stable home, then would return to New York and finally put this place—and all its painful memories—behind him.

After reaching the shelter of the front porch, he dropped his bag on the floor, then glanced at the faint light from inside glowing through the dank curtains. He frowned down at his clothes. Thick clay caked his dress shoes and lower pant legs, and water dripped from his hair and soggy shirt, plopping onto the wood planks beneath him.

Lord, he could hear Emmy now. *Not in my foyer!*

Wouldn't do to tick her off first thing. Mouth twisting, he toed off his shoes and socks, then peeled his collared shirt over his head and draped it over the rotting porch rail. The brisk kick of cool air against his bare chest made him shiver as he propped the screen door open with his shoulder and knocked on the front door.

"That you, Mitch?" The thick wood muted Emmy's shout and subsequent murmur, "Get the door, would you, please?"

Footsteps thumped inside, drawing closer with each creak of the floorboards. The rustic lanterns mounted above him lit up, and the large door swept open.

He'd expected Emmy, frowning and disapproving, along with the flood of memories that assailed him every time he entered the place. Instead, a younger woman stood before him. Tall, with a slim build and wavy blond hair framing deep green eyes and a small smile.

The polite greeting he'd reluctantly prepared for Emmy stuck in his throat as his attention strayed to the soft curves of her mouth. Those pink lips parted and her tanned complexion reddened as her gaze drifted over his naked chest.

"E-excuse me," she whispered, looking away briefly. She shifted from one foot to the other, then faced him again, attention locked on his face. "Are you Emmy's grandson . . . Mitch?" At his nod, she held out her hand, her smile fading. "I'm Kristen Daniels. It's nice to meet you."

Hesitating, he lifted his hand, clasped her smaller one and squeezed. Calluses lined her palm, but the back of her wrist was soft and smooth beneath the sweep of his thumb. Her warm, gentle hold was a soothing comfort to his cold, wet grip. A rare find in this hell of a so-called home.

Shivering slightly, she tugged her hand free and

took a step back from the door. "Emmy's been expecting you."

Mitch caught himself following her and froze. Sharp metal cut into his bare foot as it pressed against the threshold, but the warmth in the woman's soft voice lingered on the stale air that emanated from the house, wrapping around his chilled body and tugging at something buried deep within him.

It was the first time he'd found himself actually wanting to enter the dilapidated structure, and strangely, at the same time . . . he'd never wanted to escape more.

CHAPTER 2

"Oh, my sweet Mitch, it's about time you came home."

Mitch stiffened as Emmy rushed over as fast as her tapping cane would allow, pushed past Kristen and wrapped her arms around his waist as she pressed her cheek to his chest. He glanced down, and errant strands of her gray hair tickled his nose.

"I've missed you," she said.

He patted her shoulders awkwardly. His hands tangled in the strings of her long apron, his fingertips grazing the hard, angular bones of her back, where plump, cushiony flesh had once been. He gentled his touch, shivers chasing themselves up his spine at the evidence of how much her aging frame and strength had deteriorated.

As a child, he'd resisted when she'd cradled his flaming face—usually bruised or bleeding from one of his father's rampages—against her neck, rocking him back and forth in her lap and whispering, "Cry, sweet boy. It's okay to cry. I won't let him hurt you again."

But she had. Every time Emmy had kicked his father out, he would return months later, repentant, claiming to be sober, and she'd welcome him right back into their lives. Then, after a few weeks, his father would return to his old ways, and it would all begin again.

"Let go, Emmy." Mitch tugged her arms from him, then nudged her back to a steady position.

The flash of hurt on her face conjured up guilt he normally ignored. He supposed she had tried her best to protect him and Carrie. As much as she could, considering her overly sympathetic view of his father. Her love for her son—and her desperate need to redeem him—had always been her biggest weakness.

"I'm cold and wet," Mitch tacked on gently as moisture glinted in her eyes. "My car got stuck in the mud, and I had to walk through the rain. You'll catch a chill."

She pressed a trembling hand to her chest, her fragile throat moving on a hard swallow, then grunted. "Well, I'd hug you harder, but I'm mad at you."

Surprisingly, a small laugh bubbled up and escaped his lips, easing the tension in his limbs. "Good to see you, too, Emmy."

Her dark scowl lightened a bit, and she straightened. "Did you send some suit out here to talk me into selling?"

"I—"

"'Cuz if you did, it didn't work." Emmy poked a finger at him. "And just so you know, it won't ever work." She spun around, then headed toward the kitchen, saying over her shoulder, "That's my new hire, Kristen, by the way. Introduce yourself. Then grab a towel, dry off, and join us at the kitchen table.

We've held supper for over an hour, waiting on you to get here."

Mitch sighed as she stomped around the corner. The swift breeze of her departure swept over his damp skin, and the soft light from the kitchen barely reached the dim foyer.

Same old Emmy. Same old dank, drafty house.

"She was worried." Kristen shrugged, as if in apology. Her long hair slipped over her toned arms, brushing the curve of her breasts beneath a thin tank top. "She was staring out the window off and on while she cooked, watching for you."

He ducked his head, an ache seeping into his chest at the thought. Causing Emmy discomfort wasn't his end goal, but given the circumstances, there was no way it could have been avoided.

"I didn't mean to make her worry," he said.

But who was she to call him on it? A stranger with no knowledge of him, Emmy, or the history of this place?

Bristling, he raised his head and studied Kristen. Her calm demeanor and clear, steady gaze belied the grim atmosphere surrounding them. And her presence added more complications to an already difficult situation he was not looking forward to handling. Not to mention, the sensation of her soft touch still lingered on his sk—

"Why are you here?" One blond eyebrow rose at the abrasive sound of his voice. He rubbed his palm against his wet pant leg and tried for a more civil tone. "I don't mean to be rude. It's just . . . I don't know what Emmy may have told you, but surely you can see the prospect of a job here is nonexistent."

She slipped her hands in her pockets and glanced down at his bare feet.

He fought the urge to curl his toes and slide them away.

"Emmy explained that things are difficult for her right now, and I could see for myself just how difficult when your friend visited earlier." Kristen's lashes lifted as she shot him a brief disapproving look. "But she's insistent that I consider staying and working for her. She says she needs help fixing up the house, planting crops and—"

"Have you accepted the position?"

She frowned. "I told her I don't think I'm right for the job, but—"

"That's good, then." He blew out a heavy breath and reached into his back pocket. "I saw your license plate outside, and I imagine you had quite a drive out here. I'd be happy to pay you for your time."

"That's not necessary."

Her look of affront made his fingers freeze around his wallet. "I'm sorry. I didn't mean to offend y—"

"I'm not offended." A muscle ticked in her delicate jaw as she studied him. "Emmy invited me to dinner and offered me a room for the night. That's payment enough."

She stared at him for a moment, the guarded look in those beautiful green eyes making him long for the hint of warmth that had entered them upon her initial greeting.

"I told Emmy I'd help her set the table." With that, she turned and left.

Mitch dragged a hand through his wet hair. Lord, wasn't this just his luck? The first woman he'd met in months who stirred his interest seemed more impressed with his grandmother than with him. And deservedly so, since here he stood, a soaked, uncouth jerk being everything but gallant.

Grimacing, he retrieved his bag from the porch and shut the front door. After changing into a dry oxford dress shirt and khakis in the downstairs bathroom, he stowed his bag in the hallway and joined them in the kitchen.

It was the same as he remembered. Rich wood paneling lined the walls. Dark hardwood floors, scuffed and worn, contrasted sharply with the worn white cabinets and countertops. A large wood table took center stage, draped with a lacy tablecloth and loaded with deep dishes of fried chicken, cabbage, creamed corn, and lacy corn bread. The only pleasurable aspect of Hart's Hollow Farm had always been Emmy's cooking, and judging from the decadent aromas, it seemed that hadn't changed.

Emmy moved from seat to seat, folding cloth napkins by each place setting, and Kristen followed, arranging gleaming silverware in appropriate places and shooting him glances. Ice clinked inside a glass pitcher, and then a small girl with curly brown hair and a furrowed brow carried it slowly toward the table, tea sloshing over her small hands.

"Oh, gracious!" Emmy scrambled around the table and took the pitcher. "Thank you for helping, baby, but I think this is a mite too heavy for you."

The little girl's expression fell. She looked down and picked at the hem of her shorts.

Mitch's heart clenched. After squatting on his haunches, he held out his arms and asked softly, "Is that my sweet Sadie?"

She perked up, her head lifting and her blue eyes widening as she smiled. "Uncle Mitch!"

Sadie barreled against his chest, rocking him back on his heels. He laughed and squeezed her tight. She was taller than he remembered from two months ago, and, man, it was good to hear her voice again. "I believe you've grown a few inches since I last saw you."

"I have," she piped, pulling back and brushing her bangs away from her eyes. "And one of my tooths is loose." She touched a fingertip to her lower baby teeth and rocked one back and forth. "See? Nana says when it comes out, the tooth fairy will visit."

"I'm sure she will. So be sure to put it under your pillow, okay?"

She nodded.

Her cheerful chatter was a welcome relief. For weeks after Carrie's death, Sadie had barely spoken, and eventually, Emmy had stopped handing her the phone when Mitch called to see how she was doing. There was no hope of conversation when the other party remained mute.

Smoothing a hand over Sadie's hair, Mitch stood and glanced around. "Where's Dylan?"

Emmy motioned toward the hall. "Washing up. He'll be here in a minute." She leaned over the table and nodded, seemingly satisfied that all was ready, then waved a hand in the air. "Y'all grab a seat."

They did, Sadie climbing into the chair beside Mitch, Emmy sitting at the head of the table, and Kristen taking a seat in the empty chair by Emmy's side.

"Come on, Dylan," Emmy called. "Everyone's waiting on you."

Slow footsteps approached down the hallway, and then Dylan entered the room. He stood motionless in the doorway, darting glances at each of them. His shoulders hunched, and he made no move to join them.

Mitch rose from his seat. "Hi, Dylan."

He looked up but didn't speak, his mouth tightening into a thin line.

"It's good to see you again," Mitch added gently, though the boy still looked as lost and withdrawn as he had at Carrie's funeral two months ago. "How've you b—"

"I'm not hungry." Dylan jerked his chin in Emmy's direction. "I'm going to my room."

"No." Emmy spoke low but firm. "You'll join us at the table, please. You need to eat, but even if you choose not to, we'd like your company all the same."

"What company?" Dylan's chin trembled. "There's nothing to talk about, and there's nothing to do. There's nothing out here but dirt and weeds."

"I'd like to introduce you to our guest, Ms. Kristen," Emmy said. "I know you're lonely out here, son. That's why I want you to—"

"I'm not your son." Dylan returned her stare, the amount of anger and pain flashing in the depths of his blue eyes more than any child of ten should bear.

Throat tightening, Mitch shook his head. "Let him go to his room if he wants, Emmy. He doesn't have to stay on my account."

"Who said it's just on your account?" Emmy frowned at him. "There are three other people besides you at this table, and when we break bread, we do it together. Whether you like it or not, this is still my house. My house, my table, my rules, Mitch."

"Yes. I'm well aware of your rules," Mitch said quietly. "But he's been through a hard enough time as it is. Surely you can make an exception just this once?"

"There are no exceptions in this family." She balled her fists beside her plate. "When one of us hurts, we all hurt. Together. We stick together no matter what. We don't leave each other behind. That's how it should work. Not that I expect you to understand, seeing as how you don't abide by that rule—especially considering the stunt you pulled today."

Mitch glanced at Sadie, then Kristen, and their red cheeks and uncomfortable posture made him cringe. "Emmy, for God's sake," he whispered, "let's not do this now."

"Don't do that. Don't you use His name in vain in my house. And you're right. We won't do this now." She jerked a hand toward the empty seat beside Kristen. "Dylan, sit down. I'm here, Mitch is here, and Carrie's here. We're eating supper together. As a family should."

Mitch closed his eyes, the stricken look on Dylan's face staying with him anyway. "Sadie." He leveled a look at Emmy. "Her name is Sadie."

"What?" Emmy's hands jerked around her place setting. They smoothed her napkin, straightened her silverware, slid her glass two inches to the left.

"Sadie is the one who's here." He struggled to keep his voice level. "Carrie is not."

Emmy stilled. A deep flush blotched her neck, then rose to her face, her mouth opening and closing silently.

The air grew thick around the table, the only sounds the steady drum of rain on the roof and the torrents of water splashing down the large window pane above the sink.

Sadie slid out of her chair, then walked to Emmy's side, her bare feet padding across the hardwood floor. "It's okay, Nana." Tears in her eyes, she lifted to her toes and kissed Emmy's cheek. Then she crossed the room, took Dylan's hand, and blinked up at him. "Isn't it okay?"

Dylan looked down at her, nodded jerkily and let

Sadie lead him to the chair beside Kristen. He sat, and Emmy's clenched fists unfurled.

"I'm sorry, Dylan," Emmy said, her voice thick.

He slumped farther down in his chair and didn't respond.

Emmy picked up the pitcher of tea and moved it toward Dylan's glass. Her hand shook, splashing tea onto the white tablecloth, and a renewed surge of guilt hit Mitch.

"Here," he said. "Let me."

He eased the pitcher away from Emmy with a steady touch and returned her hesitant smile with one of his own. A truce reached. At least for the moment.

Mitch stretched across the table and filled each glass in turn. When he reached Kristen's, she lifted it closer.

"Thank you," she said.

He looked up briefly from his task and met her eyes. Some of the warmth from their initial meeting had returned to her expression. It moved over him and lightened the stifling weight pressing on his chest. "You're welcome."

Emmy said the blessing, and then the meal commenced in silence, save for forks clinking against plates, cups thumping periodically to the table, and an occasional cough from Sadie. Every so often, Dylan and Sadie would stare curiously at Kristen, but other than a slight stiffening of her shoulders, Kristen didn't seem to react. Instead, she ate slowly, a noticeable tremor in her hand as she gripped the fork subsiding toward the end of the meal.

Afterward, they dumped the scraps from their plates in the trash and set the dishes in the sink.

"Can I be excused now?" Dylan asked.

Emmy nodded, and he left, not sparing anyone a second glance.

Mitch sighed. "It was a long drive down from the Atlanta airport. Think I'll call it a night. Are the kids still using the bedrooms on the first floor?"

"Them and me," Emmy said. "Since my knee started acting up, I can't make it up and down that staircase as easy as I used to." She grabbed a dishcloth from a drawer, then looked at Kristen. "We tend to turn in early here, since we start the day at sunrise. We can talk shop in the morning. Why don't you go grab your pajamas, Sadie? Soon as I wash up these dishes, I'll run your bath."

"Yes, ma'am." Sadie took off, too.

"Oh, I'll take care of the dishes," Kristen said. "It's the least I can do after such a delicious meal. I enjoyed it, Emmy. Thank you."

Kristen smiled again. Bigger than when she'd met him at the door. She had dimples, cute indentations, which Mitch managed to catch a momentary glimpse of before she took the dishrag from Emmy, then faced the sink and turned on the tap, presenting her slender back to him.

"Would you show Kristen to the upstairs guest room?"

Mitch returned his attention to Emmy, who was looking at him expectantly. "I'm sorry. What?"

"I asked if you'd show Kristen to one of the rooms upstairs when she finishes," Emmy said. "I started cooking when she arrived, and haven't had a chance to show her around yet. Use the back bedrooms. Those are the only ones with clean sheets on the beds."

He glanced at Kristen, the mention of a bed so near the sight of her long hair and shapely hips stirring warm thoughts, which he struggled to quell. "Of course."

Kristen looked over her shoulder, her mouth tightening and her eyes cooling as she watched his face. "I'll need to grab my bags. They're still in my car."

Mitch cleared his throat. "I'll bring them in, then help you clean up."

By the time he had trudged through the mud and returned with the bags—dry this time, thanks to one of Emmy's umbrellas—Kristen was alone in the kitchen, washing the last of the silverware. Mitch dried the dishes, then stowed them in their proper places, while Kristen wiped down the kitchen table. He was careful to keep his eyes on what he was doing, rather than let them linger on her graceful movements.

When they finished, he hefted her bags in his hands, but she immediately tugged at them.

"I'll get those," she said.

"I don't mind."

"I appreciate your bringing them in, but I can manage from here."

The determined set of her jaw made it clear she intended to do just that, so he released them, grabbed his own bag from the hallway, then led the way upstairs. Each step creaked with their footfalls until they reached the upper landing, where he stopped in front of a bedroom on the left.

"This will be yours for the night." Mitch pointed to a closed door to his right. "Bathroom's there, and I'll be across the hall if you need anything."

"Thank you."

She entered the bedroom, set her bags on the wood floor, then flipped on the overhead light. The shiny strands of her hair rippled across her back as she turned her head, taking in the bare walls, empty nightstand, and queen-size bed.

"Kristen." He waited until she turned and faced him. A bulb flickered in the fixture, crackling with an electrical hiss and casting a shadow over her pretty features. "I'm sorry for the unpleasant scene earlier, but what Dylan said was true. There's nothing out here. Certainly no chance of a profitable future."

"I don't mean to pry, but . . ." She bit her lip. "Who's Carrie?"

"My sister. And Sadie and Dylan's mother. She passed away two months ago."

He waited, abs clenching, for the inevitable churn of anger, disgust, and pain to resume in his gut. The kind he always felt at a reminder of Carrie's death, her wasted future and the childhood of fear they'd lived on this farm.

There was no way in hell he'd allow Sadie or Dylan to experience the same. Hart's Hollow had never been a real home for him or Carrie, nor would it ever be a suitable one for the kids. It wasn't the place for them. It wasn't a place for anyone.

"I'm sorry to hear that," Kristen whispered.

"After I talk some sense into Emmy," Mitch bit out, "I plan to leave and return home as soon as possible. You'd be better off doing the same."

A haunted look entered her eyes, her words so quiet he almost missed them.

"If I had one." She lowered her head, the shadows beneath the hollows of her cheeks deepening, as she closed the door between them. "Good night, Mitch."

* * *

Soft light touched Kristen's face, glowing gently behind her closed eyelids and tugging her into awareness.

"Mmm." Sighing softly, she stretched her arms overhead, curled her fingers into the cool sheets, then opened her eyes.

A single tendril of rosy sunlight slipped through the lace curtains lining the double-hung window opposite the bed. It moved slowly across the dark bedroom floor, then up over the white bedding, warming her chest and neck.

There were no sounds of movement in the hallway or from downstairs, just the rhythmic chirps of crickets and the low croaks of frogs from outside. Judging from the weakness of the light trickling in, she thought the sun hadn't fully risen yet, but the storm had ended.

She smiled as a vibrancy she hadn't felt in ages hummed in her veins. Seemed a full belly, a soft bed, and utter exhaustion had been the perfect combination for a peaceful night's rest.

Emmy had been right. Turning in early made for getting up before sunrise. Kristen had crawled into bed around nine last night, and if she had to guess, she'd say it was around six in the morning now. Pretty close to the same schedule she'd stuck to at the Perrys' family farm in Adel.

Her smile slipped, and she turned her head on the pillow to stare at the closed door. Only, there had been very little family drama on the Perrys' farm, no children . . . and no estranged grandson sleeping in a bedroom across the hall from her. A magnificent male with clear blue eyes, thick brown hair, and a sculpted chest, which her fingers still itched to—

Enough.

After flinging back the sheet, Kristen rolled out of bed, then turned on the overhead light and picked through one of her bags for clean jeans and a T-shirt. It was time to shower and dress, thank Emmy for the great meal and a good night's sleep, and move on. Whatever issues existed between Emmy and Mitch were their own—and certainly none of her business. And though her heart hurt for both of the kids at having lost their mother, she had no desire to be around them. After last night, she didn't particularly care to become any more embroiled in the sticky situation at Hart's Hollow than she already was—no matter how sympathetic she felt toward those children . . . or how attractive Mitch might be to her lonely libido.

She left the bedroom, leaving the door cracked to allow a bit of light into the hallway, then crept into the neighboring bathroom. The bathroom was large by anyone's standards, though it was actually two smaller rooms. The room closest to the door featured a wide vanity with a deep sink, and the adjoining room had another vanity, a toilet, and a shower.

After slipping into the adjoining room, she shut the door, then retrieved a clean towel and a bar of soap from the vanity. She frowned, her hand hovering on the cabinet door. There were many economy-sized packages of bar soap—so many, they filled over half the storage space—all still sealed and stacked neatly in rows. It would take a family of four years to make it through all that.

Kristen shook her head and proceeded to shower. Twenty minutes later, clean and dressed, she slipped out of the bathroom and headed for the bedroom, only to stop abruptly in the hallway.

The sun was up, but its bright light struggled to penetrate a dingy window at the opposite end of the hallway. Grime caked the glass panes so thickly that the bare walls and the hardwood floor of the landing remained dark and gloomy.

Kristen moved to the smudged window, tossing her dirty clothes in the bedroom along the way. After locating the locks on the window, she snapped them open, then pulled up on the sash. But it didn't budge. She tried again, pressing her shoulder to the glass and putting her back into it. Her arms strained with the renewed effort, and just when she was about to give up, the window creaked, groaned, then swooshed upward.

A cool breeze rushed in, weaving through her damp hair and sweeping through the hallway at her back. She inhaled, held the air down deep in her lungs, and closed her eyes. Her face warmed beneath the sun's rays, and birds' happy chirps peppered the clean air around her.

Opening her eyes, she looked down at the scenery below. The driveway, still damp from last night's rain, wrapped around the green front lawn in a ribbon of red. Dew glistened on the thick grass and the leaves of the large oak trees, and the fields beyond were darker than yesterday, the soil rich with moisture.

Kristen's smile returned. "Beautiful."

Whatever its faults, Hart's Hollow Farm still showed signs of life. They lingered on the fragrant sweetness of the air and were strong enough to penetrate the heavy atmosphere inside the house. Though it'd take a monumental effort to revive the place.

But Emmy had spirit and drive. The kind Kristen couldn't help but admire. And despite the odds, if the situation here was less complicated, she'd be almost tempted to consider—

"Good morning."

Startled, she opened her eyes and spun around.

Mitch stood outside his bedroom door, as tall, broad shouldered, and handsome as she remembered. He wore the same blue button-down shirt and khakis from last night. His chestnut-toned hair was slightly mussed, dark stubble lined his jaw, and a morning huskiness tinged his voice, stirring a delicious sensation low in her belly.

"G-good morning." She shrugged slightly and gestured over her shoulder. "I'm sorry. The view . . . I wanted to get a better look. I hope I didn't wake you, prying the window open."

"No." He shook his head. A wavy lock of hair tumbled over his forehead, and he pushed it back with a tanned hand. "I'm an early riser. Thought I'd get a head start on dragging my car out of the mud."

Nodding, she shifted awkwardly on her feet. "I suppose I should—"

"How long do you plan to—"

They both stopped. Remaining silent, Kristen smiled and gestured for him to continue.

He mirrored the motion, the sensual curves of his mouth lifting in a grin. The action brightened his eyes, but a hint of sadness still hovered in the blue depths. Enough that a strange sensation moved through her arms, making her long to reach out, cradle him close and offer comfort.

"You and Kristen both up, Mitch?" Emmy's call echoed up the wide staircase.

Mitch turned his head and looked down. "Yeah."

"Then y'all come out to the porch," Emmy said. "I got something to show you."

Kristen left the window, gripped the dusty staircase rail and looked down, too. She caught a glimpse of Emmy's back as she left, the screen door creaking open, then shut, on her departure.

"We've been summoned." Smile wry, Mitch sighed, then stepped back, sweeping his arm toward the stairs. "After you."

They walked downstairs and onto the porch, but there was no sign of Emmy. Just wet oak leaves scattered along the bare wood-planked floor.

"I'm over here."

Mitch shrugged, then led the way toward Emmy's voice. Kristen followed, keeping her eyes fixed firmly ahead and not on the strong swagger of Mitch's lean hips and thick thighs as they walked along the wraparound porch to the side of the house.

Emmy, her jeans muddy and her gray hair escaping its bun, stood just around the corner, by a small white table, holding a stainless-steel coffeepot. An assortment of muffins filled one woven basket sitting at the end of the table; green grapes and sliced apples were piled high in a glass bowl next to it; and a plate of big, beautiful strawberries was positioned at the opposite end.

Lifting a mug from the table, Emmy asked, "Do you drink coffee, Kristen?"

Kristen nodded, her stomach growling at the aroma. "Yes, please."

Emmy poured the rich brew generously, handed it to Kristen, then pointed at two glass jars with spoons nestled inside them. "Sugar and cream are there. Mitch?"

He frowned but nodded. As Emmy grabbed another mug, he asked, "How long have you been up, Emmy?"

Her lips pursed. "Oh, since about four. Kids aren't up yet. Figured I'd go ahead and start breakfast anyway."

"You should've woken me," Kristen said, stirring in a bit of cream. "I'd have been happy to help."

"Yeah?" Emmy smiled as she handed Mitch his coffee. "Well, I'm bribing you with breakfast, so that would've defeated the purpose."

Kristen sipped the strong brew, and a hum of appreciation escaped her as the flavor filled her senses. "Bribing me for what?"

Emmy's smile widened. "Look over there."

She pointed to her left, toward the back side of the farmhouse, where rows upon rows of lush green plants sprouted from raised beds covered with black plastic. Sunlight glinted off puddles along the dirt paths between the beds, and from this distance, the plants' dewy leaves sparkled like crystal.

"Strawberries." Emmy's chest lifted with pride. "The reddest, sweetest berries that ever grew out of the ground." She set the coffeepot on the table, then nudged the plate of strawberries closer to Kristen. "Go on. Try one."

Kristen hesitated, glancing at Mitch, whose frown deepened, and then she picked a strawberry from the plate. She took a small bite. Sweet juice spilled from the plump flesh, rolling over her tongue and trickling down her chin.

"Mmm." Kristen wiped her face with the back of her hand and smiled. "It's delicious."

"Yeah, and if those four acres of land can produce fruit that perfect," Emmy said, "imagine what the other three hundred acres can do."

A spicy, masculine scent surrounded Kristen as Mitch reached around her, the rough dusting of hair on his brawny forearm brushing her smooth skin, and grabbed a strawberry. He squeezed the fruit gently, turned it over in his strong palm, then narrowed his eyes at Emmy.

"One decent patch of strawberries doesn't guarantee a substantial crop of any kind on this farm," Mitch said.

"Maybe not." Emmy's jaw stiffened. "But it proves it's not dead and buried. I can do this. I've already done a lot of prep for early soybean production and better corn. I just need help. Someone with strong legs and plenty of energy." She looked at Kristen. "That's where you come in."

Three hundred acres. And just the two of them? Kristen shook her head. "Emmy—"

"It's a long shot, at best." Mitch tossed the strawberry back on the table. It bounced against the coffeepot, rolled off, then hit the porch floor. "A waste of time and what little money you have left."

"What's a waste?" Emmy picked up the strawberry and dusted the dirt off with the hem of her shirt. "Fighting to hold on to our family's land? Wanting to feed people? Our fields alone could fill the bellies of over a hundred and fifty people for a year."

Mitch's mouth twisted. "There are a lot of people who'd debate you on that. Most of the corn you grow goes into making fuel and—"

"Even so, every kernel is worth the effort," Emmy said. "And if those fields produce only enough to keep one person from starving next year, they're worth plowing." Her cheeks reddened. "No one should have to go hungry. This land fed you your entire childhood, Mitch, so I don't expect you to know how it feels to not have enough to eat. But I do. I know what it's like to not know where your next meal is gonna come from, and it's not *a waste*, as you put it, to try to keep that from happening."

Kristen flinched, the reality of Emmy's words hitting hard. She'd missed only two days' worth of meals before arriving at Hart's Hollow, but the resulting weakness in her limbs and gnawing hole in her gut had been enough to want to avoid repeating the painful predicament. And she couldn't imagine how it would feel to go hungry on a permanent basis.

"Or maybe"—Emmy's mouth shook as she stared at Mitch—"it's not the land you lack faith in but me. Maybe you think that 'cuz I got a bit of age on me and move slower than I used to, I can't do the job. Or maybe, 'cuz I speak slow and plain, you think I'm just an ignorant backwoods bumpkin who doesn't have the smarts or wherewithal to pull it off."

"I never said that, Emmy." Mitch stepped back, his cheeks flushing. "Would *never* say that."

"But you're thinking it." Emmy peered up at him. "You think I don't know the other reason you finally deigned to come back here? You think I don't know you came to take those two babies away from me, too?"

Kristen's hands clenched around her mug, her attention shooting to Mitch. He avoided her eyes, but the guilty color blotching his neck and the tanned skin above the open collar of his shirt confirmed Emmy's assertion.

"There's a big world out there," Mitch said. "Sadie and Dylan deserve a chance to live in it. They deserve the opportunity to grow and thrive in a stable home. To have choices and opportunities."

"And I can't give them that?" Emmy's voice cracked. "I always fought for you, Mitch. Just like I'm fighting for them now. Can't you see I'm trying to make things right?"

Mitch stared back at her, his face turning pale and a muscle clenching in his jaw. "It's too late for that. Those kids deserve better, and you've earned a decent rest."

Throat tightening, Kristen looked away and focused on the green rows of strawberry plants in the distance. The painful throb in Emmy's voice brought tears to her eyes, blurring the view.

"I've rested enough in my life, and I'm not leaving my home or giving up the last bit of family I got left." Emmy stood straighter. "I don't use fancy phrases, because I only say what I mean. Ain't nothing wrong with speaking plain. Like a plain yes or no. So be honest, Mitch. Do you think I'm capable of propping this place back on its feet?"

For a moment, only the birds' chirps and the whisper of the spring breeze moved between them. Then Mitch answered, his tone hard.

"No."

Kristen frowned at him, the angry set of his expression making her chest ache. The circumstances on this farm were dire, sure, but how could he be so cruel? How could he stand there and dismiss Emmy—his own family—as though she meant nothing to him? As though she were . . . no one?

"And you?" Emmy was facing her now, a look of helplessness on her face and suspicious wetness lining her lashes. "You think I got enough life left in me to fix this land?"

Alone? With two children to raise? No. Kristen closed her eyes against the thought, shame welling within her at the instinctual need to run. There were never guarantees in life. No controlled, predictable outcomes. No one knew that better than she.

"Yes."

Her eyes sprang open, the lie that had left her lips as much a surprise to her as it seemed to be to Mitch and Emmy.

Shifting closer, Emmy wiped her cheeks with the back of her hand. The desperate hope underpinning her tremulous smile made Kristen ache to turn away. "And will you take the job?"

Kristen glanced at Mitch, the thin line of his mouth and disapproving plea in his expression sending a chill through her.

She faced Emmy, then forced herself to speak. "Yes."

CHAPTER 3

Mitch dug his heels deeper into the farm's sludge-filled driveway, then braced his hands against the rental car's back bumper.

"That plank you lodged in the front isn't tight enough to the tire. I can give it a kick, if you'd like?"

He cut his eyes to the left. Kristen's guarded gaze and determined stance made his tongue press tighter against the back of his clenched teeth. After his conversation with Emmy, he'd trudged out here, intent on blowing off some steam by prying the car from the mud, but not long after Kristen had followed.

"It's nice of you to offer to help," he said, "but the plank's plenty tight and I can handle this on my own."

"I'm sure you can, but Emmy asked me to give you a hand while she gets the kids up. She'd like you to bring her truck around. Said she doesn't drive as much, because of her knee. She wants you to take us to the neighbors'. Ruth Ann Hadden's, I think she said."

"For what?"

Kristen shrugged. "Said she has business to discuss, and I'm here to work, so . . ." She glanced at his staggered legs. "I can give that plank a kick, then get on the other side and help you rock it out. An extra hand never hurts, and that's what I'm here for."

He closed his eyes and stifled a groan. "Fine. But the plank's good, and it'll go better if you get in the car and give it a little gas instead."

She hesitated, the breeze twirling wisps of her blond hair across the stubborn set of her jaw, then nodded and walked toward the driver's side.

Mitch clenched his hands tighter around the bumper of the sedan, the sun-warmed metal heating his palms and temper. How—*in the space of five minutes*—had Emmy maneuvered pleasantries over morning coffee into a debate over the farm's worth? And hers as a person? Then for Kristen to jump on the bandwagon—

"Why did you do it?" He leaned around the side of the car, then glared as she froze and looked back at him, one of her slim legs poised in the front floorboard of the driver's seat. "Why did you say yes and give Emmy false hope like that?" He shook his head. "I've been nothing but honest with you, and you can see the state of the place for yourself. Why join a project you know will fail? Take a job I told you right off would be a dead end?"

A muscle in her jaw ticked. "Why is it guaranteed to be a dead end? Because you say so?" One blond brow rose. "Your word is gospel—is that it?"

"No." He scoffed, glancing up at the ceaseless stretch of blue above. "We've got enough gospel out here. I'm just stating facts. Sensible, practical truths."

"Is that why you're taking the kids from her? Because it's the sensible thing to do regardless of how it'll affect Emmy or the children?"

"You just met them. You don't know enough about any of us to pass judgment—"

"You're right. It's not my place to judge, and that's not my intention." Her tone softened. "But I know what it feels like to lose something precious. I wouldn't wish it on anyone."

She stopped, then looked down, her gaze darting over the red clay oozing up around her white tennis shoes and then settling on the interior of the car.

He studied the defensive posture of her slender frame. The dark flush in her cheeks, the tight line of her mouth.

The angry buzz in his veins quieted as he slowly straightened. "What have you lost, Kristen?"

She turned away, staring over her shoulder at the low swoop of a red-tailed hawk floating on the current over the empty fields. Her pulse fluttered beneath the delicate skin of her exposed neck, just below her jaw. "Everyone's lost something." Her slim throat moved on a hard swallow; then she faced him, expression blank and eyes empty. "Haven't you?"

"Yes, but—"

"Then let's just say we both know how that feels." A hint of desperation shook her steady words. "Can we agree on that at least?"

Mitch waited, holding her steady gaze, then watched the rapid rise and fall of her chest. "Okay. For now, we'll agree on that." He returned his attention to her face. "But believe me when I say there's more to this than you think. This farm may be precious to Emmy, but it's been nothing but mud and blood for me."

Kristen's mouth parted and the quick lift of her chest stilled as her eyes swept over his chest and thighs, then focused on his hands. A sharp sting hit the tender flesh of his palms, and he unfurled fists he hadn't realized he'd formed, the press of his nails leaving throbbing impressions behind.

"Sadie and Dylan, however . . ." He cleared the tightness from his throat. "They're precious to me, and I'd never do anything I didn't think was in their best interest. I'm only trying to make sure that bad history doesn't repeat itself. From the little you know of me, can we agree on that in good faith, too?"

He flinched. There was that word again. The one he hadn't uttered a single time in the fourteen years since he'd left this place. That blind, gullible term Emmy applied to every challenging circumstance regardless of common sense or reality.

Maybe it's not the land you lack faith in but me.

"I may not agree with Emmy," he tacked on, "but I want only what's best for her, as well."

She remained motionless, peering at him as the rumble of a semitruck approached along the worn highway at their backs and then faded in the distance. She released a slow breath. "All right."

A bead of sweat trickled down the back of his neck and seeped into the collar of his shirt. He returned to his crouched position behind the car and gripped the bumper. "Guide it toward the grass while I shove."

"I really think we should give that plank a—"

"All I need is for you to give it gas and steer." His face heated. *Damn.* Why did he have this inane tendency to act like an ass around her? He inclined his head. "Please."

Her eyes narrowed, but after a moment, she slipped into the driver's seat and shut the door, cranked the engine, and hit the gas. The tires spun erratically, flinging thick clay across his pant legs, and the exhaust pipe puffed fumes in his face. Coughing, he pushed, rocked, and slammed his shoulder into the unyielding metal for what seemed like ten minutes, to no avail, then slumped against the trunk to catch his breath.

The engine stopped, and a window rolled down on a smooth whisper. He propped his sweaty forearms against the trunk and leaned to the side.

Kristen's gleaming eyes and wide smile stared back at him. "Want me to give that plank a kick now?"

He batted away a gnat, then grunted, "Yeah."

She hopped out, walked to the front of the car and kicked the plank wedged against the left tire twice. After returning to the driver's seat, she accelerated while he shoved. With slick suction, the tire lurched from the mud, propelling the car off the driveway and onto the grassy shoulder.

Grinning, Kristen reemerged, spun toward him, then bowed.

He laughed. "You were right. I was wrong. Thanks."

"Never hurts for a man to tell a woman that. And you're welcome."

Those green eyes of hers lit up, and her expression lifted with her teasing tone, dispelling the dark shadows. Her whole demeanor brightened, conjuring up a warm welling sensation within his chest.

"Y'all 'bout ready?" Emmy stood several feet ahead on the grassy stretch between the oak trees, Sadie leaning against her hip and Dylan slouched behind her. "The kids are up and raring to go." She glanced down and smiled. "Aren't you?"

Sadie yawned. Dylan rolled his eyes.

It took Mitch five minutes to bring the truck around, four minutes to get everyone settled inside the extended cab, and one second of driving up the driveway before the trouble started.

"It's spring break," Dylan muttered. "We shouldn't have to get up at the butt crack of dawn when we're out of school."

Mitch frowned and glanced in the rearview mirror. Dylan sat in the middle of the backseat, wedged between Sadie and Kristen, attention glued to the cell phone in his hand. "Language, Dylan."

He scowled. "*Butt* isn't a cussword."

Sadie gasped. "He said it again, Uncle Mitch."

"Hush up, you tattletale," Dylan spat.

"I'm not a tattletale—"

"Oh, I've heard a lot worse in my time," Emmy said, twisting in her seat to eye Dylan. "But I'd rather not hear it from you, and I'd especially rather not hear it in my sweet Joe's truck. Put that phone up." She flicked a hand toward the truck door. "And, Mitch, open the windows. The sun's shining, the birds are chirping, and the fresh air will blow the grump right off him."

Mitch pressed the button on the door, and the windows squeaked open halfway.

"All the way, please," Emmy added, then nodded when he complied.

A strong breeze flooded the car, ruffling the gray hair at Emmy's temples and scattering dust particles around the cab. Sadie batted at her nose, then started sneezing.

"You all right, baby?" Mitch asked.

"Ye . . ." Another sneeze. "Sir."

"Move to the left a little, Mitch," Emmy directed. "That big hole's coming up on the right, and it'll knock the truck out of alignment."

He did so, palming the steering wheel and shifting the truck's path toward the left.

"Watch out for the drop at the end of the driveway. It'll be steeper after all that rain." Emmy flapped a thin hand at the worn highway as they approached. "Keep your ears open for those big trucks, too. They're few and far between, but they'll run you right over, given the chance."

He gritted his teeth and accelerated.

"And keep an eye out for deer. They—"

"Would you like to drive, Emmy?"

"Nope." She reached out and patted his forearm. "You're doing just fine."

Sighing, he glanced in the side mirror and caught Kristen's eyes on him. Her lips twitched and her shoulders shook as she turned away, lifting her face toward the swift breeze.

By the time he turned the truck onto the paved highway, a small smile had fought its way to his own lips.

Ten minutes later, Mitch took a left, then guided the truck over rain-filled potholes up a straight dirt driveway. Cornstalks about three feet tall stood in proud rows along large fields on both sides of the road. Green leaves glistened with dew above the saturated red soil and stretched toward the horizon, where the morning sun had emerged, warming the land.

"I didn't think you were in the habit of paying Mrs. Ruth Ann visits anymore." Mitch lowered his visor to block the sharp rays of the sun, then glanced at Emmy. "You sure this is a good idea? Thought the two of you had decided to keep your distance from each other."

Emmy's mouth twisted. "Wasn't my decision. I've never been nothing but polite to her." Her hands moved restlessly in her lap. "Well . . . except on the occasions she's forced me to behave otherwise. With any luck, she won't be there. Either way, it'll be fine. Right, Kristen?" she prompted, looking in the backseat.

He glanced in the side mirror.

Kristen hesitated before answering, "I'm sure it'll be fine."

"And besides," Emmy added, "I'm not going to see Ruth Ann. I'm going to see Lee."

He smiled. "Lee? He's back?"

That hadn't been the plan. Seven years older than Mitch and an admired high school quarterback, Lee Hadden had left Stellaville for the University of Georgia twenty years ago on a full-ride scholarship. He was a good guy with a good head on his shoulders, and getting out of Stellaville had been as high a priority for him as it had been for Mitch.

"Yep. Has been for nine years now, ever since Daryl died." Emmy sniffed. "Ruth Ann needed him, and he was happy to come back."

Mitch's cheeks heated. He avoided looking in the side mirror and changed the subject as he drew the truck to a halt in front of a large white house, its green metal roof glinting under the sunlight. "I see Ruth Ann's been keeping up the flower beds Daryl planted."

And not only those but also the entire estate itself. No rotting porch rails, battered shutters, or barren land here. Just a lush lawn manicured to perfection; wide, sparkling windows; and pristine wicker furniture adorning the front porch. Genteel, stately, and Southern—just like Ruth Ann.

Emmy harrumphed. "She hired some landscaping company. Never was one to get her nails dirty. That's why Lee came back. Widowed or not, she wasn't gonna dig in the dirt and plant crops herself."

Shoulders stiffening, Mitch cut the engine. "Emmy, this isn't a good idea."

"I know, I know," she huffed, thrusting open her door. "I'm not here to stir up any trouble. I just need to talk to Lee, and he's never turned me away, so come on."

He assisted Emmy out of the truck, then helped Sadie and Dylan climb down. By the time he reached her side, Kristen already stood in the driveway, squinting up at the house. A deep flush stained her cheeks, and a blond tendril of hair clung to her sweaty forehead.

After pausing, Mitch moved to the truck bed, pried the rusty built-in toolbox open, and sifted through various items before catching the flash of a red brim in the corner of the toolbox. He grinned, tugged the hat out, then beat it against his pant leg to knock off the dust.

"Here." He lifted it in Kristen's direction. "It's a bit worn, but it'll keep the sun out of your eyes."

She turned, glanced at the hat and smiled. That sweet tilt of her mouth was a replica of the one she'd presented when he first arrived—warm, inviting. It tugged at something deep in his middle. A small whirl of sensation. Equal parts excitement, desire, and anticipation. Something he hadn't felt since his teenage years.

"May I?" he asked, holding up the hat and stepping closer.

She hesitated briefly, then nodded and looked up at him. Her green eyes followed his hands as they settled the hat in place, tucked her bangs beneath the brim, and smoothed a moist curl from her temple.

His thumb—broad against her delicate bone structure—lingered on her cheek. "Better?"

The pink tip of her tongue touched the corner of her mouth and her chest lifted on a deep breath before she refocused on his face. "Yes. Thank you."

"Mitch!" Lee strode across the front lawn from the direction of the fields, smiling and waving a hand in their direction. "Good to see you, man. What's it been? Ten, fifteen years since I last saw you?"

"Thereabouts." Mitch stepped back from Kristen, then shook Lee's hand when he arrived. At just over six feet, he reached the same height as Mitch, and other than a smattering of gray in his hair, he looked the same as ever, his brawny frame still strong. "Looks like you're doing good."

"For an old man?" Lee joked, propping his hands on his hips. "I'm doing all right." He looked at Kristen and smiled wider. "I see you made it the night."

Mitch frowned and glanced at Kristen.

She shook her head. "I'm sorry . . . Have we met?"

"Yesterday." Lee gestured toward the highway. "Right up that stretch of road. You were looking for Emmy's place."

Kristen's head drew back as she looked Lee over. "Oh. I . . . didn't recognize you."

"Nah. Didn't expect you to." He shrugged. "First impressions can be deceiving. I'd just come out of the fields, hadn't shaved in days and was driving Old Beaut."

"Old Beaut?" she asked.

Lee pointed to the far side of the lawn at a beat-up truck overcome with rust. "Old Beaut. She's my farming girl. Might have some years on her, but she's strong and solid."

Nodding, Kristen smiled. "That's the best kind."

"You know it." Lee held out his hand and gripped Kristen's, his fingers squeezing hers a bit too long for Mitch's liking. "Seems you didn't take my advice about the storm."

"About getting out?" Kristen raised her brows. "I like a challenge."

"Ah." Lee leaned closer. "You're my kind of girl."

"Lee." Dragging a hand across the back of his neck, Mitch edged between them. "We're here because Emmy wants to talk to you."

Lee cocked his head. "Oh, yeah?"

"Yep." Emmy rounded the truck, with Sadie and Dylan trailing behind. "I want to talk business. Wanna see about renting your tractor, some buckets, and a piece of land."

Lee gave a slow grin, then winked. "Ah, now, Mrs. Emmy. You sure are pretty, but I'ma need a little sweet talk before I go giving that up."

Emmy guffawed. "You always were a rascal, Lee Hadden. If I was your mama, I'd—"

"Lee, who is it?"

Mitch shielded his eyes and peered up at the porch. An older woman, same age as Emmy, stood on the steps, her long skirt and lace blouse lying in neat pleats along her graceful frame, and her gray hair pulled back from her wrinkled cheeks in an elegant topknot. "Good morning, Mrs. Ruth Ann," he called out. "Hope you don't mind us stopping by this early."

She shaded her eyes, too, then smiled and stepped carefully down the steps. "Is that you, Mitch? Oh, how wonderful to see you. You're looking more and more like Joe." Her eyes swept over the group. "And you brought the little ones. I'm always glad to have—"

Ruth Ann clamped her mouth shut and stopped on the bottom step. A hard glint entered her expression as she stared at Emmy.

Mitch tensed as Emmy faced her, put her shoulders back and said, "Morning, Ruth Ann."

Chin trembling and nose twitching, Ruth Ann narrowed her eyes. "Good morning, Emmy. I don't recall us arranging a visit."

Lee walked over and put a hand on her shoulder. "Mama, Mrs. Emmy's here to visit me, and I'm glad to have her. Plus, she brought Mitch and the kids with her. Be a shame not to use the front porch on a beautiful morning like this."

Ruth Ann hesitated, eyes softening as they moved over Sadie and Dylan, then back to Mitch. "Well." She sniffed. "I would like to visit with Mitch and the children." Her smile, though strained, returned. "I have plenty of fresh pound cake and just made a pitcher of lemonade. You always loved my lemonade, didn't you, Mitch?"

Eager to appease, Mitch nodded. "Yes, ma'am. Thank you."

"In that case . . ." Ruth Ann lifted one shoulder and lifted an eyebrow at Emmy. "You're welcome to come up, Emmy."

Emmy muttered under her breath but followed Ruth Ann as she turned and climbed back up the stairs. Sadie, Dylan, and Kristen fell in line behind her. Lee paused on the bottom step and exchanged a rueful look with Mitch.

"It's been over fifty years, but they still haven't let it go, have they?" Lee turned his attention to Kristen, watched her curvy figure ascend the stairs with a note of appreciation in his eyes, then studied Mitch. "Pretty guest you've got there. That your hat she's wearing?"

Mitch nodded.

"You get a good look in those eyes?" Lee's tone softened as he glanced toward her. "There's an old soul in there. Maybe one that wouldn't mind a man who had a few more years on him than her." He smiled, tilting his head at Mitch. "Think history might repeat itself?"

Mitch stared at the slim line of Kristen's back and didn't answer.

Laughing, Lee strode up the steps and joined the others on the porch, leaving Mitch behind, hoping like hell Lee was wrong in more ways than one.

"Have another piece . . . Kristen, was it?" Ruth Ann nudged a ceramic plate of sliced pound cake across the table, then leaned back and tapped her polished nails against her wicker chair.

"Yes, no, thank you." Kristen took one last sip of lemonade and smiled, pressing her palm against her middle. "I mean, yes, Kristen is correct, and thank you for the offer, but I'll have to pass. It was delicious, but between this and the breakfast Emmy made, if I eat any more, I won't be fit for anything but napping the rest of the day."

Which she was afraid might already be the case.

Between brief introductions, idle small talk and a round of refreshments, Kristen's stomach had grown fuller and her eyes drowsier with each passing second. The increasing heat of the late morning sun slipping beneath the porch eaves and the gentle spring breeze tickling her bare arms and neck hadn't helped matters. Neither had the plush cushions of the wicker sofa she and Emmy lounged against.

"I want some more." Sadie, seated on a porch swing, leaned over and reached toward the pile of cake.

"Don't forget your manners, Sadie," Emmy said. "And not too much more, or you'll get a tummy ache."

Sadie blushed and glanced at Ruth Ann. "May I please have some more?"

Ruth Ann beamed. "You certainly may, sweetheart. Take as much as you'd like. Gentlemen, can I get you anything else?"

Dylan, lounging at Sadie's side on the porch swing, shook his head and returned his attention to his cell phone. Mitch and Lee offered polite declines from their lounge chairs.

Folding her hands in her lap, Ruth Ann pursed her lips, then slowly lifted her lashes and looked across the table. "Emmy?"

Kristen clutched her glass tighter, cold condensation seeping into her palm. Despite being in each other's company for just over fifteen minutes, the two women hadn't exchanged words with each other directly yet. And the tension had been easy to pick up on—even for a newcomer. But despite Mitch's misgivings about the visit, so far, it seemed to be going well.

"No, thank you." Emmy set her still-full glass of lemonade on the small table. "It's kind of you to have us."

Ruth Ann issued a small smile, then gestured toward Mitch. "I hadn't heard you were coming home, Mitch. How long do you plan on staying?"

"Just until Monday." The thin material of his shirt

stretched across his broad chest as he eased back in his chair. A hoarse note entered his voice, and his big hands curved around the sides of the wicker armrests. "I came back only for the weekend, primarily to check on Emmy and see how Sadie and Dylan were doing."

Kristen studied his polite expression. The only change was a slight tightening of his strong jaw, but it was enough to stir an ache within her. She looked away, straightening his hat on her head, her fingertips drifting to her temple, where the touch of his calloused thumb still lingered.

"I was so sorry to hear about Carrie," Ruth Ann said, glancing at the children.

"Thank you." Mitch reached out, squeezed Dylan's shoulder and smiled at Sadie, then deftly changed the subject. "I'm looking forward to spending some time with these two while I'm here."

A wistful look crossed Ruth Ann's face. "Seems like you inherited your grandpa Joe's love of kids, too. When your father was young, Joe always enjoyed taking him fishing and hunting."

Kristen stole another glance at Mitch. His relaxed posture had stiffened again.

"Anything to show off his son," she continued. "Why, David was only five when Joe—"

"No need for the reminiscing, Ruth Ann," Emmy said, straightening in her seat and casting a sidelong glance at Mitch. "He knew his dad well enough, and I've told him all there is to know about Joe over the years."

Ruth Ann smoothed her skirt and picked at one of her nails. "Yes, but you may have overlooked a detail or two. I knew Joe as well as you did, and a well-rounded view of a person never hurt."

Emmy's mouth thinned and a small tic started below her right eye, but she remained silent.

Ruth Ann sighed, then tilted her head at Emmy. "What brought you in Lee's direction this morning?"

"Business." Smiling, Emmy patted Kristen's wrist. "Me and Kristen are hittin' the ground running today, and we want to offer Lee a partnership. Right, Kristen?"

She stilled. Emmy hadn't discussed anything other than riding to the neighbors'. There'd been no talk of borrowing tractors, buckets, or land, and there had certainly been no firm plans of offering anyone any kind of partnership—just an "Ask Mitch to bring the truck around and let's go" directive.

Kristen shifted awkwardly in her seat, studying the unspoken urging in Emmy's eyes and the intense scrutiny in Ruth Ann's. "I . . . yes."

"I see." A guarded tone entered Ruth Ann's voice. "How long have you and Emmy been designing the intricacies of this new business endeavor?"

She swallowed a hefty swig of lemonade before answering. "Not long."

Ruth Ann nodded. "I'd imagine, considering you just arrived yesterday."

"Word travels fast here." Kristen looked at Lee.

"I may have mentioned you were looking for work at Emmy's place." He grinned and leaned forward, then propped his elbows on his jean-clad thighs. "It's not every day I bump into a pretty stranger on this old stretch of highway. You can't blame a man for wanting to relive the moment in the telling."

Kristen smiled. Emmy had been right. The man was definitely a big tease and more than handsome. He was as tall as Mitch, his muscular frame filled his chair, and the rippled strength of his arms was just as defined as the other man's, but he didn't stir her interest quite like Mitch.

Chancing a glance at Mitch, she caught him watching her, and the steady gaze of his blue eyes evoked flutters in her belly. She shrugged. "I appreciate the compliment, Lee, but—"

"I'm not sure how much work there'll end up being for Kristen," Mitch said, returning his attention to Lee. "Or Emmy, for that matter. Hart's Hollow is on its last leg, and the county is about to seal the deal on that new bypass. Last I heard, it's projected to cut across the center of our land."

"That's not true." Emmy balled her hands into fists on her thighs. "That decision ain't final yet, and I got a trick or two left up my sleeve. Namely, showing 'em at the next meeting in Peach Grove on Monday night that our land is too valuable to pave over. As a matter of fact, we've already grown four successful acres of strawberries, which are ripe and ready to pick. That's why I need the buckets." She turned to Lee. "I remember you saying you had a bunch left over from when you grew 'em a couple years ago. We'll buy the lot off you if you can spare them."

Lee nodded. "I no longer have a use for them, so I'll sell them to you at half price. You can use my road sign, too, if you want. You'll just need to paint over our logo and add your own."

"Lee, don't," Ruth Ann said. "What if you decide to try again next season?"

He waved away her concern. "I barely made it work the last time I tried it. I was stretched too thin between the corn and the cotton. Couldn't be in two places at once. And you remember how much you complained about all the extra traffic up and down the driveway when I opened the fruit stand?" He shook his head. "The return wasn't worth the investment."

"For you alone, maybe." Emmy pointed a finger at his chest, then waved it toward Kristen. "But this time around, it won't be a one-man operation. I'll have help, and it'll be a guaranteed success. Right, Kristen?"

All six pairs of eyes shifted to her and bored into her face. Oh, man. What had she gotten herself into? A little white lie was one thing, but these were piling up by the dozen.

Nodding, she forced her dry tongue to move. "We'll do our best."

"This is ridiculous," Ruth Ann said. "Out of the question."

"If you have a mind to take a shift at our stand once in a while," Emmy put in over Ruth Ann, "I'll cut you a percentage of the profit."

Lee propped his chin in his hand and mulled it over for a moment. "And where do the tractor and the land come into play?"

"The land?" Ruth Ann's mouth dropped open.

"That's right," Emmy said, "the land. Just a piece. That stretch you've already strip-tilled." She gestured toward Ruth Ann's gaping mouth. "And I wouldn't keep that up if I were you. You'll catch a fly." She faced Lee again as Ruth Ann sputtered. "All I'm asking is to rent the tractor and the twenty acres I sold to you back in the day. I got extra corn I want Kristen to plant so I can up our profit and have a more persuasive argument in this bypass nonsense. And I'll pay you extra for the work you already put into it."

"No." Ruth Ann shook her head. "You didn't sell that land. Joe did. And he sold it to me."

"I didn't come here to argue, Ruth Ann. I've got as

much pride as anyone else, but the fact is, I'm at my last gasp here. Do you want a bunch of asphalt-grinding semis tearing past your bedroom window at night? 'Cuz that's what'll happen if they get ahold of my land." Emmy sighed. "I'm not asking for something that was never mine. Joe sold that lot to Daryl a year before he passed to keep us afloat when we were struggling. He would've never done it otherwise. Daryl was a good man. He assured us he'd give us the chance to earn it back."

"No," Ruth Ann repeated. "Absolutely not. I forbid it."

"You forbid? Would you have forbidden Joe if he'd asked?"

Kristen winced and glanced at the children. Sadie grabbed another slice of pound cake and started chewing, while Dylan looked up from his phone, his head swiveling toward Emmy, then Ruth Ann, and back.

Mitch held up a hand. "Emmy, you've gotten your ans—"

"I would never have forbidden Joe anything." Ruth Ann's face flushed a fiery red. "I knew Joe better than anyone—including you."

"Oh, for goodness' sake. Can we please get past this?" Emmy's right eye twitched faster. "We were friends once. Long before I married Joe. And we're both widows now, so what's to stop us from fixing this?"

"You broke my heart, Emmy." Voice shaking, Ruth Ann slowly stood. "Joe was my first love. If you hadn't started chasing him, *I* would've been his wife."

"Now, Mama." Lee scooted to the edge of his chair. "Let's not go dragging all this u—"

"I know you loved Joe." Mouth tight, Emmy nodded. "But the fact was, he didn't love you back—not in that way at least—and he made that plain to you from the start. He couldn't control who he loved any more than I could."

Mitch cleared his throat. "That's enough, Emmy."

"How would you know?" Ruth Ann huffed. "You didn't give him a chance to choose."

"Oh, that ain't true." Emmy shoved to her feet but stumbled and grabbed the back of her chair, favoring her left leg.

Kristen rose and cupped her elbow. "Maybe we should come back another time."

"If anything," Emmy said, speaking over her, "it was the other way around, Ruth Ann. We were all good friends. It's just one day . . ." She spread her hands. "One day, things changed. That's all." A haunted look entered her eyes. "Sometimes things just change."

"They never changed for me. I always loved Joe—right from the first."

"And what about Daryl, huh?" Emmy asked. "Oughtn't you have loved your own husband more than mine?"

Ruth Ann sucked in a horrified breath. "I did love Daryl. How dare you imply otherwise, you . . . you . . . !" Her slender frame shook, and a vein throbbed in her neck, her temper getting the best of her. "Damn devil."

Silence fell over the porch. Cheeks flaming, Kristen shifted from one foot to the other and glanced at the others.

Mitch and Lee were poised on the edge of their chairs, looking on in dismay. Wide-eyed, Sadie sat perfectly still, both hands clutching pound cake and crumbs dangling from her lips, as she stared. Dylan smiled, lifted his cell phone higher, and focused the screen on Emmy and Ruth Ann.

"I think that's enough visiting for today," Mitch said quietly.

The cell phone buzzed as Dylan zoomed in.

Mitch thrust out his palm. "Hand it over."

"But—"

"Hand. It. Over."

Dylan issued a sound of disgust but placed the phone in Mitch's hand.

Standing, Lee winced. "I'm sorry about this, Mitch."

"Don't worry about it." Mitch nudged Dylan off the swing, then Sadie. "Thank you for the refreshments, Ruth Ann, but it's time for us to go."

Sadie stopped by his thigh. She looked up, garbling around a mouthful of cake, "She said a bad word, Uncle Mitch. The real bad one. Worse than Dylan."

He smoothed a broad hand over her hair. "I know, baby. Please get in the truck with your brother."

Mitch waited as she followed Dylan down the front steps, and then he walked over and took Emmy's other elbow. "Time we got going." Expression strained, he looked over Emmy's head and asked in a sardonic drawl, "Right, Kristen?"

Urging Emmy forward on trembling legs, Kristen had to admit that in this instance, she agreed with Mitch.

CHAPTER 4

"Paint it white. Then add *Hart's Hollow Farm: Fresh Strawberries*," Emmy said, framing her hands and punctuating each phrase in the air.

Kristen looked up from her seated position under a tree on the front lawn and curled her fingers tighter around the wooden sign balanced on her lap. "Do you have any spray paint? It'd be faster to spray it."

"No spray." Emmy tugged two paintbrushes, one large and one small, from her waistband and tossed them on the grass, beside several paint cans. "Use those and dress her up as best you can while I help finish washing the buckets. Mitch said he'd get that sign on posts before he leaves tomorrow. If we don't get it painted now, it won't be dry by then."

She ambled off and joined Mitch by the porch. He grabbed a dirty bucket from a large pile on the lawn, dipped it in a small metal tub filled with sudsy water, scrubbed hard, then handed it to Emmy. She sprayed it off with the water hose and passed it to Dylan, who rubbed it dry with a towel and stacked it with dozens of clean ones on the porch steps.

Yesterday, hours after Emmy's bitter round with Ruth Ann, Old Beaut had rumbled up the farm's driveway just as they were clearing dishes from supper, its bed filled to the brim with dusty buckets and a large sign. Lee had hopped out, apologized for the unpleasant scene earlier, and made Emmy a counteroffer regarding the strawberry endeavor.

In exchange for the buckets and the sign, Lee would take a bigger cut of the profits instead of cash, saving Emmy money up front and making money only if she did. It was the respectable thing for a neighbor to do, he'd explained, then offered assurances that he'd ask Ruth Ann to reconsider renting Emmy the twenty acres of land. Though he had made it clear it was a long shot.

Emmy had quickly agreed, thanked him, then put them all to work unloading the truck and washing buckets. Save for seven hours of sleep, they'd been washing ever since.

"I'm tired." Dylan puffed his matted bangs out of his eyes, and a bead of sweat rolled down his red cheek, the late afternoon air having grown hot and sticky. "It's Sunday. It's supposed to be a rest day. Isn't that what you always say?" he asked, glancing at Emmy.

"Not when there's buckets to wash and fields to plow," Emmy said as she sprayed the hose again. "God understands and forgives farmers."

Dylan scoffed. "We've been doing this forever, and I'm sick of it." He glared at Mitch. "When can I get my phone back?"

Mitch paused after dipping another bucket and dragged his forearm over his face. He wore jeans and a thin T-shirt instead of his usual khakis and collared shirt, and it did nothing to dampen his appeal. "When you've earned it."

"When will that be?"

Mitch leveled a stern look in Dylan's direction. "When you do as you're told without complaining." His jaw hardened. "And when you learn that it's cruel to take pleasure in other people's pain. You had no business recording that argument between Emmy and Ruth Ann."

Dylan shrugged. "I thought it was funny, and I couldn't upload it to anything anyway, because the Wi-Fi's so slow out here."

"The thought shouldn't have even crossed your mind." Mitch frowned. "I was surprised at that. You've always been kind and considerate to others, Dylan."

The boy looked down and twisted the toe of his shoe in the grass, muttering, "What does that ever get anyone?"

Mitch started to speak, then shook his head and returned to his task.

"It got us buckets," Kristen said, then stilled as Mitch and Dylan turned in her direction. "And a sign."

Though she wasn't looking forward to the idea of painting it. She hadn't touched a paintbrush in years and had planned on never doing so again. Yet here she was, getting paid to paint. The task was a world apart from her previous career for sure, but it still managed to uncoil that dread lurking deep in her middle.

Tipping down the brim of her hat, she hid her face from Mitch's scrutiny, then bent forward and dragged the paint cans and brushes closer.

Leaves rustled and a branch creaked overhead. Kristen glanced up just as Sadie shimmied toward her across a low branch, her arms and legs wound snug around the rough bark. She'd kept a moderate distance for most of the day, drying buckets for a while with Dylan, but when Kristen sat on the grass and began sanding the sign smooth, she'd climbed a tree and watched from above. She had asked Kristen questions occasionally, her cute face often hidden behind a clump of leaves, and had shown no reaction to the curt responses she received.

"What color you gonna paint the words in?" Sadie asked, her long hair cascading around her shy but curious expression.

A knot tightened in Kristen's chest as the excited lilt of Anna's voice whispered through her mind. *What color should I use for the flowers, Mama?*

She pulled in a strong breath and popped the tops off the cans. "I thought I'd use red."

"Because it's for strawberries?" Sadie loosened her grip on the branch, slid both legs to one side, then hopped down. She moved close, and her soft breaths brushed the back of Kristen's neck as she leaned over and studied the materials. "Can I help?"

Mine doesn't look as good as yours. Will you help me?

Be patient, Anna. Try again.

Chills spread across Kristen's skin despite the heat, making her hands shake. She grabbed the large paintbrush and dunked it in the white paint. "I won't need it, but thank you."

"I can do it." Sadie's voice drew even closer as she squatted beside Kristen. "I'll be careful, I promise."

Look, Mama. Eyes stinging, Kristen pressed the paintbrush to the wood. The memory of Anna poised in front of a small canvas, looking over her shoulder and smiling, superimposed itself on the sign. *I did it almost as good as you, didn't I?*

Kristen's throat tightened. Why hadn't she helped Anna that day? Exchanged teaching an artistic skill for the feel of Anna's warm, healthy hand in hers one more time before it was lost to her forever?

Sadie touched the back of her hand, her small, unfamiliar fingers a painful press against Kristen's flesh. "I can—"

"I said no!"

Sadie jumped to her feet, her face turning pale and her chin trembling. Tears welled onto her lashes.

Stomach dropping, Kristen winced as she backed away and whispered, "I'm sorry, Sadie. I—"

Sadie spun around, then ran across the front lawn into Mitch's outstretched arms. He hugged Sadie close, murmuring low words of comfort and frowning at Kristen. Emmy stared in her direction, too. Only, her expression probed rather than admonished.

Face burning, Kristen put her head down again and resumed painting the sign with rough strokes. *Nice. Real nice.* Not only had she made Sadie cry, but she'd also made an absolute fool of herself.

Her mind raced and her mouth opened, then closed, as she wanted to explain. But how could she? There was no way to rationalize or defend the selfish pain that sometimes flooded her at the sight of other kids smiling, laughing—heaven help her, just *playing*—when Anna wasn't. When Anna never would again.

"Come on, Dylan," Emmy said, dropping the hose. "The sun's dipping and it'll be dark before long, so I guess you can knock off early and get a cool drink." She started for the steps, holding out her hand. "Sadie, how 'bout some sweet tea?"

After shooting Kristen one last glance, Sadie slipped out of Mitch's hold, took Emmy's hand, and entered the house. Kristen continued painting, but the low snaps of twigs underfoot alerted her to Mitch's approach.

His rough work boots stopped by her tennis shoes; then he sat on his haunches, his jeans pulling taut across his muscular thighs, and his damp T-shirt clinging to his wide upper body. He plucked a long blade of grass from the ground, held it with one tanned hand, and dragged his broad fingertips from one end to the other.

"You want to tell me what that was about?" he asked.

Kristen dunked the paintbrush into the paint again and attacked the lower half of the sign. "Not especially."

A low sound escaped him, half laugh and half frustrated growl. "I figured as much." The whisper of paint strokes moved between them. "You know, Sadie might be young, but she's intelligent and mature for her age. Living with my sister . . ." His boot moved as he shifted his weight from one leg to the other. "Well, I imagine she became overly sensitive to what was occurring around her. Had to because she never knew what mood her mother would be in at any given moment." He hesitated, then said, "Carrie was an addict."

Kristen froze, the burning sensation pricking at her eyes traveling lower to constrict her chest. She'd never felt smaller or more insensitive in all her life.

"I didn't mean to hurt her." She set the paintbrush

down and looked up at him from beneath the brim of her hat. "But I could see I did, and I'm truly sorry for that."

He nodded slowly, his blue eyes roving over her face. "Have you been around kids much? Younger brothers or sisters maybe?"

Kristen grabbed the paintbrush and started painting again.

The sign slipped to one side of her lap, and Mitch nudged it back. "Do you have family waiting on you back in Cook County? Parents or—"

"No." She dragged the brush harder, paint speckling her jeans. "There's no one. You?"

"It's just me back in New York. Did you grow up in Cook County?"

Desperate to escape the hot seat, she dropped the paintbrush and met his eyes. "Are you going to take them?"

He blinked, his brow furrowing. "Take what?"

"The kids. Sadie and Dylan," she clarified. "If you're so sure this farm is going under and you're that concerned about their welfare, are you planning to take them home with you?"

His face flushed, and he moved his legs, shifting his balance again. "For a little while, once I talk Emmy around, but not permanently."

"Why not?"

His mouth opened soundlessly, and he shook his head. "I'm not equipped to raise two kids right now. My apartment is too small, my work hours are too long, and I wouldn't be able to give them the undivided attention they deserve."

"So you're going to take a chance on their finding a better home?" A foster home, maybe? Or even a children's home, like the one she grew up in, where she wished and dreamed someone would come for her, only to walk out alone years later? "Without Emmy?"

He twisted the blade of grass around his finger, and his fingertip turned red. "Anything stable would be better than here."

"How would you know that for sure?"

He raised a brow and returned her stare. "What makes you so certain it wouldn't?"

A screen door slammed, and Emmy reemerged onto the porch, the cane she leaned on tapping against the steps as she walked toward them and Sadie and Dylan trailing behind with cups of sweet tea. "Before my knee gives out for the day, I'd like to show Kristen the field she's gonna be responsible for. Y'all feel like taking a short ride?"

Mitch tossed away the blade of grass, and Kristen heaved the sign off her lap, and then both of them stood at almost the same instant.

Kristen bit back a smile. It was hard to tell which one of them was more eager to change the subject.

"I'll drive," Mitch said, heading for the truck. "Which field?"

"The one Lee's going to wrestle away from Ruth Ann for us."

Mitch sighed. "You heard him say that was a long shot."

Emmy smiled. "And you heard him say he was gonna try anyway. Have faith, Mitch. Now, bring that truck around."

The seven-minute drive to the back of Emmy's extensive property passed in silence except for the occasional squeak of shifting gears and the acceleration of the engine. The whir of the air conditioner, the sporadic rock of the cab as the tires dipped over potholes, and the glare of the setting sun's rays streaking across the horizon had the kids leaning their cheeks against the cool windows, struggling to stay awake. Kristen sat between them, her head lolling against the headrest on more than one occasion.

"Stop right here."

Her eyes sprang open at Emmy's command, and Mitch drew the truck to a gentle halt. They all climbed out. Mitch lowered the tailgate, and Dylan helped his sister climb onto it, then joined her, settling beside her and swinging his legs.

"Stay put," Emmy said. "We'll be back shortly."

Kristen fell in step at Emmy's side while Mitch led them off the dirt road to the field. He glanced back several times, his somber gaze watching Emmy's slow movements, then lingering on Kristen's as she maneuvered between ridges of soil.

The day was slipping away, the sunlight thinning to sharp lines that glared over the thick tree line. It lengthened the shadows between the neatly plowed rows of red soil, which stretched as far as her eyes could discern. A hawk, which she'd glimpsed often around the area, drifted in slow circles over the field as the evening breeze approached.

Kristen inhaled, the faint scent of honeysuckle tickling her nose and the clean air filling her lungs.

"What do you think, Kristen?" Emmy asked.

"It's big. Twenty acres, you said?"

"Eight hundred, seventy-one thousand, and two hundred square feet, to be precise." Emmy smiled. "Or roughly twenty football fields minus the end zones. That's how Joe liked to put it."

Mitch stopped between rows, sat on his haunches, and scooped up a handful of red dirt. Clumps of damp clay fell off the sides of his palm as he squeezed it gently, looking into the distance.

"How 'bout it, Mitch?" Emmy asked.

He uncurled his fist and shook his hand, watching the red clumps fall back to the ground, then stood. "It's still too wet. Needs at least two more days of sun before it's ready, and that's only if you manage by some miracle to get ahold of this land." He walked back toward the truck, calling out over his shoulder, "It's late, the kids are tired, and I imagine Kristen is, too. We need to head back to the house soon."

Kristen watched him reach the truck and hop onto the tailgate with the kids; then she turned back to the field, tracing the path of the sun's thin rays as they strolled across the red earth.

"What do you see?"

Kristen glanced at Emmy. Her blue eyes, measuring and weighing, stared back at her. "I'm sorry?"

"I said, what do you see?"

Shoving her hands into her pockets, Kristen rocked back on her heels. "Dirt. Lots of it."

Emmy grunted. "You can do better than that." She reached out, tugged Kristen's hand from her pocket and, leaning heavily on her cane, pulled her to a squatting position. "Here." She placed Kristen's hand on the ground, then pressed her palm tight to the soil. "What do you feel?"

A frustrated laugh broke past Kristen's lips. "Dirt. Why? Am I supposed to feel something different?"

Emmy gave her a sharp look, her mouth thinning into a tight line. "That's not for me to say."

Kristen sighed, looked down at the red ground beneath her hand and softened her tone. “Soil.” She curled her fingers around a loose pile of earth. “Moist and cool.”

“Lean into it,” Emmy said, then nodded as Kristen did so. “What’s below?”

Kristen stared, the red dirt blurring in front of her. The feel and smell of the earth against her skin was the same as it had been the day she’d sprinkled it onto Anna’s grave and said good-bye for the last time. Something broke deep within her. Widened into a gaping hole.

Don’t cry, Mama.

“Nothing.” Kristen blinked hard and tried to steady her voice. “It’s dark and empty.”

So dark and so empty, her chest ached to sink into it, and her limbs longed to curl in on themselves and absorb the black stillness. To grasp deep for something no longer within her reach.

“Hollow,” she whispered.

Emmy struggled to her feet.

Kristen cupped her elbow, helped her rise, and stayed by her side. They looked on as dusk enveloped the land, smearing the sky with lavender, gold, and pink. With a cry, the circling hawk changed course and floated off toward the trees. The air cooled; the damp field darkened beneath the cloak of approaching night; then the rhythmic chirps of crickets and frogs emerged, pulsing all around them.

“A hollow,” Emmy said, “is just another place for something new to grow.”

New York, an exciting project and an abundance of opportunities to nurture and stretch creativity? Or backbreaking work, endless squabbles with Emmy, and a slow erosion into obscurity?

Mitch grabbed a sledgehammer, positioned a steel signpost anchor by the edge of the farm's driveway, and hammered it hard. It cut through the grass and into the ground. He hit it several more times to secure it, then tossed the sledgehammer down and dragged his hands over his face.

The answer to his dilemma should be simple. A person would have to be insane to choose the latter. But there was nothing simple about this instance. Not when he factored in Sadie and Dylan.

"Are you ready for this?" Kristen stood by Emmy's truck, which she'd parked nearby, sliding a long wooden pole from the bed and over the tailgate. "I brought the sign, too."

Then there was Kristen to consider. Where she fit into all of this, he wasn't quite sure, but her questions yesterday had stayed with him all night, making him toss and turn. And had left him questioning whether leaving this afternoon, without Emmy's goodwill or a solid plan for Sadie and Dylan, was the right thing to do.

"Yeah." Mitch waited as she carried the pole toward the anchor—knowing better than to offer help—then strode over and lifted the sign from the truck bed. He hesitated. The eye-catching whirls of green vines surrounding large red strawberries on the sign caught his attention. "This is good." He studied it more closely, his gaze tracing the intricate design. Impressive work, especially in such a small window of time. "Better than good."

After visiting the field yesterday, they'd eaten dinner; then Emmy had gotten the kids settled in bed, while he and Kristen had cleaned the kitchen. Kristen had slipped off when they'd finished, saying she needed to finish the sign. She'd looked exhausted, dark circles stamped beneath her eyes, but there'd been a note of determination in her voice, so he hadn't argued. He hadn't seen her again until this morning, when she'd come down for breakfast and offered to help him wash the rest of the buckets, then hang the sign.

"You did all this last night?" he asked.

She nodded, a strand of blond hair escaping her ponytail, gleaming beneath the morning sunlight, as she dug around for metal mounts in a toolbox on the ground. "There was a portable fan on the porch, which I used to dry it faster. Hope that was okay."

"Of course." He waved a hand. "But this . . . all of this last night, you say?"

"Yeah. Emmy wanted it dry and ready to put up before you left and before we headed to the meeting this afternoon. I promised I'd finish it, so I finished it."

"Just like that?"

Her shapely arms stilled, and she raised a brow at him from her bent position. "Yeah. Just like that." Shrugging, she grabbed a hammer and stood. "It's no big deal. I just slapped some paint on it."

"Believe me, slapping some paint on it would not turn out like this for most people."

She turned away. The hat he'd given her obscured her eyes, leaving him staring at the smooth curve of her cheek and the graceful line of her neck . . . *again.*

He carried the sign over. "Have you done this type of thing before?"

She crouched by the pole, positioned one mount, then hammered in a nail.

He waited until she had finished securing the other three mounts, then asked, "Painting professionally, I mean?"

She dropped the hammer, lifted the pole, and slid it into place on the anchor.

He gritted his teeth as she grabbed the drill and squatted. "What did you do before you started working farms? Did you—"

The high-pitched spit of the drill cut off his question and echoed across the grounds and the empty highway in front of them. She cocked her head and narrowed her eyes up at him as she finished securing the pole.

After kneeling beside her, he placed the sign on the ground, holding her stare. She proceeded to ignore him, of course, and continued to drill away. Her toned biceps flexed with each push of the drill as she leaned forward for a better angle. The action tugged the hem of her shirt loose, exposing a creamy expanse of flesh above the waistband of her jeans and drawing his attention to the smooth curve of her backside.

Clearing his throat, he jerked his eyes away and refocused on her face. It was the damnedest thing—this pull she had on him. Not just the way her body tempted him, stirring a latent hunger within him, making his blood rush. But the piercing way she looked into him, those green eyes delving deep beneath his skin, plundering his thoughts and emotions but sharing none of her own.

She finished securing the last mount, cut the drill off, then tossed it aside. The tight-lipped look she tossed in his direction—the exact opposite of the welcoming smile she'd flashed at Lee yesterday—made his jaw clench.

That was another aggravation to add to the list. Irrational jealousy.

He shook his head. "You are the most . . ." *Elusive? Intriguing?* "Frustrating woman I've ever met."

"*I'm* frustrating?" After pressing her hands to the ground, she swiveled around and faced him. "What about you?"

"What about me?"

"I feel like I'm being given the third degree every time you show up." She frowned. "Why is it you always throw a thousand questions at me?"

"Maybe because I want to get to know you better."

"You know my name. You know I'm working for Emmy. What more is there to know?"

"A lot. Maybe I find you interesting."

"Oh, okay." Her mouth twisted. "Shoulda known. The most standard line in the book of men. Got any more?"

"And maybe," he added, "I find you attractive." He studied her balled fists on the ground, the lithe strength in her graceful frame and the passionate spark of her eyes. "No . . . Scratch that. You're the most beautiful woman I've ever seen up close." He grinned. "Except for Heather Andrews, maybe."

She stayed silent, her gaze drifting toward his mouth, then asked, "Heather Andrews?"

His grin grew. "She was five years older than me and knew algebra like the back of her hand. Had long red hair, told the best jokes, and gave the softest kisses on earth." He laughed. "I know only because I finagled a seat beside her on the school bus every day. I had the biggest damn crush, and she must've known, because on the last day of her senior year, she kissed me good-bye right here." He tapped his left cheek. "I was thirteen and felt it for days."

Smiling, Kristen sat back on her heels and scratched her chin. "Hmm." Her fingertips left behind a smudge of dirt. "As beautiful as Heather Andrews, huh?"

"Well, you've got her beat in the mystery department." He reached out and rubbed her chin clean with the pad of his thumb. "As for the kiss," he said, focusing on the gentle bow of her lower lip, "I can't say how that'd compare without firsthand experience."

Though, if the pleasurable tingles dancing over his skin were any indication, he'd bet his last dime he'd feel Kristen's kiss for a lot longer. And in a whole lot more places as a thirty-two-year-old man.

"But"—noting her blush, he lowered his hand—"to be fair to Heather, I'd also have to take into account the way you constantly assume the worst about me." He looked away, striving for a wounded tone. "How you always turn your back on me. Drill right over me when I'm talking."

She laughed. "Okay, okay. I won't turn my back on you anymore, and I won't—" Her chest lifted on a swift breath when he faced her, and her attention returned to his mouth. "I won't drill over you while you're talking."

He smiled and held out a hand. "Shake on it?"

She put her hand in his, allowed him to pull them both to their feet, then said, "Yes. I've done it before."

"Done what?"

The tip of her tongue swept over her bottom lip before she answered. "Painted." She motioned toward the sign. "Professionally, I mean."

He studied her expression. "When did—"

Brakes squeaked as a small sedan slowed on the highway, then turned and stopped in the entrance of the driveway behind him. A voice called out from the open window, "Mitch, do you have a moment?"

Ruth Ann. He silenced a groan. It figured that the second he made an inch of progress with Kristen, he'd be deterred.

"Excuse me." He smoothed his thumb over Kristen's soft skin once more before reluctantly releasing her hand and walking over to the car. "I always have time for you, Mrs. Ruth Ann."

"Thank you." Ruth Ann got out, nudged her sunglasses farther up her nose, and glanced over his shoulder. "Good afternoon, Kristen." After Kristen returned the greeting, Ruth Ann returned her attention to Mitch. "I hope I'm not interrupting anything."

"No, ma'am." Mitch gestured toward the sign still lying on the ground. "We're just putting up a sign for Emmy."

Her mouth pursed. "Strawberries?"

He nodded.

Sighing, Ruth Ann removed her sunglasses and snapped them closed. Her eyes were red rimmed and puffy. "I came to apologize to you for my behavior Saturday. It was silly, rude, and entirely inappropriate. I'm very sorry it happened. I stayed in church an extra hour yesterday, praying, but I didn't feel any better about it. I understand if you think less of me."

Mitch smiled and squeezed her shoulder. "Don't give it another thought." A wry laugh escaped him. "Emmy has a way of bringing out the best in all of us."

Ruth Ann patted his hand, then looked down. "But it was my fault for overreacting. And in front of the children . . ." She closed her eyes and shook her head. "I felt awful about it. Just awful."

"Oh, I think your pound cake went a long way toward consoling Sadie, and Dylan got a good laugh for the day. Matter of fact, that was the first real smile I've seen on his face in months." He released her and stepped back. "Like I said, don't worry about it."

Ruth Ann looked up, a small smile forming. "You have always had a big heart, Mitch. As big as Joe's, I think." She tapped a polished nail against the rim of her sunglasses. "Which is why, for your sake and Joe's," she stressed, "I've agreed with Lee to allow Emmy to rent the twenty acres."

He drew his head back, an uncomfortable ache spreading through his chest. "I wasn't lying when I said this farm is on its last leg, Mrs. Ruth Ann. Giving Emmy that lot of land won't do anything but prolong her problems. That bypass will be paved no matter what she does."

She nodded, a look of resignation crossing her features. "I told Lee that's how you'd feel about it. But I also told him I didn't want Emmy going around declaring I was the reason for her downfall."

Ruth Ann glanced over his shoulder again, and he followed her line of sight, watching as Kristen, who'd moved out of earshot, began attaching two hooks to the pole.

"Plus, Emmy's not the only one working this land now," Ruth Ann continued. "It wouldn't be right for me to take away an opportunity for someone else based on how I feel about Emmy."

"The two of them alone won't be able to make a go of it," he said. "Not with two kids to take care of and a house falling down around their ears. Emmy's not as spry as she used to be."

And she was getting worse by the day. He'd seen her limp more often than not throughout the weekend, her moods were growing more unpredictable, and she'd called Sadie Carrie on more than one occasion since he'd arrived.

Those things taken individually might not have bothered him too much, but taken as a whole . . .

"I'm worried about her," Mitch said, wincing when he realized he'd voiced the thought aloud.

"As any good grandson should." A suspicious wetness lined Ruth Ann's lashes. She put her sunglasses on. "Emmy is lucky to have you."

She turned and headed toward her car.

"My grandpa's been gone for over thirty years now, Mrs. Ruth Ann," Mitch said. "And when this farm goes under, Emmy is gonna need a friend. Do you think you could find a way to forgive her?"

Ruth Ann stopped, then asked quietly, "Can you?"

He stiffened. "I don't know what you mean."

"Don't you?" She looked over her shoulder, her expression unreadable behind the thick sunglasses. "Emmy and I were as close as sisters for years. We were family by choice if not by blood. When I realized we'd both fallen in love with Joe, I decided not to pursue him and asked her to do the same for the sake of our friendship. Sounds selfish and stupid, and it was. But I was young, Joe was my first love, and Emmy, for all intents and purposes, was my sister. I loved Joe enough to know that I couldn't be around him and Emmy together and not hurt. And I didn't want her to go through that if Joe looked my way instead of hers. Our friendship was more important. I told her all of that, but she threw me over instead. Just tossed me away for the love of a man." A sound of dismay left her lips. "That hurt far more than losing Joe ever did."

"I don't see how that has anything to do with me," Mitch said gently.

"The way I see it, Emmy did the same to you, didn't she? Worse, even." Her voice softened. "Your father was a troubled man, Mitch. Everyone could see that, even Joe. He loved his son every bit as much as Emmy did, but he was willing to admit David had problems, whereas Emmy wasn't. Had Joe still been alive, things would've been very different for you and Carrie growing up." She lifted her chin. "Emmy had a choice. David was a troubled man. You were an innocent boy. Who deserved her love more?"

Mitch thrust his hands into his pockets and swallowed past the thick lump in his throat. "It wasn't that simple."

"No. Neither is forgiveness, no matter what those delightful childhood fables tell us. Which might be why I haven't heard you say you're staying to console Emmy when she fails." She tilted her head. "Or have you changed your mind?"

When he didn't answer, Ruth Ann thanked him for seeing her, said her good-byes and left.

Mitch watched her drive away, her tires stirring up a red cloud of dust, which drifted over the field. The ground was drying rapidly, the sun shone bright, and it wouldn't be long before the soil would be ready for planting. He looked up the red driveway toward the house, where he imagined Emmy had already begun gathering her things for the afternoon meeting in neighboring Peach Grove, favoring her good knee and urging the kids to get ready. Sadie would be all smiles, but Dylan would probably give her a hard time.

He glanced over his shoulder.

Kristen had finished attaching the hooks and had added two small chains. She hung the sign, straightened it, then stepped back and looked it over. A hesitant smile, similar to the one she'd sported the night he'd met her, slowly appeared.

Before he could rethink it, Mitch pulled his cell phone from his pocket, dialed a New York number, and waited for Brad to answer.

CHAPTER 5

"And that's where the Andrews used to live." Kristen eased her foot off the pedal and slowed the truck around a curve, glancing toward the single-story house Emmy pointed at from the passenger seat. "As in Heather Andrews?"

Emmy's brows rose. "Thought you weren't from around here. How do you know the Andrews family?"

"Oh, I don't." Kristen's mouth twitched as she refocused on the sedan traveling in front of them. "I think Mitch might have mentioned the name earlier today."

Roughly an hour ago, in fact. Right after he'd told her she was the most beautiful woman he'd ever seen up close. Then he'd smoothed his rough thumb over her chin in a tender caress that still lingered. A smoldering look of hunger had darkened his blue eyes when he'd studied her mouth, and she could swear she still felt his warm, husky whisper sweeping over her skin.

As for the kiss, I can't say how that'd compare without firsthand experience.

Cheeks scorching, Kristen rolled her lips to stop the mouth twitch from stretching into a full-blown smile. Had it all been just a line? Possibly. But the man sure could deliver one. Either way, she really hadn't cared right then. Just so long as that slow, delicious tingle in her middle—one that hadn't emerged in what seemed like forever—hung around a bit longer.

And there was a good chance it would, seeing as how Mitch had decided to stay. For a little while at least. Though she wasn't altogether sure that would be a good thing.

Sunlight glinted off the back bumper of the sedan as Mitch eased it to the left to avoid a pothole. Kristen followed his lead.

Earlier, after hanging the sign by the driveway, she'd climbed back in Emmy's truck and waited for Mitch to finish a phone call. He had joined her shortly, then had driven them back to the house, asking along the way if she minded following him into town in Emmy's truck. He said he had spoken to a colleague and had taken an extended vacation from work, which meant he needed to return the rental car to a local dealership this afternoon. She'd agreed. After they made it inside, Mitch had informed Emmy that he planned to stay for a little while and had asked whether she minded if he attended the county meeting with her.

To say Emmy had been overjoyed would be an understatement. And she was still on cloud nine as they drove to the dealership.

"Glory be, it's a miracle." Emmy clapped her hands together and chuckled, almost bouncing in her seat. "I still can't believe Mitch changed his mind and decided to stay. Oh, it'll be like old times. I'll have a chance to talk to him again. Really talk. And we'll have help, Kristen. Lots of it. Mitch has always had the magic touch when it comes to planting. He takes after Joe in that respect. And we can—"

"He's only staying through the summer," Dylan grumbled from the backseat. "It's not for good."

Kristen glanced in the rearview mirror. Dylan, still grieving the loss of his cell phone, scowled out the window at the passing scenery. Sadie, who had yet to make eye contact with Kristen since yesterday's incident, brushed a pink comb through her doll's hair silently.

"Aw, fiddlesticks." Emmy shrugged. "He'll change his mind once he gets settled back in. I'll make him feel right at home again." She tossed a look over her shoulder at Dylan. "We'll have family dinners and evening chats on the porch." She smiled at Kristen. "You'll see. It'll be great having Mitch around. Fun. Cozy."

Not too cozy. Kristen shifted in her seat, braking at a traffic light. Or cozy at all, for that matter. The very last thing she needed to do was become embroiled in Mitch's drama with Emmy. She was here to work, not flirt with a handsome, charismatic man who was related to her boss.

Or . . . hurt a tenderhearted little girl with her selfish emotional outbursts.

A wave of remorse rolled through her as she glanced at Sadie again. She'd lost at least two hours of sleep last night replaying the unpleasant incident and felt more and more like a heel. It would not, she'd promised herself, happen again. Regardless of the circumstances.

And what had occurred with Mitch this afternoon was a slip—albeit a big one—but one she didn't plan on allowing to happen again, either. Not wanting to be rude, she'd agreed to be civil to Mitch, even friendly. But that was it. No more talks of attraction or whispers of comparing kisses, and no more slow, delicious tingles—especially considering he slept in a bed right across the hall from hers.

Kristen frowned, the thought of his tanned, muscular limbs entangled with hers, his dark blue eyes smoldering down at her with hunger, and his calloused palms sweeping tender caresses over her skin shooting a wave of heat through her middle.

Oh, gracious. Get ahold of yourself, girl. She blew out a slow breath. It was necessary to keep her distance. But, if she was being honest with herself, it was a downright shame, too.

"Something wrong?" Emmy peered at her.

"No." She tightened her hands around the steering wheel and accelerated when the light turned green. "Just taking in the view."

And that wasn't altogether a lie. The small town of Peach Grove bustled much more than Kristen had anticipated for such a rural area. It was after five, and a steady rush of cars, trucks, and large tractor trailers poured down each side of the narrow two-lane road.

"Well, allow me to show you the highlights," Emmy said. "That right there"—she pointed to a cluster of small brick buildings with colorful cloth awnings on the left—"is the hottest shopping strip in town. The makings of a perfect Saturday are to be had there. You start at the Dutch Restaurant and Bakery. People come from miles around for their blueberry and cream cheese sweet rolls. Then you skip next door to Essie's Odds and Ends and browse the antiques for a hefty flowerpot. Now, I don't care for babble mouth Bertha's salon in the middle—she gabs more than she cuts—but a lot of people do. Then you round it off with a stop at Jake's Hardware, pick out some hot pink petunias, take 'em home, plant 'em, then kick back on the porch and wait for the hummingbirds to come dance around."

Kristen grinned. "Do you do that often?"

"Once every June to break in the summer." Her smile slipped and she grew quiet before saying, "Only there's one store missing." She nodded toward the other side of the road. "Used to be Joe's older sister ran a one-stop shop over yonder, behind the ice cream parlor. Inherited it from her parents."

An abandoned building slumped in the back of an empty parking lot overrun with weeds. The only remaining brick wall still standing had a faded soft drink emblem on it and ragged window frames housing jagged shards of broken glass. Several piles of broken bricks and blocks of concrete stood haphazardly around it, and a young boy—*around Dylan's age maybe?*—circled the debris on a skateboard.

"Cindy Sue had just about anything a body could want in that store," Emmy said, her voice shaking. "Groceries, toys, a bit of this and that. She sold her crafts there, too. Had wind chimes, pottery, and the most beautiful birdhouses I've ever seen. Made 'em out of gourds Joe grew and gave to her." She turned her head and strained for another glimpse of the ruins through the back windshield. "Cindy Sue was a great neighbor. Gave several families free groceries during tough winters, when they had to choose between food and heat. And she was a good sister-in-law and an even better friend to me. That was decades ago, though. She had a heart attack at thirty-nine. Never saw forty." Her voice broke, and she sniffed. "Store closed down, and that was that."

"I'm sorry," Kristen whispered.

Emmy faced the road again and gazed sightlessly at the traffic ahead. A tear seeped out of the corner of her eye and rolled down her wrinkled cheek.

Chest constricting, Kristen said, "I remember seeing a gourd rack on your farm when I first arrived. By the driveway, I think. Do you use it anymore?"

Emmy didn't answer. Just kept staring. A second tear joined the first and settled in the corner of her mouth.

"Emmy?" Kristen followed Mitch's sedan into a turning lane and flipped on her left blinker when his started flashing. "I asked if you still use the gourd rack at the farm."

No response.

When the traffic cleared, Mitch turned into a dealership parking lot, and after making sure the road was still clear, Kristen did the same.

"Emmy, are you oka—"

A transfer truck barreled around the sharp curve and laid on the horn, forcing her to slam on her brakes.

Emmy latched on to her arm as the abrupt stop jerked them all forward. "Oh, careful. People drive like their hair's on fire nowadays, and it's gotten worse lately."

The large semi tore by well above the speed limit, missing them by inches, the whoosh of air in its wake rocking Emmy's truck. Pulling in a deep breath, Kristen checked that the kids were still safely strapped in the backseat, steadied her shaky hands around the steering wheel, then completed the turn.

Emmy scrubbed her cheeks and sat up straight. "Did you ask me something earlier?"

The sad note in her tone was gone, a slight thread of confusion having taken its place.

"Yes." Kristen carefully parked beside Mitch, watching as he walked over with powerful strides. "The gourd rack. I asked if you still use it."

"Nah." Emmy unbuckled her seat belt. "I got no idea where Joe's gourd patch is. That was his place, you know. We both had our own quiet spots to think things over. Besides, it's probably grown over and useless now. Was nice when he had them, though. Those purple martins loved 'em, and the birds kept the pests down, too."

Mitch opened Kristen's door before she had a chance to, and his eyes raked over her, Emmy, and the kids. "Y'all all right?"

Emmy waved a hand and shoved her own door open. "Yep. Some lunatic tried to run us over, but we're fine."

Mitch looked Kristen over again, his intense gaze stirring warm flutters that spread throughout her body. "Sure?"

She nodded and swung her legs out. "We're good."

His big hand engulfed hers, and he assisted her as she slid down. Then he opened the back door and helped Sadie climb out. The gentle grip of his long fingers left behind a strong, comforting sensation, which Kristen savored longer than she should have.

"I'll run in, give Jeff the keys, and then we'll head to the community center," Mitch said, heading for the front entrance.

"Wait. We'll come with you." Emmy grinned at Dylan. "You got that flyer I asked you to make?"

Dylan didn't crack a smile but held up a piece of paper. There was a picture of a huge strawberry in the middle with an advertisement to "pick your own" at Hart's Hollow Farm.

Emmy's smile widened. "Oh, that looks perfect.

Lead the way, Mitch. Think you can talk that friend of yours into doing you one more favor?"

Mitch frowned. "Jeff's already doing me a plenty big one by getting that car back to Atlanta. What do you need?"

"Fifty color copies of this flyer run off on that fancy doodad of his."

"What for?"

"To slap up around town, of course," Emmy huffed. "Can't get customers out to the farm if we don't invite 'em. Kristen, grab one of those buckets of strawberries out of the truck bed and, Dylan, put on your best smile. We're gonna make an exchange and get some free advertisement while we're at it."

Mitch shook his head, and Dylan looked put out, but everyone did as they were asked. It took only a few minutes for Emmy to sweet-talk Jeff, the dealership's energetic and cheery owner, into making copies of the flyer in exchange for the strawberries. Shortly thereafter, they left the dealership, drove to the community center, and walked inside.

"They've redone the place," Mitch said, hovering on the threshold of the conference room and glancing around. "New screen and projector. Tables, chairs."

New beige carpet, too. Kristen breathed in a lungful of the fresh fiber smell, the low hum of idle conversation and the cool air filling the wide space making her limbs sluggish.

"Ah, Mitch," a deep voice boomed. A tall, robust man, dressed in a suit and standing in a small group by a large mahogany table, walked over, hand outstretched. "Good to see you. I heard you'd dropped in for a visit."

"A long visit," Emmy clarified, giving a satisfied smile as Mitch shook the man's hand. "He's staying."

"Oh?"

"Yeah. Just for the summer," Mitch explained. "Took a leave of absence and had a lot of vacation time I decided to use up." He stepped to the side and ushered Kristen forward. "Charles, I'd like you to meet Kristen Daniels. She's helping out at Hart's Hollow."

"Nice to meet you, Kristen." He shook her hand. "I'm Charles Holt. An old friend and former classmate of Mitch's."

Kristen smiled. "Good to meet y—"

"Mitch!" A brunette with a pretty grin, who appeared to be around Kristen's age, rushed over and hugged Mitch. "This is a surprise. I didn't expect to see you around here again until at least Christmas. How's life in New York? Still designing those fancy high-rises?"

High-rises? Kristen studied Mitch's broad frame with fresh eyes. The dark pants and white dress shirt he'd donned in place of his sweaty jeans and T-shirt looked boardroom ready, even without a tie. His strong hands—*those of an architect?*—hung steady and sure by his sides, and his demeanor had altered slightly since they entered the community center. He seemed more formal. Reserved.

Mitch smiled, stepping back as the young woman released him. "I'm getting by. Kristen, meet Iris Jackson. She's another former classmate and—"

"Troublemaker." Iris laughed. "Mitch always covered for me when I misbehaved in Mrs. Landrum's class." She gave Kristen a once-over, then said, "I thought I heard someone new had settled in at Hart's Hollow. Are you Mrs. Emmy's new hire?"

"Yes," Kristen said.

"Oh, that's great. It's always nice to have someone new join the Adams County fold. If you decide you need a break from the farm, look me up. Peach Grove might be small, but there's plenty of fun to be had if you know where to look." Iris leaned close and winked. "And I can give you all the juicy dirt on Mitch."

Kristen avoided Mitch's eyes. "Thank you, but I don't know that this will be a permanent position."

"Well, look who it is."

Thankful for the distraction, Kristen moved aside as another man greeted Mitch. The small group began to reminisce. Before long, they were chatting and laughing in jovial tones, like most of the other people in the room. And, like most of the others, they were all dressed formally save for two other couples around Emmy's age and a young woman who was flipping through a thick notebook.

Kristen tugged her T-shirt down lower over her worn jeans, smoothed a hand awkwardly over her ponytail, then inched across the room to the kids. For the first time in a long time, she found herself wishing she had more clothing in her bags than standard outdoor-work wear. And she was equally uncomfortable with the idea of being pulled into the Adams County fold, as Iris had put it. The community was obviously close-knit and full of entanglements, which she didn't need.

"Good evening, everyone." A woman moved to the front of the room and smiled. "I'm Dana Markham, a consultant with the Georgia Department of Transportation, and I'll be leading Adams County's first Citizens Advisory Committee meeting tonight." She spread her arms toward the table. "It's about that time, so if you'll all have a seat, we'll get started."

Kristen looked at Dylan, who glanced at the doors

behind them, a look of mournful resignation in his eyes, which she had to fight herself not to return.

"Dylan, there's room on the bench in the back if you and Sadie would like to sit with my son," Charles said. "You and Zach are in the same grade at school, aren't you?"

Dylan cast a quick frown at Charles's son, who looked just as enthusiastic to be there as he did, a skateboard propped against his shins. Then he presented to the older man a polite—if strained—smile. "Yes, sir. Come on, Sadie."

The kids sat on the bench, and Emmy and Mitch headed for the packed table. All the wide leather chairs surrounding the table, except for two, were taken or reserved with purses or stacks of paper, which people moved before sitting.

Kristen turned and walked toward the door.

"Kristen." Her steps slowed as Mitch's low voice sounded behind her. "Where are you going?"

She whispered over her shoulder, "There isn't room, and I'm not a member of the committee, so I thought I'd wait outside."

"Oh no." His hand curled loosely around her upper arm. The tangy scent of his aftershave teased her senses as he leaned close. "You're in this, right?"

Heart tripping, she stopped and faced him. His charismatic demeanor affected her more than she had expected, and she stumbled, her breasts brushing his chest, as she turned. The masculine heat radiating from his sculpted length beckoned her to press against him and nuzzle her cheek against the smooth skin at the base of his throat.

"I-I'm in what?"

His gaze drifted over her mouth, then down to her

chest. Lean cheeks flushing, he glanced around, released her arm slowly, then stepped back. "You're in on this plan to save Hart's Hollow with Emmy," he prompted quietly. "As in, according to you, my word and ill-fated predictions aren't gospel, remember?"

"But this is a county meeting," she whispered. "I'm not a permanent resident, so I shouldn't be here. And"—she lifted her chin toward the packed table—"there isn't room."

"We'll find room." He cupped her elbow, the rough pads of his fingers sliding over her skin, sending frissons of pleasure through her that were even more tempting than she'd imagined. "I'll make a place for you, Kristen."

His words were soft—so soft she barely heard them. But she did, and the unspoken possibilities she imagined behind them . . .

The hopes and dreams she'd let go of long ago, which she caught herself searching for in his voice . . .

Kristen spun toward the exit. "I'm just gonna slip out."

The double doors thudded shut before she could take a step. The woman who'd welcomed the group earlier smiled, released the doorknobs, then returned to the front of the table and said, "Lights, please."

Darkness engulfed the room as the ceiling projector clicked on and beamed a colorful image of Peach Grove's welcome sign onto the wide screen.

Mitch lowered his head, his warm lips brushing Kristen's ear and a smile in his voice. "Too late now."

Getting two hardheaded people to agree had been a feat in itself, but getting fifteen Adams County residents with conflicting agendas to budge an inch toward a compromise had proven to be more than Dana Markham could handle.

"If you could all please just quiet down for a moment, I can better explain." Dana leaned over the packed table and waved her hands in the air, an expression of something akin to despair crossing her delicate features.

Mitch took in the angry red faces and frustrated postures of those seated around him. Most he recognized—Al and Stephanie Jenkins, owners of a cattle operation and several acres near Hart's Hollow Farm, local mechanic Terrance Smith, and Peach Grove Elementary teacher Elena Martinez were all familiar faces. As was Peach Grove's mayor, Bud Watson, who sat beside Charles and Iris.

"Now, I'm just not going along with anything other than our original plan." Bud sat back in his seat and crossed his arms over his generous belly. "The residents of Peach Grove want a bypass, and I'm here to see that they get it."

"That's not true." Terrance stabbed the table with a blunt fingertip. "This resident doesn't. The majority of my customers are ones driving through town on long commutes, looking for quick fixes to their vehicles along the way. I can't count how many tires I've replaced on semis. They're my biggest business."

"And our worst nightmare, Terrance." Elena tucked a dark curl behind her ear, eyes narrowing. "Do you have any idea how many close calls we've had during the school year? Those trucks are too big for these small roads—especially on stretches by our bus stops. A five-year-old child is easily overlooked on a sharp curve from the limited vantage point those drivers have." She shook her head. "It's not worth the risk."

"Not to mention the increase we've had in noise

and car accidents," Charles said. "Within the past six months alone, wrecks have tripled at the corner of Main Street and Canterbury Lane." He motioned toward Mitch. "You just blew back into town, Mitch. What do you think? Traffic gotten worse since you were last here?"

No doubt. Had it not been for Kristen's quick reflexes earlier, that damn transfer truck would've run her, Emmy, and the kids right over.

Mitch dragged a hand over the back of his neck and glanced at Emmy. She sat beside him, blue eyes narrowed up at him. Kristen sat on the other side of Emmy, her hands curling over the armrests of the chair he'd borrowed for her from a neighboring room, her gaze apprehensive.

As a matter of fact, traffic wasn't the only thing that had gotten worse—so had Emmy and her defiant refusal to face reality. He'd been back in town for only a weekend and in this meeting for half an hour, but it was clear the majority of Adams County residents disagreed with Emmy in regard to the bypass. And he was beginning to regret his decision not to return to New York. Staying for an extended summer would only encourage her, and at the moment, he had no clue what he'd hoped to accomplish by calling Brad as he had on the spur of the moment. What in the world had he been thinking?

"Well . . . I can't say it's gotten any better." Mitch blew out a heavy sigh as Emmy stared him down. "One of those semis you mentioned almost took Emmy's truck out on the way in."

Emmy glared. "Now, that was just one of those things. Happens from time to time when you drive."

"That may be so." Mitch frowned. "But if it hadn't been for Kristen's quick response, things would've turned out very differently. Traffic has gotten a lot worse during my last visits, Emmy. I won't downplay that to help you win an argument."

Emmy's angry stare bored into Mitch. He dragged a hand through his hair, his neck tingling under her scrutiny.

"There." Charles nodded. "You see?"

"So what y'all are saying is that we reroute all that trouble through people's backyards?" Al asked. "Chop down trees kids climb? Bulldoze through herds of cattle? Pave over streams and unblemished land?"

"Nothing that dramatic, but something has to be done." Charles's voice rose. "The roads in Peach Grove have become congested to the point that traffic is a danger to pedestrians and drivers alike. And with the new cyber security facility expanding in Augusta, just thirty miles up the highway, through traffic is only going to increase. Are we supposed to just sit by and watch it get worse? We're talking about people's welfare and quality of life here, Al."

"So am I, but I'm also talking about conservation," Al said. "Those woods you're proposing we mow down are home to deer, foxes, turkeys, rabbits, squirrels, you name it. Rural communities like ours are some of the few places where people can still enjoy nature unspoiled in their backyards. And those trees aren't just shelter for wildlife. They produce the oxygen that fills your lungs." Chin trembling, Al reached out and covered his wife's hand with his own. "I'm talking about people's welfare and quality of life, too. Stephanie and I have raised cattle on my family's land for years. It's our livelihood. I was born in the same house we raised my kids in. Our neighbors just received the Centennial Family Farm Award, which means their farm has been in their line for over one hundred years, and their land is on the map to be paved. You want to be the one to take their heritage from them?"

Charles sighed. "Our intention is not to take anything away from anyone, but we have to face the fact that things have changed. We have too many small farms going more and more into debt every year, using up land that could be utilized in other ways to better serve our communities and economy. Corporate farms have been successful in neighboring counties, and there's talk of vertical farming and even autonomous farms being possibilities. Adams County will never grow or attract new business if we don't expand. It's time to face that reality and initiate improvements. We're just looking to the future. Progressing."

"By throwing out the old and bringing in the new, huh?" Emmy asked.

Mitch tensed.

"You've forgotten something, though," Emmy continued, locking eyes with Charles. "Our farms may be small, but together, they make a difference." She looked at Al. "Those barbecue ribs they serve at the Dutch Restaurant, where do they come from?"

"My cattle," Al said, pride in his eyes.

"And the blueberries they use for the sweet rolls?" Emmy asked, glancing at the other end of the table. "Where do they get those?"

"My mother's land." A young woman, around nineteen or twenty, lifted her chin. Bright lights from the projector glinted off moisture in her brown eyes. "Well, mine now. Me and my sister are scheduled to deliver another load next week."

Mitch studied her familiar features. "Are you Susan Yarrow's daughter? Jenny?"

She nodded. "Mama passed away last year, so it's

just me and Nancy running the place now. Nancy has one more year of high school before she'll be able to work full-time. I just have to keep the place afloat for this year and the next. Then things will get better." Voice shaking, she sniffed and squared her shoulders. "The crops are good so far, and if we get to keep our land, we're gonna make it."

"Of course you are," Emmy said, voice husky. "You're a strong woman and a dang good farmer, Jenny. Your mama would be proud." She glanced around at each person sitting at the table. "Now, I ain't here to stir up trouble or hold the county back from progress. But I'm old enough and stubborn enough to have earned my say. All I'm asking is that you think about what that asphalt will be cutting through if the bypass is built. It'll cut through woods, creeks, and crops. Peaceful land. And the soil . . ." She spread her hands. "That soil is a bridge between our past and our future. It holds our history, artifacts, and fossils. I mean, they've found pieces of prehistoric pottery in a cornfield up in North Georgia. Who knows what's waiting to be found here? It ain't a big stretch to think Adams County has treasures of its own."

Her elbow brushed Mitch's arm as she turned and met Kristen's eyes.

"That soil is a bridge between death and life," Emmy continued softly. Her voice shook as Kristen ducked her head, her teeth nibbling her lower lip. "If done right, when one crop fades, what's left behind helps the next one grow. There's comfort to be found there. I never feel closer to my sweet Joe than when I'm standing in a field full of healthy fresh growth."

"Me too," Jenny added. Her chin trembled. "It

might sound stupid, but the fields are the only place Nancy and I still feel close to our parents."

Emmy smiled gently. "When we plant, that soil carries water and nutrients to roots. It gives birth to new life. Bears sweet corn and fresh fruit to fill bellies for miles around. Over the next twenty years or so, the world's population is supposed to increase by over two billion people. There'll be over nine billion to feed with less farmland available than we have now. Who's gonna feed all those people? And how? Solely through vertical or autonomous farming?" She faced Mitch, her cheeks flushed, gray hair curling at her temples, and eyes pleading. "When we talk about paving over small farms, we're talking about breaking the backbone of our families. Of our communities. And even beyond. All I'm asking is for us to hear Mrs. Markham out and think it over. Give those of us who want one a chance."

Mitch stilled and glanced at Sadie and Dylan. They both stared back, Dylan with a guarded expression and Sadie with wide-eyed innocence, clutching her doll. Lord, he wished it were all that simple—just an easy choice between family and business. Right and wrong. Good and bad. But the problem was, in tiny Adams County and on Hart's Hollow Farm, those lines had a tendency to blur, and no matter what was decided, one side would lose.

"Please," Emmy said.

The desperation in her voice sent a fresh wave of guilt through him.

"We all appreciate and value the concerns and sentiments you express, Emmy," Charles said quietly. "We've all mourned our neighbors' losses and will continue to do so. But emotion and a handful of Adams County farms won't solve the problem."

"Then why don't we do as Emmy suggests and hear Mrs. Markham out? Get another perspective?" Kristen's thick lashes lifted, a spark of determination in those gorgeous green eyes and firm resolve in her tone. "You did say that the Department of Transportation was still considering two options and that a decision hasn't been made yet, right?"

Shoulders sagging with relief, Dana nodded. "Yes, thank you. That's what I've been trying to get across for some time. Lights, please." She picked up a stack of papers, waited until the overhead lights blinked on, then straightened. "We've conducted surveys throughout Adams County over the course of several months—many of which you've participated in. We studied those results closely and were able to identify the most pressing concerns citizens have so far, as presented to you in the slideshow. You were chosen to join this committee in order to represent those concerns. There are many parties involved in this project. Some consultants, like myself, represent environmental considerations and public involvement, while some are focused on engineering issues and costs. But the goal for all of us is to find a solution that will address as many of your concerns as possible. One that is financially feasible and will most benefit the community as a whole."

She lifted the stack of papers higher. "I've compiled a packet for each of you. In it, you'll find two plans. We ask that between now and our next meeting, you take a look at them, think them over, and discuss them with neighbors who share concerns similar to yours."

Mitch sat back as Dana handed the papers to him, and then he took one packet and passed the rest to Emmy. For the next several minutes, only the rustle of papers, the creaks of chairs, and random sighs filled the room.

"So the second option you're proposing," Mitch said, closing his packet and glancing at Dana, "is widening the highway to four lanes through Peach Grove and adding roundabouts on each end of town."

"That's the gist of it." Dana motioned toward Elena. "Roundabouts are tremendously useful in slowing traffic, which should curtail the high speeds of trucks through downtown." She directed her gaze to Terrance. "But this approach will still bring the same amount of through traffic, which will, in turn, bring added clientele to local businesses."

Bud tossed his packet on the table and shook his head. "And it will still leave the problems of congestion, dangers to pedestrians, and noise levels generally unresolved."

Dana inclined her head. "That is a valid point, and one the Department of Transportation is still carefully weighing."

"But our land would be safe." Emmy smiled, hope lifting her features.

A sense of dread seeped into Mitch's chest. He shifted closer to her side and placed a hand on her forearm. "Emmy, this is just a second option and not necessarily the approach that will be taken."

"From what you know, Dana," Iris said, leaning forward, "would you say the Department of Transportation is still more inclined to choose the bypass?"

Dana hesitated, her gaze skittering over the faces around the table. "Yes. For the moment, the bypass is the favored option."

Charles, Bud, and Elena eased back in their seats with satisfied nods. Emmy's smile faded.

"We'll meet again on the first of July to gather final input from the committee, and the Department of Transportation will announce a decision shortly thereafter." Dana smiled. "We thank you for attending tonight and look forward to seeing you again at the next meeting."

The meeting officially adjourned, and everyone gathered their belongings, then lingered around the room, chatting in groups and casting guarded glances at others. Mitch helped Emmy stand and get her bearings.

"Well, that was promising," Emmy declared, grinning and beckoning Sadie and Dylan over.

Mitch scoffed. "Which part, Emmy?"

"All of it. At least they're throwing something other than a bypass in the mix now."

"Emmy . . ." A frustrated breath left him, and he rolled his shoulders before continuing. "You saw how opposed the mayor is to the new suggestion, and you heard Dana say the bypass was still the favored option."

"So?" Emmy shrugged. "It can fall out of favor just as fast. Especially once we dig into planting." She frowned up at him. "Clouds were high and dry today, and winds were blowing in. Kristen's field should be ready with one more day of sun, yeah?"

"I suppose, but—"

"Then that's settled," she said. "We'll plan on Kristen planting her corn Wednesday, and once she gets the hang of it, she and I'll split up and tackle the rest of the fields. We'll have a couple months of nurturing, and then we'll harvest quality crops so we can plead a better case at the next meeting."

Mitch bit his tongue and turned away. Good Lord,

the stubborn woman had no idea what she was up against.

"Can we go now?" Dylan asked, trudging up.

Sadie skipped behind him, clutching her doll to her chest.

"Nope. We got flyers to hang and strawberries to pass out." Emmy ruffled Dylan's hair, then took Sadie's hand and walked to the door, announcing along the way, "Anyone interested in some fresh strawberries is welcome to swing by my truck on the way out. I brought a free bucketful for every member of the committee."

Bud's eyes narrowed. "Are you trying to bribe us, Mrs. Emmy?"

"Nah. Just thought your wife might like a sweet batch for the shortcake she makes. It's about that time of year, ain't it?"

Bud returned Emmy's stare, his mouth twitching, as he rubbed his belly, and then he slowly followed her to the door. "I suppose I can't argue with you on that. Highlight of my day is a good dessert." He paused on the threshold. "But that's got nothing to do with my decision on this bypass."

"Of course it doesn't," Emmy chided. "I'm just giving you a taste of what Hart's Hollow Farm has to offer nowadays."

She left, and the others soon followed. Mitch moved to the window and watched the group gather around Emmy's truck. Dylan climbed in the bed and passed out buckets. Emmy's smile grew wider with each thank-you.

Shaking his head, Mitch shoved his hands in his pockets. Why in hell had he let a few choice words from Ruth Ann shame him into staying? Why hadn't he just left when he had the chance? All any of this would do—including his staying—would be to encourage Emmy's hopes, then intensify her misery over the unavoidable outcome.

"What a mess," he whispered. "What a depressing, dead-end mess."

Something soft brushed his elbow, and a light, sweet fragrance drifted near.

"Not necessarily." Kristen had joined him by the window and had adopted the same pose. "Nothing is ever certain." A thread of pain laced her quiet tone.

Her gaze was fixed on the activity outside, but he couldn't tear his attention away from the shadows dimming her bright eyes or the sad tilt of her lush mouth.

His palms ached to cradle her face, and his lips tingled with the need to drift light kisses along her smooth forehead and flushed cheeks. He longed to coax the soft corners of her pink lips up and hear her fleeting, cheerful laugh again. Taste the sweetness of her mouth with his own.

All of this reminded Mitch of exactly why he'd chosen to stay.

CHAPTER 6

"So, what do you think?"

Kristen tipped her head back farther and took in the large tractor in front of her. The soft early morning sunlight barely peeked above the flat land in front of them, casting a hazy glow through the clear windows of the spacious cab and highlighting the deep green body and yellow trim. Enormous black tires—eight of them maybe?—supported the massive piece of machinery and raised it high off the ground, and she'd have to climb five steps to reach the driver's seat.

"What do I think?" Kristen shook her head and whistled low. "It's a beast."

A deep chuckle sounded at her back, and cheeks warming, she spun and faced Mitch. He stood a few feet away, propping his fists on his lean, jean-clad hips as he looked up at Lee's tractor. The action raised his chin, exposing the strong column of his throat, and stretched his blue T-shirt across the ropy bulk of his shoulders and chest.

"A beast, huh?" His voice was still husky with the

lingering effects of sleep, but his eyes brightened when he glanced at her. He smiled wider and dragged a hand through his hair, tousling the dark waves. "It looks that mean to you?"

Uh-uh. Her eyes clung to the sensual curves of his sculpted mouth. *More like tender, charming, and . . . sexy.*

Belly tightening deliciously, Kristen jerked her cap lower on her forehead and cleared her throat. Dear sweet heaven, the man was pure sin. "Not mean, exactly."

She rolled her shoulders, glancing at Emmy and the kids, who stood nearby. Emmy grinned back at her. Sadie rubbed her eyes as she leaned against Emmy's leg. Dylan sat on the grass, raised his knees, and propped his chin on them, seemingly uninterested and unimpressed. As usual.

"It's just . . . intimidating," Kristen added.

After the meeting on Monday night, they'd posted the strawberry flyers around town and returned home. Yesterday Kristen had picked strawberries and filled buckets for the strawberry stand with Emmy and the kids, while Mitch had finalized negotiations with Lee to rent the tractor, then had driven it back to Hart's Hollow.

"You've never driven one before?" Mitch asked.

"No." Seizing the distraction, she moved closer to the tractor and gripped the edge of one of the large tires. "Nothing like this. The Perrys used only old-school equipment. Simple, low to the ground. Mr. Perry preferred to do the field work himself, and they weren't big on new technology."

"Neither was I," Emmy said, walking to Kristen's side. "But once Lee showed me what this thing could do, I changed my mind pretty fast. This bad girl can even drive herself if you ask. People act like self-driving vehicles are something special, but we've had that technology on farms for years." She placed her foot on the tractor's bottom step, reached up toward the handgrips, then frowned at Kristen. "Think you can give me a boost?"

"Oh, no." Mitch strode over, cupped Emmy's elbow and eased her back. "I don't want you straining your knee climbing in and out of that thing."

Emmy scowled. "I have to. At least for today. Someone's gotta show Kristen how this thing works, so she can do it herself. Then I can get started on the other fields in our tractor. We got to have two tractors in the fields in order to get the corn and soybeans planted within the next two weeks."

"Why two weeks?" Mitch swept his muscular arm out toward the farm's back lots. "Kristen will start with her field, I'll help her with the other cornfields, and then we'll start soybeans around mid-May, like you usually do."

"I told you before, I got a new plan. I'm shifting gears and going with early production to up my yields. And to pull it off, I have to get that indeterminate seed in the ground by the end of April."

"That's not a plan, Emmy. That's a gamble. There are too many variables and risks with early planting. You'll be harvesting the soybeans at the same time heavy rains usually tear through here. You'll have only a ten-day to two-week window to harvest. Plus, you have to worry about stinkbugs, root-knot nematodes, extra monitoring . . ." He issued a sound of frustration. "Why don't you just stick to the status quo? Do what you've always done? Especially since this is the last season you'll—"

Regret in every line of his expression, he bit his lip and looked away. His eyes met Kristen's.

"The last season I'll what?" Emmy's jaw hardened as she glared at Mitch. "Plant? Harvest? Or own this farm?"

Kristen touched Emmy's arm. "Emmy, you told me yourself that Mitch has the magic touch out here. He's giving us the heads-up on things to watch out for, but it's nothing we can't handle." She raised her brows at Mitch. "He's just trying to help. Right?"

Mitch sighed, then glanced hesitantly at Sadie and Dylan before saying, "I'm sorry, okay, Emmy? But I'm only being honest. You want me to lie to you?"

"Nope. I want you to tell me the plan's amazing—and my plan *is* amazing."

"It's risky."

"Amazing," Emmy repeated. "And thirty years ago, when you were my sweet, handsome little boy, you'd have believed it, too." A teasing light entered her eyes as she faced Kristen. "Why, when he was just a toddler, he'd stride out to the fields right after me. Chest out, shoulders proud, and diaper swishing. I could tell he was gonna be a heartbreaker even then."

Mitch tipped his head back, closed his eyes, and groaned. "Good Lord."

Kristen rolled her lips, stifling a smile.

Snickering, Dylan lifted his head, the second real hint of amusement Kristen had seen shining in his expression. "That right, Uncle Mitch? Diaper and all?"

Mitch opened his eyes, narrowed them at Dylan, then stalked off toward the back of the tractor. "All right. I'll show Kristen how to work the tractor, while you handle the strawberry stand. When we finish, I'll start on the rest of the fields with the other tractor." He pointed at Dylan. "Up and over here. You're gonna help load the planter."

Dylan's smile fell. "Why me?"

"For that crack earlier. And because I'd like your company." Mitch headed for the shed behind them. "Come on."

Emmy turned to Kristen and grinned. "Think I ticked him off?"

Kristen studied the tight set of Mitch's broad shoulders as he walked toward the shed. He glanced back at them, and his handsome face flushed a deeper shade of red.

"Yeah," she whispered, a laugh escaping her. "Embarrassed him, too, I think."

"Good." Emmy nodded, then called out toward his retreating back, "And he can just get happy in the same britches he got mad in, 'cuz this is gonna work." She patted Kristen's arm. "Bring him in for lunch. Ready to head back to the house, Sadie?"

Sadie hovered, wide awake now, watching Mitch and Dylan heft large seed bags out of the shed, her big blue eyes following their every move. Her shoulders slumped, and her heart-shaped mouth drooped. "Yes, ma'am."

Just go about your business, a small voice whispered inside Kristen. *No need to get involved.*

Maybe. But she could be kind, couldn't she? Could include the little girl just this once to make up for hurting her the other day. What harm could it do?

"Sadie?" Kristen picked at the hem of her jeans, then licked her lips. "Would you like to help us for a little while before you sell strawberries? The bags are too heavy for you to lift like Dylan, but I'm sure there's something else you can do."

Sadie blinked up at her, nibbling at her lips with a guarded expression.

"Of course there is." Mitch tossed a bulky seed bag on the grass and lifted his chin at Sadie. "We'll need someone to pull the bags off the hoppers after they've emptied. Make sure all the seeds made it in. You'd be perfect for the job."

A broad smile broke out across Sadie's face. One last quick glance up at Kristen, then she bounded toward Mitch, her long brown hair rippling out behind her.

Mitch's gorgeous eyes lifted and met Kristen's. He watched her for a moment, then mouthed, "Thank you," and grinned. His warm, approving gaze teased a smile from her in return.

And that alone made getting involved, just this once, more than worth it.

Over the next hour, Mitch, Dylan, and Kristen hitched up the planter—a wide green and black frame with twelve yellow buckets and two large tanks—and dumped opened seed bags in each hopper as Sadie pulled the empty bags away, and then Mitch and Kristen filled the tanks with liquid fertilizer. When that was complete, they took a step back to catch their breath.

The sun had cleared the horizon, its rays beaming across the bare fields in the distance, drying the dew on the grass beneath their feet and seeping past Kristen's clothes to heat her skin. Sweat trickled down her back, and a gnat stung the corner of her eye. She batted it away, then wiped the droplets of sweat from her upper lip with the scooped collar of her shirt.

"Good man, Dylan. You did a great job. Mind taking Sadie back to the house for me?" Mitch ruffled Dylan's hair, then squatted and hugged Sadie. "What a big help you were, sweet Sadie."

Beaming, Sadie wrapped her small arms around his neck, kissed his cheek, and skipped to Dylan's side. "Thanks, Uncle Mitch."

"Think I could drive the tractor some?" Dylan asked.

"Not this one," Mitch said. "Tomorrow, once I get Emmy's tractor ready, you can give it a whirl."

Dylan nodded, something that looked very similar to excitement lighting his eyes. "Okay. Come on, Sadie."

They left, Sadie clutching Dylan's hand and humming.

"Time to hit the field." Mitch blotted his flushed face with the tail of his T-shirt, flashing the toned expanse of his sculpted abs and a small sprinkling of dark hair that arrowed down toward his lean, jean-clad hips.

Skin heating even more, Kristen spun around and walked to the tractor's steps.

"Hold up."

She stopped, one foot on the bottom step.

"You're gonna need this." He stopped, grabbed an empty seed bag, and held it up. "Lee's seeds and fields are different, and he just added a new receiver, so you're going to have to reconfigure the equipment. Take a look and tell me how many seeds per pound."

He tossed the bag to her, and she caught it, then turned it over a time or two until she found the information. "One thousand, six hundred and ninety-five." A gnat tickled the corner of her mouth. She puffed out a breath to dislodge it. "What do we need that for?"

He smiled. "To set the vacuum."

"Vacuum?"

"Yep. For pulling the seed." He walked over and motioned for her to precede him up the steps. "Tear that bit off, chuck the bag, and I'll show you a thing or two."

A thing or two turned out to be about a thousand things. After they sat in each of the two leather seats inside the air-conditioned cab, Kristen in the driver's position and Mitch by her side, there was a receiver and modem that needed attention, and two small monitors and one tablet mounted by Kristen's seat. Information had to be entered, and measurements calculated, then confirmed once more outside the tractor with a measuring tape. Accuracy was critical.

"So the planter will know when to start and stop planting when it's supposed to," Mitch explained.

The GPS and maps had to be cleared and reset, and displays on the monitors had to be rechecked to ensure each field of data populated correctly.

"All right." Mitch motioned toward a large panel with an assortment of buttons. "Let's fire up the seed units and give 'em a turn or two."

After being walked through another brief review of all the buttons' functions, Kristen pressed one to turn the seed units, then jumped as a series of loud beeps filled the cab.

Mitch laughed. "Easy. It's only doing what you asked it to." He reached out, and his strong fingers moved over one of the monitor's touch screens. "One measurement's a bit off. Let's work on that again."

After making more adjustments to the equipment, Mitch led her through the steps to fold up the planter and put the tractor in transport mode. "When we get to your field, I'll show you how to make sure the planter's level. For now, let's take a ride." He gestured toward the dirt driveway on the right. "You remember how to get there from here?"

Kristen hesitated, her hands tightening around the steering wheel. "Yeah, but you trust me with this thing? Maybe you should get us there first, so I don't . . . I don't know . . ." She glanced at the wide road winding around Emmy's front lawn and cringed. "Hit Emmy's house."

His deep chuckle reverberated in the cab. "You chickening out on me?"

"Heck no." Grinning despite her racked nerves, she sat up straighter and moved the transmission knob forward. "I got this. You just sit back and enjoy the ride."

He laughed harder, leaned back, and crossed his arms behind his head. "Well, hell. That I can handle."

Maybe it was his suggestive tone and the devilish gleam in his eyes. Or maybe it was the bulge of his biceps; his strong, sprawling frame; and his spicy masculine scent. Whatever it was, it kicked her heart rate up a notch, set her cheeks aflame, and had her laughing just as hard.

A little while later, they arrived at Kristen's field—safely and without bulldozing Emmy's house, *thank the Lord*—and Mitch reviewed several steps before they lowered and unfolded the planter and turned on the seed units again.

"Let's hop out and check the planter," Mitch said.

She followed Mitch's lead. As he demonstrated ways to ensure the planter was level, she tore her eyes from his jeans, which clung in an appealing way to his attractive backside and, instead, listened carefully.

"You need to make sure seeds are coming out of all twelve exit points at the right angle," he said. "If you don't have uniform seed depth, emergence and height will be affected, which means lower yields." He shook his head. "And this year, Emmy's betting her bottom dollar on what comes out of this ground."

After they returned to the cab, Mitch set up a few auto features in order for the tractor to take over most of the work. Then Kristen sucked in a deep breath, focused on the empty field in front of her, and reminded herself of how important it was to succeed.

"Too much at once?"

She glanced at Mitch, whose expression was patient and kind, and shook her head. "No. I just want to get this right for Emmy."

"Well"—Mitch stretched across her toward the controls—"in that case, you forgot the most important part."

He pressed a button, and static emerged from the cab's speakers. A few movements of Mitch's long fingers over the controls and a steady beat filled the cab.

"Country?" She laughed. "Is that a prerequisite for planting a field?"

"Nope." He stretched an arm along her seat's headrest, his boyish grin stirring warmth low in her belly. "I'm all for vibrant, hard-hitting rock at the end of the ride. But to start off right, you gotta inject a bit of soulful guitar into the air." He tapped his chest with a fist. "It feeds the soul and the seed."

It wasn't hard to imagine Mitch as a charismatic

young man, energetic and adventurous, working and exploring the farm. Or even driving a date to an empty field lit up with stars, turning on the music, and flashing that charming smile.

"Did you ever sneak out here and rock out when you were young?" she teased.

His grin slipped, and his voice faded to a low murmur as he replied, "Once upon a time. When I was able to."

She watched him closely. His previous lighthearted tone had disappeared, and his expression was closed. It was the same look he'd had when he'd confronted her about agreeing with Emmy and taking the job.

This farm may be precious to Emmy, but it's been nothing but mud and blood for me.

A cold shiver crept over her damp skin. It had been obvious since he'd arrived that he was still struggling with the loss of his sister. Her lips twisted. She was acquainted well enough with grief to pick up on that. But other than his brief comment about Carrie's addiction the other day, he'd given no details about his family history or his childhood here. What had happened to make him hate the farm so?

She longed to lean against him, settle her cheek on his chest, and ask him to unload his burden. Share his secrets.

But . . . that would also mean sharing her own.

Seeking to shift the mood, she cleared her throat and tapped the steering wheel with her fingertips. "Was this one of the fields you, uh . . . streaked across as a toddler?"

A burst of laughter left his lips, and his lean cheeks flushed. "Really? After all the hard work I've put in showing you how to run this thing, that's the thanks I get?" He cocked an eyebrow at her and looked at the top of her head. "Careful. You might offend me to the point that I reclaim my hat."

"Oh, I don't think I'd go along with that." She tapped the hat down firmly on her head. "I've grown kinda attached to it."

His smile widened, and she returned it, holding his gaze for a few moments before facing the field and easing the tractor forward.

Over the next few hours of planting, the wind picked up, sweeping over the red soil in waves, stirring up clouds of dust, which billowed out behind them and sparkled in the bright sun. Wispy clouds drifted high above them in a wide blue sky. Green trees in the distance bent and swayed almost in time to the soothing music, and the rhythmic bounces of the tractor had her leaning back against the welcoming strength of Mitch's outstretched arm on more than one occasion.

It was almost as if the land itself was in tune with them, lifting and lowering with their breaths, lulling them into a tranquil silence of contemplation.

Once upon a time . . .

Kristen smiled as she recalled Mitch's words, drinking in the beauty surrounding her and breathing in the slight aroma of honeysuckle and freshly turned earth trickling through the air vents into the cab. At the moment, Hart's Hollow did feel magical. As though, at one time, it might have been sturdy and spacious enough to hold any dream that could be imagined, and to offer the promise of it coming true. Or at least to make it seem within reach.

She swiveled her seat around to check the planter through the window and watched with drowsy eyes as it moved along behind them. Something tickled her neck, and she could almost swear she felt Mitch's big hand glide lightly over her hair, his long fingers brushing through the strands. But when she turned around and smiled at him, he just nodded, complimented her, then resumed staring somberly at the land ahead.

Two weeks of checking fields, loading planters, and driving tractors across hundreds of acres for fourteen-hour stretches under an increasingly scorching sun and in stifling air could wilt the best of men. But Kristen wasn't a man.

Mitch eased back in his chair at the kitchen table, looked across at her and smiled. The bright sparkle in her green eyes, her cute freckled cheeks and her excited smile awakened every inch of his body. No. She was a strong, tenacious woman who'd thrived taking on the daily battles of grit and grime. And now she was fresh from the shower, scrubbed clean, damp hair curling sexily around that luscious mouth and smelling sweet, and it was damn near all he could do not to ease around the table and beg for a little of her attention.

"And this one." Kristen pointed a slim finger at one of the photos Emmy had scattered over the table, between emptied supper plates. "Is that Joe?"

Emmy, seated beside Kristen, shifted Sadie in her lap and leaned closer. "Yep. That's my Joe, all right. He's on the same tractor Dylan drove last week." She picked the photo up and held it out across the table. "See, Mitch? It was bright and shiny at one time."

He took the picture and studied it. The focus was off and the edges were worn, but the blue frame of the tractor and Joe's young, smiling face were clear. "How old was Joe in this one?"

"Hmm . . ." Emmy's brow wrinkled. "Around his midthirties, I think." She toyed with her napkin, twisting it between her fingers. "Was during the eighties when we got that tractor brand new. Joe was proud. He loved that tractor."

Dylan leaned over in his seat, bumping Mitch's arm, and looked at the photo, too. "He looks like you, Uncle Mitch."

"Yeah." Mitch examined the blue eyes and the wide smile staring back at him, the sincerity in Joe's expression a far cry from the hateful sneer and bleary gaze his own father had sported. "Guess I do favor him some."

"Some?" Emmy smiled. "You're the spitting image. Just as handsome and just as strong." She reached across the table, her smile slipping, and squeezed his forearm. "And just as giving. Thank you for all you've done these past days, Mitch. We never would've gotten all that seed in the ground without you."

He dropped the photo back on the table, patted her hand, then gently tugged his arm free. "It was the least I could do." He spread his hands toward the dinner dishes, which still housed leftovers of grilled pork chops, fried okra, and sliced tomatoes. "Supper was delicious, as usual. If I'm going to eat your food and sleep under your roof, I ought to be putting myself to work."

The lift of her happy expression fell. "You're entitled to those things. This is your home, too, Mitch."

Ah, hell. If he could physically manage it, he'd kick himself in the butt for his thoughtless words. But . . . he couldn't force his tongue to move in agreement. Hart's Hollow had never really been a home for him. It'd been a stark, barren place, with fear and pain saturating every square inch of mud. No matter how much he hated hurting Emmy's feelings, he couldn't find a way around that sad fact.

Lately, he'd disappointed her on a routine basis. Every day last week, after he'd finished in the fields, Emmy had met him at the front door, hooked her arm through his, and ushered him inside to reminisce over piles of old pictures stored in shoeboxes under her bed. He'd hoped she would spend the time he freed up for her resting or, at most, selling strawberries at a leisurely pace. But there had been no strawberry customers, and she'd kept busy working in her garden, cleaning house, and cooking two, if not three, big meals every day.

And every day, her eager greeting had dimmed a bit more at his obvious lack of enthusiasm for painful memories he'd rather ignore.

Mitch waved a hand toward the opposite side of the table. "Wasn't just me doing all the work. Kristen worked as hard, if not harder, than I did." He met Kristen's eyes and savored the pink rising in her cheeks and her shy smile before gripping Dylan's shoulder. "And Dylan. He knocked out two fields last week. Showed me up more than once with the way he wielded that tractor around with dead-on precision."

That had been more of a surprise than Mitch wanted to admit. Not that he didn't think Dylan capable of hard work and attention to fine detail, but he hadn't expected the unsolicited sweaty high fives at the end of the workday. Or anticipated the steady growth of pride and self-assurance in Dylan's stride each evening, as they'd trekked from the fields to the house with the sun setting at their backs.

No. That had been more than a pleasant surprise.

"Wish spring break wasn't over." Dylan slumped

back in his chair and thumped his half-empty glass of tea. "I could've stayed home this week and done the big fields by the road with you instead of going to school."

Emmy's smile resurfaced. "I'm proud of you, Dylan. You've done a great job. You like working the farm, huh?"

Dropping his head to the side, Dylan shrugged. "It's all right."

"Better than a cell phone?" Mitch asked.

Dylan sprang upright again and shook his head. "No way. Can I have it back?"

"Well, let's see." Mitch rubbed his chin. "What do you think, Kristen?"

She looked up, holding another photograph, as Dylan glanced her way and stiffened. "I'd say . . ." That gorgeous grin of hers emerged, dimples and all. "I'd say he's earned it."

Dylan spun back to face him, thrust his hand out and smiled.

Hemming and hawing, Mitch crossed his arms behind his head. "Gimme a minute, all right? I might grab it for you after my stomach settles. After all that planting, I'll need the extra rest to regain my strength."

"Aw, man." Dylan slumped back in his chair, but the smile stayed. "Whatever. When do you think we'll see the crops come up?"

"Kristen's corn should be showing right about now," Mitch said, glancing her way.

"This soon?" Kristen leaned forward, rubbing the pads of her fingers together. "Could we take a look?"

He dragged his eyes away from the sexy tilt of her pink lips and nodded. "Tomorrow good enough? It's too late to head out there tonight."

And strolling around a starlit field with Kristen would only conjure up a million other indecent ways he'd rather spend the next couple of hours with her. Those were thoughts a gentleman had no business pondering.

"Will you wait till we get out of school tomorrow?" Dylan asked. "I want to go, too."

"Me too." Sadie scooted forward on Emmy's lap and bounced excitedly. "Can I go with them, Nana?"

"Oh, heavens," Emmy groaned, stilling Sadie's movements. "Course you can, angel. We'll all go. But you got to jump back in your chair now. My knee's had about all it can take."

Smiling, Sadie slid off of Emmy's lap and walked toward the kitchen. "Can I help you put up the dishes?"

"Sure." Emmy braced her palms on the table and winced as she struggled to rise.

"Oh, let me, Emmy." Kristen stood, gathered up several dirty dishes, then placed them in the sink. The window above it was open, and the steady chirps of crickets drifted in on the cool breeze, along with the soft rumble of thunder in the distance. "Where's the dishwashing liquid?"

Emmy gave a grateful smile and pointed at a cabinet. "Bottom shelf."

Mitch eyed the white lines by Kristen's pinched mouth, then nudged Dylan. "Help Kristen out with the dishes, please."

He nodded, collected the rest of the plates and joined Kristen and Sadie at the sink. Mitch watched them for a few minutes, noting how Dylan's smile lingered as he waited for Kristen to wash the first dish and hand it to him. When she did, her hands carefully dodging Dylan's, he glanced up at her and blushed.

"Thank you, Ms. Kristen," he whispered. "You know, for the phone."

Her blond curls slid across her slim back as she turned and whispered back, "You're welcome."

Mitch smiled, glancing at Sadie, who hovered by the fridge, staring at Kristen. Her curious gaze clung to every movement of Kristen's hands; skimmed her tall, graceful frame; then drifted up to study her face. Sadie stepped toward her once, then danced in a circle and returned to lean against the fridge.

Mitch's mouth tightened, and a heavy feeling settled in his gut. Sadie was desperate for attention, love, and support. Not just the spring and summer kind, but a permanent, reliable presence that she wouldn't hesitate to embrace. To trust. Something she and Dylan had never experienced and had no hope of securing on this farm.

"Here." Emmy pushed a stack of pictures across the table. "Take a look at those. You've never seen this batch."

Reluctantly, Mitch glanced at the glossy photos, then sifted through them. There were several more of Joe, a few of Emmy, and one of him and Carrie. They were young—he couldn't have been more than nine at the time—and he was leaning against one of the oak trees in the front yard, while Carrie hung upside down from a low branch above, her long hair brushing his shoulders.

He touched his thumb to Carrie's smile, a pricking sensation hitting the back of his eyes. Lord, he could count on one hand the number of times he'd seen her smile like that, but he couldn't remember the particular day captured in the picture. He obviously hadn't shared that moment of joy, because his own expression in the photo was stiff—not angry, just . . . resigned.

"And here's one of me and Cindy Sue." Emmy shoved another colorful picture in his hand. "Oh, she'd be so proud of what a wonderful man you've become. I'm in one of my favorite dresses—wore it all the time when I was young and slim like Kristen. Cindy Sue helped me make it, you know. She was so good with her hands." She tapped the table and swiveled in Kristen's direction. "We'll have to swing by her shop soon, Kristen. I want to introduce you."

Mitch's fingers tightened around the picture.

Kristen glanced over her shoulder, head tilted. "Introduce me to who?"

"Cindy Sue." Emmy smoothed her napkin.

Kristen frowned. "But I thought . . ." Her voice trailed away, and she looked at Mitch, the realization in her eyes adding to the heavy pull of pain within him.

"Emmy." Mitch returned the photograph to the stack and watched the slow, repetitive movement of Emmy's hand. "Cindy Sue's shop isn't open anymore."

The movement stopped; then she patted the napkin. "Only on the weekend."

"No, Emmy." When he spoke again, Mitch softened his tone, his chest tightening at the confusion clouding her eyes. "It's not open at all. Hasn't been for years."

Emmy blinked. "No. No, it's not open."

She said the words, but a thread of uncertainty still lingered in her voice.

Mitch moved to stand. "Emmy—"

"No, don't get up." She pushed off the table and stood, leaning heavily on her chair and shaking her head. "Sounds like a bit of rain's heading this way. That's just what those seeds need, and it makes for good sleep. Seems I'm wore out tonight, and it's 'bout time I get these tired bones in bed, in case we have some strawberry customers tomorrow."

He stood anyway, then hesitated as Emmy waved Sadie over.

"Come on, Sadie girl. You need a good night's sleep to get up for school in the morning. We'll wash up, and I'll read to you till you drift off."

Smiling, Sadie darted over and hugged Emmy's waist.

Mitch moved toward them. "Emmy, I think we need to talk."

"Don't worry." She reached out and patted his cheek, her gaze tired but admiring as it drifted over his face. "My sweet Mitch is home. My strong, beautiful boy. I'm gonna sleep good tonight."

He stood still, arms hanging at his sides, as she and Sadie walked out of the kitchen and around the corner, out of sight.

Kristen's soft voice sounded at his back. "Dylan, why don't you head to bed, too? I can handle the rest of this."

Dylan's light tread moved across the creaky hardwood floor; then he hovered in the hall. "Can we still go with you to check Ms. Kristen's corn tomorrow?"

Forcing a smile, Mitch nodded. "Yeah. We'll wait till you and Sadie get home from school."

Dylan smiled, then left. The breeze from the window pushed at Mitch's back, and the sweet scent of Kristen's shampoo enveloped him as she drew near.

"You need some rest, too, Mitch. I can handle this."

He looked down at his side, and finding the sight

of her soft, warm hand too inviting to resist, he slipped his fingers between hers and squeezed. "Thank you."

She squeezed back once before sliding her hand free and stepping back. "You're welcome."

Mitch watched her return to the sink, dip her hands into the sudsy water, then scrub another dish. A drizzle began outside, small droplets of water pinging against the raised windowpane, and the sharp scent of rain filled the room.

An aching need for comfort, deep and searing, spread through his limbs, and he forced his feet to move away. "Good night, Kristen."

CHAPTER 7

"A little farther this way. Watch your step." Kristen smiled, adjusting her grip on Emmy's arm and moving her feet carefully across the loose clumps of soil beneath her.

Humid heat seeped through the dark cloth covering her eyes, and the tang of dirt and distant rain in the air touched her tongue as she licked her lips. A giggle bubbled up from her belly, and she closed her mouth, trapping the laughter in her throat.

Good grief. It was silly and ridiculous to get so excited over something so small. But she had to admit that ever since dinner last night, when Mitch had mentioned that her corn should be showing, she'd thought of little else. All day, while she and Mitch had serviced and cleaned Lee's tractor, she'd caught herself gazing over her shoulder toward her field, peering past the thick clouds on the horizon to see whether she could spot any signs of life from afar, knowing full well she wouldn't at that distance. Mitch had been forced to nudge her out of her reverie at least four times during the workday.

Emmy had seemed to pick up on that embarrassing fact. She'd tossed amused glances in Kristen's direction as she picked more strawberries and filled buckets, which, unfortunately, no one had come to buy yet. Then, after Sadie and Dylan had been dropped off by the bus and had come running up the driveway a half hour ago, Emmy had made a game of blindfolding Kristen before they all piled into the truck and drove to the field.

"It's not every day you get to see your first crop spring from the ground," Emmy had said. "It's special and should be treated as such."

"Now," Emmy announced, kneeling and then pulling Kristen to a squatting position. "Give me your hand."

Kristen complied, grateful for the confident note in Emmy's voice.

Despite last night's confusion, Emmy seemed more solid after a long night's sleep. She'd even slept an hour later than usual this morning, which Kristen could only assume should help matters.

She stilled, hearing Mitch's heavy footsteps behind her and feeling the towering heat of his presence above her. He'd looked so weighed down last night, after Emmy's confusion, his eyes heavy and his shoulders sagging. So much so, she'd been tempted to wrap her arms around him and pull him close.

But . . . that wasn't her place or concern. Though, increasingly, she had to force herself to remember that. She was here to work, and her focus should be on producing a healthy crop for Emmy—not on romantically entangling herself with Mitch. Nor should she be ruminating over Emmy's mental slips. It wasn't for her to say, but that was probably all last night's confusion had been. Emmy had overexerted herself and exhausted her mind. It happened to everyone on occasion.

Still, forcing herself to concentrate on the business side of the farm hadn't removed the unsettled feeling that had spread through her after Emmy's incident. Or diminished her desire to touch Mitch, whisper words of comfort and ease his mind. To offer strength and support for Emmy and the kids, too, however tiny or insignificant her help might be to them in the long run.

"What do you feel?" Emmy asked after pressing Kristen's hand toward the ground.

Kristen touched the soil, moist and warm beneath her fingertips. The brief rain showers of last night and this morning had loosened it. She drifted her hand farther across the flat ground, her stomach dropping at the absence of any obstruction, then jolting back up when a soft object brushed against her skin.

"Something small." Kristen curled her fingers gently around it. Her heart pounded hard, echoing in her head. "Flexible, fragile."

Emmy untied the blindfold at the back of Kristen's head and whispered in her ear, "New life."

The cloth fell away, and Kristen blinked, then focused on the tiny green seedling cradled against her palm. It was barely more than a sprig, less than four inches tall.

"This," Emmy continued, "is the cotyledon." She guided Kristen's pointer finger to the lowest part of the plant, where a tiny green stalklike leaf protruded from the ground. "It doesn't emerge very far, but it's the seed leaf, part of the embryo." Guiding Kristen's finger farther up the seedling, she stopped at the edge of one of the three small leaves. "See this rounded tip? That means this is the first leaf. And we call the place where it meets the sheath here a collar." Her tone softened. "It's at the V-two growth stage, just a baby still. When the collar shows up on the third leaf, it'll be at V-three."

"And when I see it on the fourth leaf," Kristen prompted, "it'll be V—"

"Four," Emmy said at the same time. "And so on, till you reach V-ten. After that, you'll start to see tassels, silk, then kernels." She smiled and cupped Kristen's elbow. "Now, help me up, please, and we'll take a look around."

Kristen did, glancing at Mitch and returning his warm smile, and then she slowly turned to take in the expansive field surrounding them. Rich red soil was the most visible element, but the delicate tips of thousands of corn seedlings danced in the breeze along perfectly formed parallel lines that met the horizon. The gray clouds, drifting low, sheltered them in a cool cocoon, providing a respite from the late afternoon heat.

"This would've made Joe so proud." Emmy slipped her hand in hers, a slight tremor running through it. "*You* would've made Joe proud, my dear girl."

A soothing sensation unfurled in Kristen and poured through her veins, filling a little of the emptiness inside her. She leaned closer to Emmy, the older woman's solid warmth and approving tone making her heart swell. Stirring a deep longing she'd buried with Anna.

What would it be like to have this? To start every day with someone at your side, standing on firm, stable ground where you felt like you belonged? To be a part of something bigger than you could ever become on your own?

"There are so many," Sadie shouted happily from the edge of the field, Dylan at her side.

"Yep," Mitch called back, a hint of pride in his voice. "Ms. Kristen's first crop. I think this calls for a celebration."

Kristen's skin heated, and that delicious tingle stirred in her belly.

"Can we go to town for some ice cream?" Dylan asked, smiling.

Sadie bounced in place. "Ice cream," she squealed. "Can we, Uncle Mitch?"

"Before supper?" Mitch made a concerned face. "I don't know."

"Oh, come on, Uncle Mitch," Dylan said. "It's Friday. We don't have school tomorrow. We can eat supper later."

Mitch smiled at Kristen, the teasing light in his eyes lifting the shadows from his expression and sending a renewed surge of pleasure through her. "What do you say, Kristen?"

She grinned. "I say, you can buy me two scoops."

The drive into town didn't take long, and the increasing clusters of storm clouds above provided a blanket of shade across the landscape. The cooler air prompted Kristen to ask Mitch to lower the windows. He did, and a swift breeze swirled through the cab, lifting Kristen's hair from her face and settling sweetly in her lungs. She turned her head and admired the passing scenery.

Wide ditches sprinkled with tall grass blurred by, and beyond that, every now and then, the distant hills would flatten and a field would emerge. One as big as hers. And as rich with potential.

Her smile grew.

"What kind of ice cream are you gonna get, Ms. Kristen?"

She glanced to her right, where Dylan smiled up at her. He sat in the middle of the backseat this time, between her and Sadie. Seemed her assistance in rescuing his cell phone had gone a long way in thawing his chill toward her.

"Oh, I don't know. What kinds do they have?"

"All kinds," Dylan said. "Chocolate, vanilla, rocky road, mint, bubble gum—"

"Bubble gum?" Kristen shuddered.

"Yeah. It's good. You pick out the big pieces, put 'em in a napkin, then chew them after you finish the ice cream." He clapped his hands. "Two treats in one."

Mitch laughed, meeting her eyes briefly in the rearview mirror. "It's an acquired taste. I used to love it as a kid."

"I might give it a whirl." Kristen leaned forward and glanced at Emmy, who sat in the front seat. "What kind will you get, Emmy?"

"Hmm?" Emmy raised her chin as they reached Peach Grove's city limits, straining for a better view. "It's up on the right. There's a big dip in the driveway, so go slow."

Mitch nodded. "I will, Emmy."

She tapped a finger in the air. "Take this next turn."

"Yes, ma'am," he murmured, returning Kristen's smile in the rearview mirror.

Mitch took the turn, eased the big truck over the rut in the driveway, then parked on the side of a small white building with THE SCOOP displayed in a playful pink font across the front veneer.

"All right," Mitch said, cutting the engine. "Let's get some ice cream."

They got out, and Sadie and Dylan led the way with excited skips to the front entrance. Kristen followed, surprised at how packed it was both inside and outside the small business. Several people sitting at booths could be seen through the windows, and more were seated outside, at high tables lining the front and sides of the shop, licking ice cream off cones, spooning sundaes, and chatting in small groups. The parking lot was full of cars and trucks, and a cheery tune trickled out of speakers attached to the building, putting a light spring in her step.

Mitch walked beside her. "What do you think? Place worth the trip?"

"For ice cream?" She laughed. "Always. Don't you think so, Emmy?"

Kristen's steps slowed at the lack of a response from Emmy, and Mitch stopped, then glanced behind them.

"Emmy?" he called. "What are you doing?"

She stood several feet behind, still by the truck, her back to them. Her posture was different. There was a rigid tilt to her sloping shoulders, and she had assumed a readied stance, with one foot forward and the other back.

Kristen stilled, her skin prickling. "Emmy?"

Mitch walked toward her, saying over his shoulder, "Hold up, kids."

A rhythmic pound and whoosh echoed across the parking lot. Two boys on skateboards sped out from behind the ice cream parlor, then circled back to the familiar ruins of a building. One jumped off his skateboard, grabbed a brick from a nearby pile, and threw it at the jagged remains of a window in the one wall still standing. The glass shattered, and broken shards crashed to the pavement.

Emmy raised her fists, her shouts echoing off the ice cream parlor.

"Oh, no," Kristen whispered.

By the time she reached the truck, Emmy was doing her best to edge around Mitch, who spoke to her in low, placating tones.

"Emmy, please—"

"They shouldn't be here," Emmy yelled, pacing and waving a fist at the boys. "You shouldn't be here!" She spun around, and her eyes widened at Kristen. "Look what they're doing to Cindy Sue's shop. Look!"

Stomach churning, Kristen glanced at the two kids. Oblivious to Emmy's shouts, one boy circled back on his skateboard, focused on the pavement in front of him. Emmy shoved past Mitch and limped toward him, then snagged the boy's elbow as he passed. The skateboard jerked to a halt, and the boy stumbled in her grip.

"You get out of here and don't come back," Emmy yelled, shaking him. "You hear me?"

"Ow! Let go."

Mitch jogged over and struggled to pry the boy out of her grip. "Emmy, let him go."

Kristen joined him and pulled at the gnarled fingers of Emmy's other hand, but the feel of thin skin and fragile bone made her stop and gentle her touch.

Emmy yelled louder as she strained against them. "Cindy Sue? Come out here."

"What's going on?"

Cringing, Kristen glanced back at Dylan, who ran toward them. Sadie hovered a few steps behind. They both stared wide-eyed and pale-faced at the scene before them.

"Wait there with Sadie, please," she said, striving to keep her tone calm and renewing her efforts to free the boy.

Emmy was inconsolable. Her fierce grip tightened, her knuckles turning white.

"Emmy," Kristen begged. "Please let him go."

"They've ruined it." Emmy's eyes, panicked and confused, settled on the decaying building. "What's Cindy Sue going to do?" A tear rolled down her cheek, and her voice broke when she added, "She's worked so hard. Been good to so many people." She shook the boy harder. "You don't do a body like that, you hear? You don't just throw someone away."

The boy's face contorted with pain. "Get off me, you crazy bitch."

"Shut up," Dylan yelled, moving toward him. "Don't call her that."

"Dylan, go back to the truck," Mitch said firmly. He nodded at Kristen when they finally managed to pry Emmy's hands from the boy and move her away. "You're Zach, right? Charles's boy?" He eyed Zach's upper arm. "You all right?"

Rubbing his arm and scowling, Zach nodded.

"I'm sorry about this. Go on home." Mitch turned back to Emmy and held her thrashing arms at her sides.

"You don't do a body like that," Emmy shouted.

"She's crazy," Zach spat, snatching up his skateboard.

Mitch's tone hardened. "Go home, Zach."

Low voices and hushed murmurs mixed with the peppy music still streaming from the ice cream parlor's speakers.

Kristen glanced around, and when she saw that people had abandoned their tables outside the ice cream parlor and had gathered behind them to watch the disturbance, her face heated. Dylan, red faced, hovered nearby, shifting from foot to foot. Sadie clutched the neckline of her T-shirt with both hands, mouth trembling and tears streaming down her face.

Kristen looked at Mitch, and the helplessness in his eyes as he struggled to restrain Emmy's angry movements made her chest tighten.

"What can I do, Mitch?" she asked softly, taking a hesitant step forward.

Cheeks pale, he shook his head. "I don't know. Just stay back."

"Cindy Sue?" Emmy craned her neck and peered past Mitch. "Come out here."

Mitch's tone was firm. "Emmy, she's not there."

"I have to go to her. She might be hurt. All that glass . . ."

"She's *not* there."

"You let me go," Emmy screamed. "You suits are all the same. Selfish. Hateful. Useless—"

"No one is there, Emmy." Mitch's hands tightened their hold on her shoulders. "No one. They're gone. Do you hear me? Everyone is gone."

Her arm shot out, and her hand slapped Mitch's cheek, the sharp crack of flesh striking flesh rocking Mitch back on his heels.

Kristen gasped. "Emmy!"

"Nana, don't," Sadie cried, tearing past Emmy and

barreling into Mitch. She wrapped her arms around his waist, her small shoulders racked with sobs.

Red blotches rose on Mitch's left cheek. He released Emmy and lifted his hands, palms out. His fingers shook.

"You don't throw someone away." Emmy turned, stumbling a bit, and stared blankly at the people gathered behind them. "You don't just throw 'em away."

The group of bystanders fell silent, and Sadie's cries echoed across the parking lot, mingling with the heavy rush of traffic on the road behind them.

Vision blurring, Kristen swallowed past the tight knot in her throat, then held out a shaky hand. "Come with me, Sadie."

The little girl lifted her head and looked up at Mitch, her breath coming in ragged bursts.

"Go with Kristen," Mitch said, staring straight ahead, his voice unrecognizable.

Sadie let go of him and turned. Red rimmed her eyes, and she had a look of desperation on her face as her gaze darted around the crowd of strangers who surrounded them and stared.

Kristen dropped to her knees, spread her arms, and whispered, "Over here, sweet Sadie."

Relief flashed through her expression, and she ran into Kristen's arms, small hands clutching her neck and legs winding around her waist. Kristen stood, holding Sadie, and walked back to the truck. She stopped to grab Dylan's hand along the way.

They climbed into the backseat of the truck, and Kristen hugged Sadie close to her side, watching through the windshield as Mitch slowly walked Emmy back. When they reached the truck, Mitch opened the passenger door and waited while Emmy put a hand on the seat and stared.

"You need some help, Mitch?" a male onlooker asked quietly.

Mitch didn't turn around, just shook his head, his eyes averted toward the truck's floorboard. "No. She just needs a minute."

Eventually, Emmy climbed in. Mitch shut the door and rounded the truck, got in and drove past the onlookers out of the parking lot.

The first few miles were silent except for Sadie's muffled sobs against Kristen's shirt and the slow drum of light rain against the hood of the truck. Dylan slumped against the closed window, fists balled on his knees. And Mitch stared straight ahead, his strong jaw clenched, the bright red mark spreading across his cheekbone.

"What did I do?"

Kristen froze as the sound of Emmy's shaking voice filled the quiet cab.

The passenger seat creaked as Emmy turned to study Mitch, her mouth trembling and eyes wide. She glanced at the backseat, and her gaze moved over Dylan, then Kristen, and stilled on Sadie.

Her face crumpled. Her voice breaking, she asked, "Oh, what did I do?"

Mitch shifted gears, slowing the truck, then pulled off to the side of the road.

Kristen straightened. Her breath quickened at the tense, angry set of his mouth. "Mitch . . ."

"I'm sorry," Emmy said, looking at him in frightened confusion, tears pouring from her eyes. Her chest lifted and lowered in jerks, and her hands moved aimlessly over the sides of her seat. "I'm so sorr—"

"Shh." Mitch leaned toward her, his big hands cupping her face, his broad thumbs sweeping over her wrinkled cheeks. "You have nothing to apologize for. You hear me, Emmy? Not a thing." He kissed Emmy's forehead, wet lashes and hands, cradling them in his own. "Not a thing."

Shoulders sagging, Emmy closed her eyes. "I—I want to go home."

Mitch kissed her forehead once more, whispering against her skin, "Then that's what we'll do."

He started the truck, pulled back onto the worn highway, and continued driving. The windshield wipers squeaked in a steady rhythm for the rest of the ride. Kristen studied Mitch's reflection in the rearview mirror along the way. She knew that the stoic strength he exhibited masked his real feelings, as it was so reminiscent of the brave face she'd struggled to maintain years ago, while sitting at Anna's bedside after yet another new treatment, listening to the words of a tight-lipped doctor with skeptical eyes.

Hope for the best, but nothing is certain.

They were halfway up the farm's driveway before Kristen realized that she'd rested her damp cheek against the top of Sadie's head and that the little girl had fallen asleep in her arms.

Slow afternoon rain intensified as night fell. Fat raindrops pummeled the roof of the farmhouse and slapped against the window in Dylan's room. The heavy sound did nothing to drown out Mitch's thoughts or distract him from the throbbing pain in the tender flesh along his cheekbone. And it didn't stop Dylan from insisting on answers to his questions—ones Mitch was not prepared to provide.

"But what's wrong with her?" Dylan sat up in his bed, the sheet slipping down his bare chest.

When they'd returned to the farm a couple of hours ago, Dylan had hovered by Mitch's side as he'd helped Emmy to her room, and then the boy had stood by silently as Mitch had asked Kristen to help Emmy change and get settled in bed for the night. He had followed Mitch to the kitchen, had eaten the sandwich and chips Mitch managed to pull together for supper, then had taken a shower and crawled into bed early without protest as Mitch had gotten Sadie settled, too. But now he demanded attention.

Mitch sat on the edge of the mattress and cupped his hand around Dylan's ankle through the covers. "Emmy's having trouble with her memory. And with recognizing the difference between the past and the present." He swallowed hard. "Sometimes she mixes up the two."

Dylan looked down and picked at the blanket, his forehead creasing. "Will she get better?"

"I . . ." Mitch shook his head. "I don't think so. I think it'll only get worse from here on out."

"How much worse?"

"A lot. Eventually to the point that she won't be able to take care of herself."

Dylan raised his head, those blue eyes—so like Mitch's own—locked on his uncle's with piercing intensity. "Or me and Sadie?"

Mitch sat back, his hand tightening around Dylan's ankle. "Yes."

"What will happen then?"

God help him. He'd known the question would come, but he'd hoped it wouldn't arise until later. When he'd had time to rest. To think. Lord . . . to at least figure out what step to take next and prepare for how to break the news to the kids.

"We'll cross that bridge when we get to it." He held Dylan's gaze, hoping like hell he sounded more confident than he felt. "You have nothing to worry about, Dylan. I'm not going to let anything bad happen to you, Sadie, or Emmy." His throat tightened. Dipping his head, he added, "I am going to ask something of you, though. I need you to trust me. I need you to understand that whatever decisions I'll end up having to make, I'll be making them in your, Sadie's, and Emmy's best interests. And I'll need your help running this place until it's time to make those decisions."

Dylan remained silent for a minute, his guarded eyes peering into Mitch's; then he settled back against his pillow and tugged the sheet up to his chin. "Okay."

Mitch patted his ankle, stood, and walked to the door.

"Uncle Mitch?"

Mitch stopped, his hand tensing around the doorknob. "Yeah?"

"I know I told Emmy I didn't like it here—and sometimes I still don't—but . . ." Dylan's voice trailed away, its tone hesitant. "But sometimes I do, you know?"

Mitch closed his eyes, the weight of the day washing over him. The enormity of the pain, loss, and uncertainty Dylan and Sadie had already suffered in their young lives and were facing now hit him in the chest, stealing his breath. "I know." He glanced over his shoulder and forced a smile. "Now get some rest."

He flipped off the light, moved into the hallway,

then shut the door behind him. The house was still, quiet, and dark in the midst of the storm's onslaught save for a muted slant of light slipping beneath the closed door of Emmy's room. Kristen was still in there, probably sitting at Emmy's bedside, watching her chest lift and lower on deep breaths as she drifted off, and wondering just what the hell she'd gotten herself into by coming here.

Wincing, Mitch rubbed his temples with his thumb and forefinger, then moved to the next bedroom. He nudged the door open a bit farther and eased his head around the doorframe to look inside.

Sadie was peaceful and still beneath the pink sheet, her long brown hair lying over her shoulder and covering her smooth cheek. Her gentle breaths moved an errant strand against her lips.

He walked to her bedside and brushed the lock of hair back, tucking it behind her ear. A small whimper escaped her before she settled back to sleep.

How would Sadie take the news? Unlike Dylan, she had always had a close relationship with Emmy and had embraced the farm right away. Even through the worst months here with Carrie, she'd always seemed at home when he'd come to check on her.

This is your home, too, Mitch.

Eyes burning at the memory of Emmy's words, he balled his shaking hand into a fist, then left the room. He forced his weak legs to carry him to the front door and out onto the porch.

A thick swath of moist, humid air enveloped him, and rain poured off the eaves in dense waves, the relentless pounding of the storm stretching for miles. A tangy mix of rainwater and clay misted the breeze and clogged his nostrils with its pungent smell.

You don't just throw someone away.

Gripping the rotten porch rail, he ducked his head and shoved it into the heavy stream of rain. The cool water rushed down the back of his neck, around his jaw, then dripped from his chin.

Why hadn't he returned to help Emmy years ago? Why hadn't he fixed this dilapidated porch so she could enjoy it while she still owned the place? Offered to help with the crops as soon as he arrived, instead of waiting for guilt to push him into it?

You suits are all the same. Selfish. Hateful. Useless.

Shoulders heaving, he clamped his lips together and choked back the guttural roar shoving its way up his throat.

Can't you see I'm trying to make things right?

He should've come back sooner. Should've talked to Emmy long before now—should've listened. Should've tried to understand.

Instead, time had slipped away, and he was alone now. Alone in deciding Emmy's, Dylan's, and Sadie's futures. Left with the challenge of salvaging what little absolution he could for himself and Emmy from the remnants of her fading memory. From what was left of her weakened heart.

"Mitch?"

He tensed at the sound of Kristen's voice. Then a broken sound parted his lips, and shame heated his face. "In all my life," he said, "Emmy's never lifted a hand against me—not even to spank me when I cut up as a kid."

Her footsteps drew close, and he could feel the warmth emanating from her slender frame.

"I can't remember the first time my dad hit me—" His throat closed. "Seemed like that's just how it always was. But I remember every time Emmy threw him out of this house because of it, and I remember every time she let him right back in. Mine and Carrie's childhood was nothing but pain, blood, and fear. I've never been able to accept that or find peace with it." The splintered wood of the porch rail cut into the soft flesh of his palms. "I don't care if Emmy forgets this damn place or my father. He was a rotten bastard, and we'd all be better for it. But for her to forget Sadie or Dylan . . ." His eyes burned. "For her to forget me . . ."

Kristen's hands were on him, smoothing over his back, gripping his shoulders, then tugging him toward her.

Giving in, he drew back from the fall of rain and buried his wet face in the curve of her neck and shoulder. Her smooth skin was warm and dry against his cold, soaked cheek, and he moved his mouth along the pulse fluttering beneath her jaw, up over her delicate chin, then hovered above her lips, their breaths mingling.

"One day she may not know me anymore." Droplets of water clung to his mouth, mixing with his tears, shaking with his heavy inhale. He focused on the pink curve of her bottom lip. It trembled. "She won't know my name. Won't know Sadie's or Dylan's."

A tear rolled over her cheek, settled in the corner of her mouth. He traced its path with the tip of his finger.

"After losing Carrie, how can I look those kids in the eyes and tell them they're going to lose someone else they love, too? How can I explain that they'll have to leave the only home—*the only family*—they've known because it's empty and dead?" He raised his eyes to hers, and the pain in their green depths pulled the knot in his chest tighter. "How do I say it without breaking down?"

Something moved through her expression, something dark and heavy; then a fiery determination lit her eyes as she speared her fingers through his wet hair and cupped the back of his head. "You won't."

She lifted to her toes and pressed her lips to his.

Her soft kiss swept through him on a rush of comforting warmth. Groaning, he slid his arms around her slim back, curled his hands into her shirt, leaned into her. He parted her lips with his tongue, delved deep and collected her sweet taste. Salty tears and the crisp flavor of rain mingled together on their tongues, and he deepened the kiss, absorbing her soft cry of pleasure.

The welcoming feel and delicious taste of her joined the pounding of the storm, and for a moment, the painful memories embedded in the land around them faded.

Mitch raised his head and dragged in a deep breath, a strong bolt of need shooting through him as her chest lifted against his, her soft breasts pressing tight to him, and as one slim leg slipped between his.

She looked up at him, her fingers sliding down the back of his neck, kneading his shoulders. Pink flushed her cheeks, and her mouth moved the smallest fraction of an inch closer to his before she stepped back, trailed her soft palm down his arm. She took his hand. "Come with me?"

He should stop this now. Should thank her for her help, apologize for taking advantage of a weak moment, then climb the stairs to his room. Avoid complicating matters further by saying good night, shutting the door between them, and grieving in private.

But his arms longed to hold her close, and his heart ached for her to hold him back.

He brushed a blond curl away from her forehead, then nodded.

Kristen led him across the porch to the lone chair around the corner, then eased him into a seated position. She sat on his knee, wrapped her arms around him, and tucked her head beneath his chin. He pulled her close and breathed her in, her soft hair tickling his nose, as they watched the heavy curtain of rain, dimly lit by the porch light's glow, lower over the front lawn.

"This place isn't empty or dead," she whispered.

Rain pounded the roof harder above their heads, and water cascaded in swift currents around them. The air grew cooler, and she snuggled closer, wrapping her arms around his biceps, her strong heartbeat heavy against his chest.

"It's spacious," she continued, "with plenty of room to grow. It's trying to now, right out there in that beautiful field we planted. The good that's left in this place is trying to push its way through the ground, and we're going to help Emmy make it strong."

Mitch closed his eyes, her reassuring words, delivered in a firm tone, washing over him.

"We're going to bring it back to life," she vowed.

CHAPTER 8

Orange, glowing heat seeped through Mitch's closed eyelids and stirred him awake. He blinked, then inhaled, and the aroma of honeysuckle and fresh dew swept through his nose and filled his lungs.

The sun was up, the bright eye rising slowly above the horizon. Its rays cut through the rain-induced mist that still lingered over the fields, and cast crystal-like shimmers across the deep puddles scattered along the red driveway. Stronger shafts of light reached the steps of the front porch, stretched over the broad floor beneath his boots, then trailed lazily over the smooth skin of Kristen's bare arm that rested against the arm of the rocking chair.

He smiled. The act stretched the tender flesh along his cheekbone, but her comforting weight pressed against his chest soothed him in this moment of discomfort. He lifted his hand, smoothed his palm over her soft blond hair, and studied the sprawling landscape surrounding them.

We're going to bring it back to life.

And strangely enough, that was how he felt. His

limbs, like his eyes, were light, filled with purpose and a renewed sense of energy. That gnawing ache in his gut had receded, a pleasant sense of calm having taken its place.

Pushing with one foot, he rocked back in the chair and eased it into a gentle rhythm. Each flex of his leg was met with a creak of weathered wood and the chipper calls of birds, the sounds an odd sort of comfort. The kind he'd never experienced at Hart's Hollow and savored all the more for it.

"Mmm." Kristen shifted against him, rubbing her cheek against his chest, and sighed. "We fell asleep?"

His smile grew. "Yeah."

She placed one palm to his thigh and one to his chest, then straightened and looked up at him. Sunlight caressed her sleep-flushed cheek, highlighting her freckles, and brightened the tender, concerned look in her green eyes.

It was enough to bring a man to his knees.

"It bruised," she whispered, trailing a fingertip across the sore flesh along his cheekbone. "Does it still hurt?"

"A bit." He caught her hand in his, brought her fingers to his lips and kissed each one in turn, grinning. "But this helps."

She smiled, all dimples, flirtatious expression and soft comfort, then cupped his jaw. Her thumb glided across the stubble lining his chin. "And this?"

A sweet ache stole through him, and he lowered his eyelids. "Yeah. That too."

"And this?" She leaned closer. Her soft lips brushed his in the lightest of kisses, but it burned right through his skin, flooding him with heat and curling his toes.

He cupped the back of her head, covered her mouth with his, and answered her with restrained urgency in his kiss. Her pleased sigh awakened him even more, stirring his body and heightening his senses.

When he drew back, allowing them both to catch their breath, she murmured teasingly, "Better than Heather Andrews?"

A rusty chuckle escaped him, and he pulled her closer. "Hell, yes." More than that. "Perfect."

He'd give anything to hold her like this all day. Explore her body, mind, and heart. Uncover all her secrets, fears, and dreams and lay out his own. But there were more pressing matters at hand, and others to consider. So he'd have to wait. For now.

"Thank you for listening last night." His voice was husky. Clearing his throat, he speared his hands through her hair and massaged the soft skin behind her ears. "And for . . ." Easing his mind? Taking away the pain? Giving him the first glimmer of hope he'd had in a long damn time? "Everything."

She rubbed his forearms, her palms rasping over his rough hair. "I meant what I said. I'll help however you need me to."

He glanced around, eyed the rotting porch rails and the paint that was peeling from the weather-beaten balusters. "We'll need to make the rounds for several weeks, check the fields, scout for weeds and pests, but I want to fix this house up, too. Maybe start with the porch. Replace the railings and balusters. I could use your help painting them, if you're willing?"

"Of course." She squeezed his wrists, eased away, then stood.

Her body heat clung to his chest and thighs despite her absence, making him smile even more.

"I imagine Emmy will wake up soon." She craned her neck and peered through the window behind him. "Would you like me to check on her?"

"Please." Reluctantly, he stood. "I need to speak with her. Thought I'd get some coffee going, freshen up, then take her some."

She nodded. "I'll let her know."

Mitch watched her walk into the house and allowed himself a small sigh of regret before following. He fixed a pot of coffee, then went upstairs and took a shower while it percolated. After shaving and dressing in clean jeans and a T-shirt, he made his way back downstairs and rummaged in several cabinets to find two ceramic mugs with delicate wildflower patterns—Emmy's favorites—washed them, then poured coffee in each.

He carried them down the hallway to the back bedroom, then paused outside the door as Kristen exited. "How is she?"

"Better." She glanced over her shoulder and said quietly, "A little embarrassed, though. She doesn't remember all of it, but enough for it to hurt." She sighed. "I thought I'd fix some breakfast. Emmy said Sadie and Dylan like pancakes. That okay with you?"

He nodded. "Thank you."

Kristen smiled as she eased past him, the slight press of her hand on his upper arm helping him take the few steps into Emmy's bedroom.

She was sitting up in bed, lavender sheet tucked across her middle and under her arms, her gray hair disheveled across her forehead. Her eyes widened on his face as he approached, and a small gasp escaped her. "Oh, Mitch." Her voice shook. "Did I—"

"Aw, now. None of that," he said softly, walking over and sitting in a chair by the bed. "We covered that yesterday."

"W-we did?" She kept her focus on his right cheekbone, her lashes glistening.

"Yeah." He held out one of the mugs. Steam rose above the rim, twirled in the sunlight that poured through the open window, and the scent of aromatic brew drifted between them. "It's black. No sugar. Just how you like it. And I found the cups J—"

"Joe bought for me," she said, finishing for him, her anguished expression receding a little. "He found them in a pottery store outside Helen when we honeymooned in the Blue Ridge Mountains. We went for a hike early one morning, stumbled on this little rundown cabin, and there they were." She pointed at one delicate flower painted on the mug. "See the white one there? The one with the yellow tip on it? That's an Eastern shooting star. Joe said that's what I was to him. Precious and hard to catch. That was back when I ran just about everywhere. When I was young and strong." She took the mug from him, grew quiet for a moment, then said, "Isn't that funny?"

"What?" he asked.

"That I can remember that morning so clearly. Like it was yesterday. Like he should still be here on this bed, next to me." Her chin trembled. "But yesterday I forgot I'd lost Cindy Sue. This thing is stealing from me. It's taking things I don't want to give. My thoughts, my words . . . pieces of my soul."

Throat tightening, he cradled his mug in his hands, the scalding heat against his palms a welcome distraction from the burning sensation in his eyes. "You know that for sure?"

She nodded, staring down at her mug. "I found out two years ago. I was forgetful. Things seemed off, and Carrie suggested I go have a checkup. I got the news and came on home." She shrugged. "What else do you do?"

Mitch focused on the long white curtains on the other side of the room. Watched them billow out and deflate with each push of the morning breeze. "There are specialists. We can ask about new treatments to slow the symp—"

"No." Her tone had hardened, and she faced him. "It's taking my time from me, too. An hour here, a day there." She shook her head. "I don't want to spend what good time I got left on waiting rooms and side effects. I want to be home with people who'll treat me like I'm still me. I want to hear Sadie laugh louder, see Dylan smile more. I want to watch that corn grow. Help you and Kristen make this land breathe again. This farm and this family give me a reason to get up every day. To try."

He scooted forward in his chair. "I'm going to stay and help you through this."

"But your job—"

"It'll wait. After I order a few things online and have them shipped, I can draw up plans here just as well as I can in New York. And I have some savings I'm going to use to make improvements here. Kristen told me she's willing to help in whatever way you need her. You can count on both of us."

Emmy turned toward the window. The curtains rippled faster on a stronger gust of wind, and outside the mist had faded from the property, providing a clearer view of the soggy red driveway, the freshly planted fields, and the solid blue sky.

"Kristen came out here to hide, you know," she said. "Not sure what from, but some people do, thinking it's a good place to disappear. Doesn't take long for 'em to find out it's not. There's just the earth beneath your feet, the air in your lungs, and the sky above. The only thing in between is you—whatever's in you—the good, the bad. Can't hide from any of it. Can't do nothing but choose what to hold on to and what to let go of." She faced him again. "Can you understand that's all I was doing with your father? I was holding on to the good I still saw in my son."

Neck heating, he looked down and tightened his grip on his mug.

"There's one more thing I want," she continued. "I want to see you feel at home here one day. I want to know that, in your heart, you forgive me."

The air left his lungs, pouring out of him and tugging him forward. "Emmy . . ." He reached out, squeezed her hand. "I want to understand. I do. And I'm going to try."

A hesitant smile lifted her lips. "I'm not perfect—never have been. I've screwed up a lot in my life and made yours and Carrie's harder. But I'd have given my life for David—just as I would for you. There was still good in him, and I couldn't just throw him away." Her shoulders lifted helplessly. "Is it okay for a parent to give up on their own child? To stop loving him? Because I couldn't. I tried, but I couldn't."

Mitch rubbed his hand over his jaw. "I mattered, too, Emmy. So did Carrie. I just . . . I feel like you were putting him over our well-being. Over the rest of the family. Sometimes there's no more hope of someone changing."

"But how do you know that for sure?" A deep sadness shadowed her expression, and her eyes eagerly questioned. "How do you know when there's no more hope?"

He moved to answer, then stopped. Recalled the pain and disgust he'd hauled up the sludge-filled driveway when he'd arrived weeks ago; examined the renewed energy and peace that had pulsed through him just hours ago on the porch, at sunrise, when he'd held

Kristen in his arms. That unexpected feeling continued to well inside him at just the thought of her. At the prospect of something fresh, whole, and pure—a chance to start over.

"I don't know." His attention strayed to the open window. The scenery outside was brighter and more welcoming than he could've ever imagined.

"I've never been able to step outside and not feel something bigger than me out there," she said quietly, her tone searching. "And I still believe miracles come along out of nowhere. Hoped for one for David and this place—no matter how ignorant, superstitious, or naive that may be to some. Where's the wrong in hoping?"

Heart aching, he looked back at her. Studied the sagging muscles in her arms, which had lost their definition, and the feisty gleam in her eyes, which defied the exhaustion lurking in the cloudy depths. And despite everything she'd lost, all the pain she'd suffered, the almost insurmountable odds and opposition she now faced, she still fought. Still dreamed. Still loved.

"There's no wrong in it, Emmy. None at all. But you've never needed anyone's permission or approval on that. You're not asking for it now, are you?"

The desperate look in her eyes faded, and defiance flooded her expression. "No."

He set his mug on the nightstand, leaned over, and kissed her forehead. "You're going to see this place become whole again. I promise."

She looked up at him and smiled, a fresh surge of tears moistening the crow's-feet at the corners of her eyes. "Thank you."

A knock sounded, and the bedroom door creaked

open. Kristen peeked around it. "I'm sorry to interrupt, but there's someone here to see you, Mitch."

Nodding, he squeezed Emmy's hand once more and made his way to the door. "Kristen and I will handle things today, Emmy. I want you to spend the day resting. No cleaning, no cooking, no worrying—just resting."

She perked up, a sassy spark lighting her expression. "Ain't he something, Kristen? Bossing me around like I'm some preschooler. Might go over better if he asked me nicely."

Mitch paused on the threshold. "Please?"

"Only 'cuz I'm comfy and got coffee."

"And you'll have pancakes in a few minutes," Kristen said. "The griddle's heating now."

Emmy settled back against her pillow, nose twitching. "I suppose y'all have talked me into it."

Laughing, Mitch shook his head, then went to the front door. Dylan stood at the window, frowning toward the porch and rubbing his sleepy eyes.

"Who is it?" Mitch asked.

"Zach and his dad." Dylan flashed him an angry look. "What're *they* doing here?"

"Probably has to do with yesterday, and we'll greet them politely, just as we would any guests." He ruffled Dylan's bed head and managed a smile, despite the knot tightening between his shoulder blades. "Where's Sadie?"

"In the kitchen. We're gonna help Ms. Kristen with breakfast."

"Good. Why don't you go on and help her out? I'll handle this."

Dylan's frown deepened, but after one more look out the window, he trudged back to the kitchen.

Mitch rubbed a hand over the back of his neck, then opened the door and walked onto the porch. Charles stood on the top step, hands shoved deep into the pockets of his khakis, and Zach hovered behind him on the bottom step, head lowered, eyeing the ground.

"Morning, Charles."

Charles stepped forward, held out his hand, and gave a strained smile. "Mitch. I'm sorry to show up so early, but I've got some errands to run today and wanted to speak to you first."

Mitch shook his hand. "Not a problem. I'm guessing you heard about yesterday."

Charles nodded.

"I'm sorry things happened the way they did. Emmy wasn't hersel—"

Charles held up a hand. "Zach has something he wants to say." He glanced over his shoulder. "Zach?" The boy started, then cringed as he looked up at his dad. "Come on up here."

Zach did, moving slowly up to the porch and studying the worn floor. "I'm sorry, Mr. Hart."

"For what?" Charles prompted, voice stern.

Zach licked his lips. "For being rude and calling Mrs. Hart a bad name." He looked up, cheeks reddening. "I shouldn't have done it. And I really didn't mean it. She just grabbed me so hard and . . ." His shoulders fell as he searched for the words.

"She hurt you," Mitch said, then smiled softly when the boy nodded. "I understand. We all say things we don't mean when we're hurting."

"I've suggested to Zach that one way to make amends with Mrs. Emmy would be to offer his time," Charles said. "I understand Dylan's been working the fields with you, and I was hoping you'd consider let-ting Zach assist you on the weekends until school releases for the summer."

"That's not necessary, Charles."

"I know, but it'd be a favor to me." Charles patted Zach's shoulder, then gripped it loosely. "Zach's a good man, but he needs to learn that you own up to your mistakes and rectify them when you can. I've told him he needs to repay his debt in order to earn back his skateboard. He's a hard worker, takes direction well, and if he's any trouble, just say the word."

"Well . . ." Mitch glanced at Zach, then looked out at the fields. They could use the help. Every pair of hands counted, especially now that he was going to tackle the house, too. And having another boy around might help raise Dylan's spirits. "Okay. If you're interested, we'd be grateful and happy to have you, Zach. You're welcome to start today if you'd like. Dylan and Sadie are in the kitchen, about to eat breakfast. Pancakes sound good to you?"

Zach stood a bit straighter. "Yes, sir. Thank you."

Mitch reached back, opened the screen door, then tipped his chin toward the entrance. "Go ahead. Dylan's in there, and I'll be right behind you."

He waited until Zach had left, then turned back to Charles. "Thanks. I appreciate the help and your understanding."

Charles nodded. "How is Emmy?"

"Better today." He looked away, watched the broad leaves on the oak trees rustle in the breeze, the sunlight flash sharply between the healthy branches. "There's no predicting tomorrow, though. I'm staying for a while, until we see how things turn out."

"If there's anything I can do, don't hesitate to call on me." After Mitch thanked him, Charles walked back to the porch rail, the floor creaking beneath his steps. "That's a good-looking crop you've got growing out there. You've put in a lot of hours."

"Kristen too. Think she planted more acres than I did."

Charles glanced back over his shoulder, smiling. "She turned out to be a find, didn't she? Becoming Emmy's right-hand and speaking up for her at the bypass meeting?"

Mitch smiled, recalling the way Kristen had jumped in Emmy's corner at the meeting. How she'd consoled Sadie in the backseat of the truck yesterday. How soothing her tone had been at Emmy's bedside last night, and how she'd offered him gentle comfort on the porch. His skin still tingled with the memory of her soft touch.

After Charles left, Mitch stood on the porch for a few minutes more, studying the balusters, railings, and Gothic trim and estimating the costs to refurbish them. He tried to focus on calculating measurements and adding up hours of labor. But his mind kept returning to Kristen's warm but wary gaze. The genuine concern and sincerity in her voice. At that moment, he realized that her tender kiss and whispered words of comfort had slipped inside his heart, making him long to be near her, to see her, to hear her. To just know she was here, partnering with him in more ways than one to make this place new again.

Kristen came out here to hide. . . .

Yeah. She had. But thank God, the universe, or random luck, he'd found her. And he was damn well going to hold on.

Certain parts of Mitch should be outlawed during Kristen's working hours of five in the morning to nine at night. Like the flex of his strong biceps as he lifted lumber. The firm, masterful movements of his long fingers as he guided wood planks along a table saw. The thoughtful set of his sensual mouth as he evaluated the detail on a freshly milled porch baluster.

And . . . *especially* . . . that gorgeous rumble of laughter that had been bursting from him more and more often over the past two weeks, drawing her ears and eyes and drumming up deliciously sinful urges that pulsed throughout her entire body.

Just like, oh, now.

"Fine."

She jerked upright from her crouch on the front porch, bumped her head on the top rail, and peered up at Mitch. He was standing and smiling down at her, legs staggered, a drill in one big hand, the late afternoon sunlight slanting sharp at his back.

Fine? Oh, boy, *fine* didn't quite do him justice. *Alluring, magnetic, irresistible?* Those were more accurate descriptions.

"I said," Mitch remarked, squatting beside her, "I think the balusters turned out fine." He cupped the back of her head and rubbed the spot above her temple that had bumped the rail. "Don't you think so?"

"Yes." It was hard to look away from his gorgeous blue eyes, and the slow grin spreading across his face prompted her to lean closer. "They're beautiful."

And that was an understatement. In the span of a handful of days, Mitch had worked wonders on the front porch. He'd used every spare bit of daylight left over after checking crops for nutrient needs or signs of damaging diseases and spraying for weeds to dismantle the porch rail, then repair each weather-damaged inch of it with fresh materials. Any original portions that were salvageable, he'd saved. Any that couldn't be resurrected had been replaced with pieces he'd painstakingly crafted for a perfect match.

At times, he'd stayed outside well past midnight, laboring under the bright flood of a halogen work light and flashing that sexy smile at her when she'd jerked awake after nodding off while priming wood on the front steps.

"You're very talented," she said, eyeing the sensual sweep of his bottom lip.

His smile widened. "I had a lot of great help. Matter of fact, there was this gorgeous woman that showed up every night and worked harder than I did."

"Sometimes." She laughed, cheeks burning. "I had a tendency to sleep on the job."

"You had good reason, what with working in the fields all day, helping Emmy in the garden and the kids prepare for final exams at school." He bent and brushed his mouth across her temple. The throb of hunger in his deep voice made her tingle when he said, "Besides, the sight of you certainly kept me awake."

Heat swirled in her belly. She grinned, dropped her paintbrush back in the pail at her side, then laid her hand on his thick thigh. "Hmm. That's good to know, seeing as how you've disturbed my sleep quite a bit." She kissed his cheek, then whispered by his ear, "You have this mischievous habit of sneaking into my dreams."

He laughed. "Good ones, I hope?"

Sitting back on her heels, Kristen studied his sculpted features and brawny frame, then looked beyond him at the renovated porch. Freshly painted columns, Gothic trim, and railings gleamed in the sunlight, each piece Mitch had lovingly crafted projecting lazy summer shadows on the new wooden floor beneath their feet. Emmy and Sadie hummed a happy tune at the other end of the porch as they stretched up on their tiptoes and washed the wide windows until they glistened. Dylan swept remnants of wood and dust off the wraparound floor and into the dustpan Zach held. They made a game of it, Dylan thrusting the trash forward with hockey-like moves and Zach zigzagging from one side to the other to capture it.

The boys' laughter and Emmy's and Sadie's slightly off-key tune merged and the scent of paint and clay in the clean air mingled with each other. Beyond them, in the distance, the crops were thriving. The corn's green stalks and leaves reached up toward the clear sky, and the red earth, gently furrowed around each stalk, cradled the two-foot-tall plants.

"Heaven," Kristen said, meeting Mitch's eyes and tilting her lips up in invitation as he dipped his head toward her. "Pure heaven."

Every hardworking, laughter-filled, desire-inducing day with Mitch over the past couple of weeks at Hart's Hollow had been wonderful. Better than she'd imagined, even.

So much so, it felt like—

"Oh, gag a maggot."

Mitch's head stopped its descent to hers. His lips twitched as he cut his eyes in Dylan's direction.

"Y'all aren't over there kissing, are you?" Dylan walked toward them, broom thumping against the porch floor along the way, and stared down at them. A disgusted expression crossed his face, but there was a happy—almost hopeful—light in his eyes. "You said we're supposed to be working. You're s'posed to be painting the rails, and me and Zach are s'posed to be sweeping."

Mitch sighed, murmuring, "So much for stealing a romantic moment." He stood. "We weren't kissing, Dylan," he said, winking down at her. "We were discussing something important."

Dylan crossed his arms over his chest. "Like what?"

Mitch cocked an eyebrow. "Like how much you and Zach have earned this week."

Dylan lost the sarcastic tone, dropped his arms to his sides, and adopted an innocent expression. Zach joined him, edging over to Dylan's side and smiling angelically up at Mitch.

Kristen bit back a laugh. For the past weeks, the boys had worked hard every Friday after school and on the weekends. They had followed Mitch's every direction to the letter in the fields, had helped Kristen and Emmy till the small vegetable garden behind the house without complaint and had picked bucket after bucket of ripe strawberries, even when buyers had been few and far between.

At first, Dylan had been slow to warm up to Zach, as he'd still been resentful about Zach's comments to Emmy. But after an apology from Zach and several hours of working together, they had begun chatting about video games during their downtime, then had progressed to hitting baseballs in the backyard and shooting water guns on hot afternoons. The sad look in Dylan's eyes was less apparent now, and he smiled more often.

"We've done good, haven't we?" Dylan asked.

Mitch smiled. "You've both done very well. Enough to earn twice this week what you earned last week." He ruffled Dylan's hair. "I'm proud of you both."

Dylan and Zach lit up, their chins lifting and chests swelling.

"And I think you deserve a break," Mitch added. "Especially seeing as how today was your last day of school and your summer vacation has officially started. So feel free to knock off for a while and have some fun."

"Thanks, Mr. Mitch," Zach said.

Grinning, the boys dropped the broom and dustpan, took off down the front porch steps, then ran around the house toward the backyard.

"What I wouldn't give for a bit of those boys' energy," Emmy said from the other side of the porch.

Kristen smiled. After the scene in town two weeks ago, Emmy had been taking it extra easy lately, leaving the field work to Kristen and Mitch and staying closer to the house. Twice during evening meals she'd seemed confused, but after a good night's rest, she'd bounced back each morning. She'd lost her temper only once, and her mood seemed to have improved.

Maybe that was what Emmy had needed all along—extra rest, some help, and time to get back to her old self again. And with Mitch staying, she was bound to get even better.

Emmy wrung out the wet towel she'd used to wipe down the windows, did the same with Sadie's, then stepped back and looked around the porch. "It turned out gorgeous. Looks better than the day me and Joe first stepped foot on it." Her eyes glistened as she smiled at them. "Thank you both so much."

"We were happy to do it," Kristen said, pushing to her feet.

"All it needs is some new furniture." Mitch glanced

at Emmy. "What do you think about a couple new rocking chairs and maybe a swing?"

Sadie squealed and clapped her hands together. "Can we, Nana?"

Emmy nodded. "I think it's a wonderful idea."

Smiling, Sadie skipped over to Kristen, her long braid flapping behind her. "Can we get a white one, Ms. Kristen? With squishy cushions?" She patted Kristen's leg. "Like the one at Ms. Ruth Ann's?"

Kristen looked down, and her spirits rose even higher as she studied Sadie's impish grin and bright blue eyes. After the incident in town, Sadie had taken up trailing after her in the afternoons. Though Sadie still kept a good foot of empty space between them, she'd walked with Kristen in the corn and soybean fields as she checked for pests, weeds, and diseases, watching as Kristen measured growth and asking questions without hesitance or reservation.

And every Saturday morning, Kristen admitted reluctantly, she'd caught herself listening eagerly for the soft telltale footfalls that signaled Sadie was close behind, and she lingered longer over her morning coffee when the little girl slept late, giving her extra time to catch up to her before she left for the fields.

It was an odd mix of new feelings—this eagerness for Sadie's presence but a nagging need to still maintain some distance.

"Cushions would be a nice touch." Kristen smiled at Sadie, then glanced at Mitch. "Is there a store in town that sells them?"

Mitch nodded. "Jake's Hardware, probably. They have rocking chairs, too. We could make the drive in tomorrow morning, if you're up to it."

"I'd love to." Kristen glanced at Emmy. "I have it

on good authority that Saturday is the perfect day to take a trip to town and break in the summer."

Emmy laughed. "If you're going to do it right, don't forget to start at the Dutch Bakery and get a—"

"Blueberry and cream cheese sweet roll," Kristen said, finishing for Emmy, a warm feeling of excitement bubbling within her. One she hadn't felt in a long time. "Then go to Essie's Odds and Ends to browse the antiques. Will you go with us, Emmy?"

Emmy remained quiet for a moment, her smile fading slightly. "No. I've grown pretty fond of sleeping in on the weekends, thanks to the two of you spoiling me." She glanced between them, her smile returning full force and a mischievous sparkle brightening her eyes. "I'll stay here with the kids so y'all can have a relaxing morning and some privacy for a change."

Kristen's face burned. She ducked her head and shot a look at Mitch, then made a face when he laughed and shrugged. They'd grown closer lately, but she'd thought they'd done a pretty good job of hiding it—especially around Emmy and the children.

Despite her best intentions to maintain a hard dividing line between her professional and personal life, the two had meshed after her night on the porch with Mitch. And how could they not? The hurt, vulnerable look in his eyes that night had called to something deep inside her. A strong urge to comfort, support, and . . . *love?*

Love. She repeated the word in her head, turning it over, inspecting the way the syllable conjured up a sweet throb in her middle that pulsated up to her chest as she studied Mitch's familiar features.

"Tomorrow morning it is, then." Mitch held her gaze, his blue eyes gentle and warm.

Kristen nodded slowly, that pleasant feeling inside her intensifying. *Heaven, indeed.*

The low rumble of an engine and the swish of tires sounded up the dirt driveway. A small sedan rounded the circular end of the drive, then drew to a stop in front of the house.

"Ruth Ann." Emmy walked to the top porch step, shifting the majority of her weight to her good knee. "First time she's driven up this driveway in at least ten years. Figures she'd show up now, when we're having such a good day."

"Emmy." Mitch's voice held an admonishing note. "Keep an open mind, all right? Maybe she's just stopping by for a friendly visit."

"Hogwash." Emmy scowled. "The woman's here to irritate me with some inane thing." Her frown deepened as Ruth Ann exited the car, shut the door, and smoothed a hand over her full white skirt. "She called me a devil."

"Well"—Mitch lifted his shoulders—"you've called her worse things, Emmy."

She looked up, brow wrinkling as she considered it, then blew out a breath. "I suppose."

Ruth Ann walked across the front lawn, made her way to the lowest porch step and smiled. "Good afternoon, everyone." She tilted her head back, and eyes widening, she surveyed the new railings, the decorative balusters, and the pristine Gothic trim. Her mouth formed into a small O. "Lee told me you were renovating the place, but he didn't mention how wonderful it was turning out." Her gaze swept over Mitch, Kristen, and Sadie, then came to rest on Emmy. "It's beautiful, Emmy. Stunning, really."

Emmy crossed her arms. "Whatcha want?"

Ruth Ann spread her manicured hands. "To pay my neighbor a visit."

"Why? It's been a month of Sundays since you stepped foot on my land, and I can't recall you ever once paying me a so-called neighborly visit since me and Joe moved in."

Ruth Ann's chest lifted on a deep inhale, and she raised her brows. "Well, I guess I just . . . missed your company."

"Missed my—" Emmy drew back and made a face. "You heard about what happened in town a couple weeks ago, didn't you?"

Ruth Ann looked away, shifting from one high heel to the other and picking at a pleat on her yellow blouse. "I don't know to what you're referring."

Emmy narrowed her eyes. "Oh, yes you do. You heard about my meltdown and decided to come over here to gloat, didn't you?" She motioned with her hand when Ruth Ann didn't respond. "Didn't you?"

"Oh, all right." Eyes flashing, Ruth Ann straightened. "I heard about what happened, but I didn't come here to gloat. I came to buy strawberries for shortcakes, and I brought the other makings for them in hopes that you'd consider putting a few together with me for the children." Her expression softened. "Like we used to do with my mom after getting out of school for the summer. Those were good memories, Emmy."

Emmy stared, her shoulders relaxing. "Good memories?"

"Yes. You and I made a lot of them during our younger years." Ruth Ann's voice shook. "Ones I found myself wanting to revisit lately, especially after I heard . . ." She shrugged, her chin trembling slightly as she shot a glance at Mitch. "That is, I thought it might help to have an old friend around. And I hoped we could come to a truce, if you're willing?"

Sadie brushed past Kristen and tugged Emmy's short sleeve. In a whisper filled with hope, she said, "I like strawberry shortcake, Nana."

Emmy glanced at Sadie, then looked over her shoulder at Kristen.

"It's a hot afternoon," Kristen said softly. "Strawberry shortcake topped with chilled whipped cream would hit the spot for me, too."

Emmy faced Ruth Ann again. "You're welcome to stay, but I don't want pity."

Ruth Ann smiled. "Good. Because strawberry shortcake and small talk's all I'm offering." With that, she spun around, went back to her car, and opened the trunk.

Kristen walked down the steps, squeezing Emmy's arm as she passed and saying to Sadie, "Let's give Ms. Ruth Ann a hand, okay?"

They did, Kristen lifting the largest box, packed with canisters of flour, sugar, and baking powder, and Sadie carrying a small box containing sticks of butter and tubs of whipped cream. Mitch carried in bowls and a large blender, then excused himself to round up the boys and check the fields.

Over the next couple of hours, Emmy, Ruth Ann, Kristen, and Sadie sliced strawberries, whipped up a sweet berry mixture, kneaded and baked biscuit dough, then began assembling individual shortcakes.

Emmy eyed Ruth Ann's hands as she dolloped generous heaps of fluffy whipped cream atop six strawberry-slathered biscuits. "You've slapped too much whipped cream on that batch."

Ruth Ann cocked an eyebrow and sucked a speck of cream off the tip of her finger. "No I didn't."

"Yes you did. They're gonna spurt out all over the place when someone takes a bite of 'em."

Ruth Ann shrugged. "So be it. Besides, some people like the whipped cream best."

"It's too much. We'll have to mix more topping to finish the others."

Ruth Ann huffed. "Why must you always make everything into an argument?"

"I'm not arguing. Everyone with good sense knows you stack equal portions of cream and strawberries to balance things out."

Wincing, Kristen set down the large spoon she was using to spread berry mixture on the biscuits and glanced at Sadie. The little girl stood on a step stool at the other end of the kitchen counter, wide eyes moving from Emmy to Ruth Ann and back.

"Emmy," Kristen said, "it's no trouble to make more topping."

"It is, too." Glaring, Emmy pointed a cream-covered spatula at Ruth Ann. "She's just doing it to get my goat."

Ruth Ann propped her hands on her hips. "That's ridiculous, Emmy. And it's just like you, always having to have the last word on everything." Her face reddened. "Just like you had to have Joe."

"Uh-oh, here we go." Emmy's voice hardened. "I knew you'd get on that before you left. You're just gonna hold on to that until I croak, aren't you?"

"You're darned ri—"

"Don't worry, Nana." Sadie grabbed a bag of sugar, dumped it into a big bowl of whipped cream, then grabbed a handheld mixer. "I'll make more for you."

Kristen sprang to action. "Sadie, don't!"

Before Kristen could reach her, Sadie flipped the mixer on high, shoved it into the bowl, and flung clumps of whipped cream and sugar all over the kitchen, herself . . . and Emmy and Ruth Ann. They were covered in it from the tops of their gray heads to their waists.

Kristen, who'd managed to duck beneath the spray of whipped cream, rose from her crouched position and cut off the mixer. She watched, frozen in place, as a particularly slimy glob slid off Ruth Ann's nose and plopped onto her splattered blouse. "I-I'm so sorry, Ms. Ruth Ann."

Shoulders shaking, Ruth Ann returned Emmy's stare across the table; then both women burst out laughing. Whipped cream fell from their faces onto their clothes and the table as they doubled over and reached out to take each other's hands.

"That's what we get for acting like two foolish children," Ruth Ann howled between bouts of laughter, squeezing Emmy's hands and trying to catch her breath. "Just look at us. I doubt he'd want either of us now."

"No, I don't think he would." Emmy's laughter trailed away. "Especially considering the way I've been treating you." She released Ruth Ann's hands and limped around the table, wiping her face. "Here you are, trying to be a friend to me again, and I start harping away."

"You've harped for as long as I can remember, and I've always loved you anyway." Ruth Ann grew silent, then reached out and squeezed Emmy's arms. "What do you say we let Joe rest for a while? And let it just be you and me again? Like it used to be?"

Emmy nodded slowly and whispered, "Like it used to be."

Kristen's eyes blurred as the two women hugged. She blinked hard, then cleared her throat and helped Sadie down from the step stool. "Sadie, why don't you go wash your face? I'll clean up in here."

Emmy released Ruth Ann. "Excuse me, Ruth Ann. I need to give Sadie a hand. Then we'll have supper. You're welcome to join us."

Ruth Ann smiled. "I'd love to."

When Emmy left, grinning with satisfaction, Kristen grabbed a roll of paper towels, handed a few to Ruth Ann to clean her face, and began wiping down the counter and the table. The afternoon sun had dipped, and it glinted through the kitchen windows, casting long shadows on the walls. Outside the rhythmic rattle of cicadas echoed around the house.

"Am I too late?"

Kristen's hand stilled against the table. "Too late for what?"

"For Emmy. How is she?" Ruth Ann had cleaned the whipped cream from her face, but a tear rolled down each cheek. "I heard her episode in town was bad."

"It was, but everyone's entitled to a rough day now and then." Kristen resumed wiping up the whipped cream. "Mitch and I have taken on the majority of the work lately, and since she's been resting, she's been much better." She steadied her voice, despite the dread unfurling in her veins. "She's going to get well. It'll just take some time."

It was silent for a minute save for the squeak of the damp paper towel that Kristen was using to scrub the countertop; then Ruth Ann spoke.

"You say that with conviction, but I don't see it

here." She touched Kristen's temple, her fingertip resting against the corner of her eye. "You've felt that thin line between heaven and hell, too, haven't you?"

Kristen froze, then straightened. "What?"

Ruth Ann wiped her cheek with the back of her hand. "When my husband fell ill with pneumonia, the doctors told me he was so weak, he didn't have long. They said I should prepare, but I didn't. Instead, I prayed—I prayed so hard—and tried to picture him well. Tried to see him getting out of that bed and us walking hand in hand out of that hospital together. That would've been my heaven, had he taken a breath in the opposite direction." A fresh sheen of tears glistened in her eyes. "But all I felt was this strange fear knot in my stomach and tighten around my heart. I hoped and prayed, even when I knew I had absolutely no control and could feel what was coming."

Kristen shook her head, unable to speak.

Ruth Ann studied her, then said, "My faith is just as strong as Emmy's, but my eyes are open. I still pray, but I also face reality. That's why I came today. Mitch told me a while back that Emmy could use a friend when things started to go bad." She bit her lip. "But it wasn't until I heard about what happened that I realized how bad off she really was. And how little time might be left to make amends."

Kristen stiffened. "Emmy will get better. Just like Hart's Hollow. We're going to see to it."

Ruth Ann studied her, a sad look of pity crossing her expression. "I hope you're right. I really do."

CHAPTER 9

The Dutch Restaurant's blueberry and cream cheese rolls had always been sweet, but with Kristen's flirtatious smile and deep green eyes facing Mitch from the other side of the booth, they tasted all the sweeter to him.

"Careful." Laughing, he reached across the table and wiped a sticky spot of icing from her chin. "It's running away from you."

She covered her mouth and giggled while she finished chewing. "Emmy was right. These are wonderful."

"She used to bring me and Carrie here every weekend when we were kids. I'd put away five or six of them on a good day." He nudged a small plate with one remaining decadent baked treat toward her. "Have another."

"Oh, no." She held up a hand. "Thank you. I've already had two, and if I eat another bite, you'll have to roll me out of here."

"Coffee, then," he urged, politely getting the waitress's attention. "At least one more cup before we head to the hardware store for the porch swing?"

Anything to entice her into lingering right here in this spot—in this moment—with him for just a little longer. Hell, for as long as he could tempt her.

"Okay," she said, smiling. "I can always go for more coffee, especially at this time of the morning. I usually need another kick of caffeine around nine."

Those cute dimples of hers were back, and her nose wrinkled just an adorable bit when she laughed. Pink tinged her tanned cheeks, and the Saturday morning sunlight poured through the wide restaurant windows, casting a golden glow along the smooth skin of her neck and bare shoulders and making her blond curls shine.

They couldn't have picked a better morning to drive into town for breakfast and shop for Emmy's new porch furniture. Though the first of June was almost upon them, the air still held a cool, springlike freshness in the earliest hours of the day, and he'd driven with the windows down, filling the truck's cab with a swift breeze, which picked up the appealing scent of Kristen's shampoo and swirled it around, teasing his nose.

She hadn't spoken much during the ride or mentioned how Emmy's visit with Ruth Ann had gone the prior afternoon. Just had sat quietly in the passenger seat, admiring the scenery and turning her head to smile at him on occasion. And it hadn't mattered. Because simply having her by his side again, just the two of them, with miles of road unrolling ahead and nothing but green, fertile fields and possibility surrounding them, had been all his happy heart could handle at the time.

Still admiring her, he sat back in his seat as the

waitress stopped by with a carafe of fresh brew. Kristen's eyes followed the other woman's hands as she filled each ceramic cup to the brim. Her thick lashes lifted, and she murmured, "Thank you," her full lips parting just enough to make him wonder how much sweeter her kiss would taste with the familiar flavor of his favorite childhood treat on her tongue.

"What did you like?" He leaned forward, resting his elbows on the table and savoring the way her gaze gentled as she focused on his face.

Her head tilted. "Hmm?"

"When you were a kid," he prompted. "What kind of things did you like the best?"

She looked down at her cup, her slim finger tracing the rim and brow furrowing. "I don't know."

"Oh, come on." He scooted closer. "There has to be something. Everyone's got at least one thing they miss."

Her finger stopped moving. She raised a brow and returned his stare. "Well, what about you?"

Mitch grinned. "That's easy." He tapped the almost empty plate. "You already know about these. And the other thing I miss is riding my bike on the back roads. Those long dirt ones with steep hills and belly-flipping drops. Ducking and dodging low-hanging limbs." He closed his eyes and remembered the feel of wind skating through his hair, down the back of his neck, and billowing his shirt. "Every mile I pumped those pedals took me farther from my dad and let me relax. Helped me lower my guard and just be me." When he opened his eyes, he saw the caring light in her eyes, and felt warm inside. "The older I got, the harder it became to catch that feeling. There were times I thought I'd never find it again."

"And did you?" She moved her hand to the table,

palm down, and slid it across to nudge his knuckles. "Ever find it again, I mean?"

He flexed his fingers, rested them on her warm wrist. "Here lately, yeah."

Her cheeks flushed. She bit her lip, but a smile broke out across her face all the same.

"So, what is it you miss?" he asked, pressing. "There has to be something."

Her smile dimmed, and she hesitated briefly before answering. "I never stayed in one place very long until I was ten. And after that, I lived in a children's home in Atlanta until I aged out." She shrugged. "It was a really nice place, with really good people who cared, but I guess it was always just a place, you know? I never really thought of it as my home."

So that was it. The evasiveness and uneasiness when he'd asked about her family, and the guarded look in her eyes when she'd mentioned having lost something precious in her life, were a result of never having had a home or a family she felt she could call her own.

The first night she'd spent at Hart's Hollow, he'd stood at the threshold of the guest room, laid out his intentions to talk Emmy around to his way of thinking, then leave. Said he was returning home as soon as possible and suggested she do the same.

She'd mulled over his words, a haunted look in her eyes, her attention drifting away from him. Then she'd said softly, "If I had one."

But there was something more. A dark pain that never seemed to leave her eyes.

"I'm sorry, Kristen." He spoke softly, rubbing his thumb across her wrist in gentle circles.

"Don't be." Straightening, she shifted to a more comfortable position on the booth's vinyl seat. "I was well provided for, had lots of adults to go to when I needed advice or support, and as a matter of fact, one of the counselors helped me find my first apartment. The first place I could truly call my own." Her gaze dropped to the table, and she slid her hand from beneath his to toy with an empty sugar packet. "It was small, but it had this beautiful window seat in the master bedroom, and in the fall, I'd crack that window open, grab a blank canvas, and we'd paint for—" She stopped, her mouth tightening, then visibly shook herself. "I'd paint every morning, before I left for work, close that window, then leave, knowing that same spot would be right there waiting for me when I returned."

Mitch hesitated, eyed the blank expression she'd carefully adopted, then asked, "When you said *we* . . . ?"

At first, she didn't answer. But after taking a sip of coffee, she said, "I was engaged for one year. I met Jason not long after I turned nineteen. He was one year older and in his second year of college. He grew up with very little family—just his mother and grandfather, from what he told me—and they never really had much, so he was on a mission to make a better life for himself." She pushed the sugar packet around with her pinkie. "I was looking for that, too, but we ended up wanting different things in the long run."

"What kinds of things?"

She picked up the packet. Twisted it around her finger. "I wanted a family, and he didn't. So I ended up walking away." There was a wealth of pain in her words. It throbbed in her tone and coated her voice.

"Do you regret it?"

Her green eyes lifted to meet his. "No. That was nonnegotiable for me."

He lifted his cup, took a deep swallow of the rich brew, then asked quietly, "Do you still love him?"

She studied his face for a minute. "We were so young and inexperienced when we met, I don't think either of us really knew what love was."

"And now?"

"I think fondly of him from time to time. I wish him well. But that's all." Her gaze dropped to his mouth. "What about you? Have you ever been in love?"

"Not in the past." He set down his cup, took her hand in his and lifted it to his lips. "But the present seems to have a mind of its own."

Her pink lips parted, a small intake of breath sounded and those gorgeous eyes of hers darkened to a deeper shade of green.

Tempted beyond polite restraint, he ignored the curious glances of nearby patrons, disregarded the distant chatter of the waitresses, and leaned across the table to press his mouth to hers. He swept his tongue along her bottom lip and relished her soft sigh of pleasure as she kissed him back. And, oh man . . . she tasted just as delectable as he'd imagined. Warm, welcoming, and tempting. All of which continued to hum through his veins after he'd released her and sat back.

"And the future?" she whispered, her drowsy lids lifting slowly.

Voice husky, he cleared his throat. "For the first time in a long time, I think it holds more than its fair share of possibilities."

They stayed there another ten minutes. He asked more questions, some of which she answered and others she politely sidestepped, but it didn't matter. The sound of her voice, her shy smile between sips of coffee, and the soul-stirring kiss were enough to keep him rooted right there, wishing, for the first time ever during a visit to Hart's Hollow, that he could stay put forever.

The thought sat well with him. As he paid the tab, he imagined what it would feel like to visit the restaurant every Saturday morning with Kristen. While he drove the truck to the hardware store, he examined how the daily grind on the farm had gained an exciting appeal over the weeks as a result of her presence. As they browsed various colors and patterns of cushions for the porch swing they'd chosen, he pictured her poised on a window seat by the stained-glass window upstairs, painting a blank canvas and bringing it to life the way she had that worn-out wooden sign they'd positioned by the driveway.

And he found himself wanting to focus more on the future. Wanting, with every fiber of his being, to make a place in his heart, in his life—at Hart's Hollow—for Kristen. And for Emmy, Sadie, and Dylan.

"What about this one?" Kristen held up a red-and-white-striped cushion. "Do you think Sadie would like it?"

The cushion was over four feet long and spanned the length of her frame, from her shoulders to her toes, and so her bright smile and excited expression were the only visible parts of her body from his angle.

Mitch smiled. "She'll love it."

Pleased with his answer, she folded the cushion, tucked it under her arm, and glanced around. "We've picked out the rockers, the swing, and the cushion. Anything else we need to look at?"

"Nope. We're all set." He nodded toward the back of the store. "Although if you don't mind staying a little longer, I'd like to take a look at the screen doors they have on display. Emmy's birthday is the last week of June, and I thought a new one would be a nice finishing touch for the porch."

"Her birthday? She hasn't mentioned a word about it."

"She wouldn't. Emmy hasn't formally celebrated her birthday in nine years." He shrugged. "Said she doesn't like anyone making a fuss over her."

"I can see her wanting that." Kristen looked toward the back of the store, then asked, "I'd like to get her something, too, though. What do you think she'd like?"

"I expect she'd be happy with anything you gave her." He took a few steps in the direction of the back of the store and then waited as she fell in step beside him. "Figure if they have a screen door I think she'd like, I'll go ahead and order one today so it'll arrive in time for the big day."

Kristen bumped her shoulder against his. "Think she'd let us throw her a party?"

"Well," he said, winking down at her, "I've always heard it's better to go ahead and do something and ask for forgiveness later rather than waiting around for permission."

She laughed. "Sounds good to me."

An hour later, they had ordered a new screen door and had purchased and strategically loaded into the truck a white hardwood porch swing, two rocking chairs, and the cushion Kristen had chosen. Mitch tied the items down with several thick ropes, then pulled out of the parking lot after waiting several minutes for traffic to clear.

"It's busy," Kristen commented, watching the traffic whisk by at a rapid pace.

"Yeah." Mitch looked at the steady stream of cars,

SUVs, and transfer trucks, and an uncomfortable churn started in his gut. "I imagine it's worse because it's the weekend."

Once they left the busiest part of downtown Peach Grove and passed The Scoop Ice Cream Parlor, the traffic thinned, and he pressed the accelerator pedal. Congested parking lots, honking horns, and the sporadic thump of music from passing cars faded into the distance as the tree line on both sides of the road thickened. For the first five miles, the only sound in the cab was the rumble of the aging truck's engine.

"What will happen to Hart's Hollow, Mitch?"

He glanced at Kristen, and the somber look on her face and the heavy tone in her voice intensified his discomfort. "If they build the bypass?"

She nodded.

Mitch faced the road again, pulled in a deep breath, and focused on the broken yellow line clipping by. "They'll tear down the house and pave over the fields. Time will pass. People will forget. Then it'll just . . . disappear." He swallowed hard. "Like it was never there."

He could feel her gaze on him, could hear her small breaths each time she started to speak, then hesitated.

"Like Cindy Sue's?" she asked.

His hands tightened around the steering wheel.

When he didn't answer, she touched the back of his hand. "Do you think that sometimes things can work out? No matter what you're up against?"

Her words were unsure, and her voice trembled. And dear God, he wanted to ease her fears. Wanted to tell her that despite what he knew of Emmy's illness, she'd recover. That she, Sadie, and Dylan would be fine no matter what became of the farm. That if he had to leave Hart's Hollow at the end of the summer, return to New York and the status quo, he wouldn't spend the next fifty years regretting that he hadn't built a new life here with what little time he had left with Emmy. With Sadie and Dylan. And with Kristen.

Only, that tight knot in his chest and every instinct he possessed screamed otherwise. And there was a small, quiet voice inside that whispered he might still be able to do something about it.

"I didn't used to think so." Mitch lifted one hand from the steering wheel, threaded his fingers through hers and squeezed them tightly. "But I'm beginning to believe it."

Every time Kristen returned to Hart's Hollow Farm, a feeling she couldn't quite put her finger on rushed through her veins, filled her chest, and moistened her eyes. She'd never experienced the sensation in her old life, but when Mitch rounded a sharp curve as he drove Emmy's old truck back from their shopping trip, and the familiar red driveway appeared, it returned full force.

The three deep ruts embedded two feet up the driveway were still there, making her smile as they were jostled in the cab while passing over them. Sunlight hit the strawberry sign by the road at just the right angle to draw her eyes, and the recognizable style of her own art widened her smile even more. Fields, previously empty, were now filled with healthy green soybean plants to the point of overflowing. And the familiar clang of a broken gourd against the metal rack greeted them as they—

"Good night above," she whispered, sitting up straighter. "Why are all those cars here?"

They were everywhere: compact cars and sedans were parked in single file down the driveway, a few SUVs straggled over the slight slope of the field to the left, and a slew of heads, striding legs, and waving arms flashed in the empty spaces between as people milled about near the house.

"I don't know." Mitch stopped the truck behind the long line of parked vehicles and cut the engine.

"We've been in town a couple of hours." She glanced at him, and the tight clench of his jaw sent a chill through her. "Do you think something happened to E—"

He'd thrust his door open, jumped out, and jogged halfway up the driveway by the time she'd unbuckled her seat belt and managed to follow, weaving her way awkwardly between vehicles.

She skidded to a stop just inches from his back at the end of the driveway. He stood frozen in place, his eyes on the scene before him and his broad shoulders blocking the view. "Mitch?"

"Look." He reached back, and his hand fumbled along her hip before grasping her fingers and tugging her close to his side. A slow smile stretched across his face. "Before long, Emmy won't have a strawberry left."

She followed the direction of his gaze to the crowd that had gathered toward the back side of the farmhouse, right at the edge of Emmy's strawberry field. There were dozens of people walking the paths between the rows of fruit, carrying white buckets—including Elena Martinez, Al and Stephanie Jenkins, and Jenny Yarrow from the Citizens Advisory Committee meeting.

A few middle-aged men in jeans and light blue collared shirts were bent over rows of plants, chatting and laughing with each other as they picked. A group of older women kneeled on blankets they'd spread on the ground, inspecting each berry closely through thick glasses, passing it to the woman seated next to them for approval, then placing it gently in a large box.

And children . . . Gracious, there were so many. Several boys and girls Dylan's age stood on red dirt beyond the field, tossing a football, with dozens of strawberry-filled buckets at their feet. Toddlers held tight to their parents' hands, some bending awkwardly to pick a berry and others chewing with happy expressions, red juice spilling down their chins.

And Emmy was smack-dab in the middle of it all, her deep belly laugh traveling across the front lawn as she spoke with a group of women.

"Well, it's about time the two of you showed up." Ruth Ann squeezed sideways between two cars, with Sadie skipping behind, long braids bouncing.

"This your handiwork?" Mitch asked, lifting his chin toward a big white van parked at the edge of the front lawn, with PEACH GROVE METHODIST CHURCH written in elegant font on the side.

Ruth Ann smiled. "No. It's Emmy's." She motioned over her shoulder to the strawberry field. "I may have called a friend or two last night, after my visit here, and told them how delicious our strawberry shortcakes turned out and that Emmy's fresh crop was the reason why."

"Just one friend or two?" Mitch teased, one dark brow lifting.

"Well"—Ruth Ann spread her hands—"one friend happened to be a minister, and the other a schoolteacher who wanted to do a good deed." She stepped closer and whispered, "I may not have always shown it, but I care for Emmy a great deal, as do a lot of other people." She waved one hand to the side. "But don't tell Emmy that. She'd throw everyone off the farm within ten seconds if she thought there was even a whiff of charity in the air, and right now she's enjoying herself."

"You always were a sweet soul, Mrs. Ruth Ann." Mitch bent his head and kissed her cheek. "Thank you for doing this."

"Oh, the thrill," Ruth Ann simpered, pressing a palm to her cheek. "Had I known that was the thanks I'd get, I'd have done it a long time ago, my dear handsome boy. What a shame I was born two generations too soon." She narrowed her eyes and lifted one shoulder coquettishly at Kristen. "Otherwise, I'd give you a run for your money, Kristen."

Mitch tossed his head back and laughed. His throaty chuckle took Kristen's mind off the heat scorching her cheeks and gave her a thrill of her own.

"Did you get the swing, Ms. Kristen?" Sadie asked, tugging at Kristen's jeans.

Kristen looked down and smiled. "We did. And we found the perfect cushion. It's red with white stripes."

Sadie's eyes brightened. "And squishy?"

Kristen laughed. "Very."

Sadie turned to Mitch. "Can we put the swing up today? With the cushion, too?"

"Sure we can." Mitch motioned toward the crowd milling about the property. "But I need to help your nana out with these customers for a while, then check the fields."

"I can do that," Kristen said. "I'll help you unload the porch swing and chairs, and then I'll check for weeds while you help Emmy. That way, we'll be able to tackle installing the swing before dark."

Mitch tilted his head, his warm gaze roving from the top of her head down to the tips of her toes. "You don't mind?"

"Not at all."

A slow grin spread across his face. After leaning close, he cupped her cheek with a broad hand and nuzzled the shell of her ear. "You're a dream, you know that?"

She lit up on the inside, and her breath caught as she whispered back, "A good one, I hope?"

"Heaven." His lips brushed her temple as he murmured her answer from yesterday, the hunger deepening his husky tone, making it all the sweeter. "Pure heaven."

A throat cleared, and Kristen pulled back, returning Mitch's grin.

"When you're ready for introductions and small talk," Ruth Ann said, mouth twitching, "just let me know, Mitch. In the meantime, I'm going to assist Emmy."

With one last knowing look, Ruth Ann left to join Emmy. Sadie, however, hovered nearby. Her wide eyes moved slowly from Kristen to Mitch, then back, her expression lifting and her smile widening.

"Can I help you check the corn, Ms. Kristen?" she asked, blinking up at her.

"Sure. I'd like that."

Blushing, Sadie hopped in place with excitement, then, hesitating, reached out and lifted her hand toward Kristen.

It wasn't an easy gesture. Kristen knew that. Since the ride home from Peach Grove after Emmy's episode, when the little girl had fallen asleep in her arms, they'd grown closer, but Sadie had continued to carefully keep her distance, and so had she. But now, looking into Sadie's cute face, full of hope and happiness, she found herself unable to take a step back.

Instead, she took Sadie's hand in hers. Sadie's small fingers curled, the warm fingertips pressing snugly against Kristen's skin, their gentle squeeze flooding her with so much warm comfort, it spilled over her lashes.

Kristen looked away, dragged her cheek over her shoulder, and glanced at Mitch. He was watching her closely, and the kind, admiring look in his eyes deepened. He walked to the other side of Sadie, took her other hand in his and led the way back toward Emmy's truck. Sadie skipped between them, swinging their hands back and forth and humming a happy tune, and Mitch met Kristen's eyes several times along the way.

I'll make a place for you, Kristen.

"Heaven, indeed," she whispered, heart swelling.

After unloading the porch swing, rocking chairs, and cushion, Kristen and Sadie climbed into the truck and left to check the fields. It took two hours to drive around and scout the soybeans. The small plants were thriving, the leaves green, healthy, and clear of pests. Light but frequent steady rains over the past couple of weeks had encouraged rapid growth in both the soybean plants and the cornstalks.

When Kristen reached her field and parked the truck, a small gasp escaped her.

"They're getting bigger," Sadie piped from the passenger seat, craning her neck to peer at the field.

"They certainly are."

The midafternoon sun, a bright golden sphere, sat comfortably a few feet above the horizon. Rays of heat beamed over the three-foot-tall stalks, and Kristen could almost feel the powerful streams of light coaxing the strong green leaves out of the red earth, beckoning each tip to unfurl and lift itself higher to the flawless blue sky tinged with a blushing pink.

Kristen climbed out of the truck and walked to the field's edge. She stood there, savoring the heat seeping into her skin, the light breeze that ruffled her hair, and the impressive green growth, which had transformed the once barren ground into a well-nourished cradle of new life.

She tipped her head back and smiled at the sky. "Gorgeous."

Kristen walked each block of rows, carefully checking green leaves for pests, taking soil and leaf samples, and monitoring for weeds. Sadie stayed close by her side, and after a while, though Kristen's legs, back, and shoulders ached, she followed Sadie's energetic lead and skipped to the end of one row.

"Wanna race to the end of that one?" Sadie asked, pointing down the last row of corn, to where it met the tree line.

Kristen grinned. "You're on." After crouching into a runner's position at the starting mark, she shot a sidelong glance at Sadie and waited as the little girl mimicked her posture. "Ready, set, go!"

Kristen took off, laughing, and slowed her strides so Sadie could catch up and eventually pass her. Specks of dirt flew up from Sadie's stomping sneakers, the tang of clay rushed into Kristen's lungs, and the breeze picked up, soothing their sweat-slicked skin and rustling leaves on the trees.

"I win," Sadie shouted before doubling over by a tree and breathing hard.

"Woo," Kristen laughed, dragging the back of her

hand across her hot forehead. "You wiped the floor with me."

"Hey, what's that?"

Kristen followed the direction of Sadie's outstretched arm and narrowed her gaze on a small clearing just visible between the trunks of several trees.

"I don't know." Kristen shielded her eyes and headed in that direction. "Let's go poke around."

They reached the clearing, a brief stretch of green ground that received a hefty dose of sunlight. An overturned rusty wheelbarrow rested on the grass by a small metal shed. High weeds grew around it, but there were a few broad leaves and small white flowers tangled within the thick growth. Beyond this, in a brown pile of litter, several rotten gourds slumped into the hard ground.

"Joe's place," Kristen said, smiling.

She walked to the shed, carefully sidestepping green vines and motioning for Sadie to do the same, then tugged on the dented metal door. It swung open with a squeak, revealing several wooden tables cluttered with leaves, debris, and . . . gourds. Dried brown gourds of all shapes and sizes, some peeling, some rotten, and some in absolutely perfect shape for an artistic hand.

Sadie edged over to a table and poked one brown shell with a fingertip. "What are they?"

"Gourds." Kristen joined her, gently brushed aside a pile of twigs and leaves, then ran her palm over a particularly large one, admiring the dark markings. "Like the one hanging from your nana's rack by the driveway." She smiled wider. "A few of these are whole, cured, and in great shape."

Sadie wound her hand around Kristen's upper arm and leaned close, eyeing the gourd. "Great shape for what?"

"For painting." She traced the natural markings with her thumb. "See these? They give each shell a life of its own. You can paint them, and once you hollow them out, they're perfect for birds—especially purple martins."

"You can make it into a birdhouse?"

"Yep. Native Americans used them that way to attract birds and keep insects down. And art . . . Oh, they made beautiful art with them. Still do." Kristen picked the gourd up, lifted it into the light streaming in through holes in the metal roof and examined it from different angles. "I think this one would make a perfect birdhouse." She envisioned a combination of red, yellow, and blue paint filling in the natural markings to complete a solid image. An image she had seen in so many of Emmy's photographs and could replicate—if Mitch was willing to help her secretly borrow a few of the pictures from Emmy's shoebox. "And it'd make a perfect birthday gift for Emmy."

"Can I make a birdhouse for Nana, too?" Sadie grabbed a gourd from the table and held it up. "Out of this one?"

Kristen nodded. "That'd be wonderful."

"How will we do it?" Sadie asked. The tip of her tongue touched the corner of her mouth as she narrowed her eyes at the gourd.

"We'll wash, scrub, and cut an entrance hole and a place for hanging it. Then we'll scrape out the seeds and let it dry. We'll soak it in a preservative, let it dry again, then paint it. After that, it'll be ready to hang."

"And the birds will come?"

"Yes." She pointed to the center of Sadie's gourd. "They'll make a nest right there."

"Once it's empty?"

Kristen nodded.

Sadie's eyes sparkled with glee. "For the baby birds?"

"That's right." The excited delight in Sadie's expression mirrored her own. Kristen reached out and smoothed a hand over the little girl's soft hair, the motion a practiced one from her past.

Something heavy returned inside her with the action. Something that had been replaced in recent days with Mitch's kisses, Sadie's and Dylan's laughter, and Emmy's approving comments. It surged forth with renewed vengeance, pricking at her conscience and welling in her eyes. It warred with the peace struggling to take root in her heart.

Kristen forced herself to speak past the thick feeling in her throat. "The hollow inside will be a perfect place for them to grow."

CHAPTER 10

Mitch gripped the handle he'd just installed on the new screen door he'd purchased for Emmy's porch, clicked the black push button latch several times to make sure it worked, then opened and shut the door to check the alignment.

"Works like a charm," he said, glancing over his shoulder.

Kristen, standing on the front lawn, near the bottom porch step, shielded her eyes against the low-hanging sun, looked up at him and flashed a crooked smile. "And it only took you two and a half hours. Impressive."

Mitch laughed. "All right, now. That included the trip to town to pick it up, haul it back, unbox it, and install it without directions and a missing part. I think that speaks volumes as to my handyman skills." He looked pointedly at Dylan, who stood beside Kristen as she slid a hand-painted gourd onto the arm of a small gourd rack. "Let that be a lesson to you, Dylan. A Hart doesn't need much to pull off great feats."

Dylan shared an amused look with Kristen, then

smirked. "Whatever you say, Uncle Mitch." He handed a cotter pin over to Kristen, then watched as she used it to secure the gourd in place. "Is that one yours or Sadie's?"

"Mine." Kristen stepped back, then adjusted the gourd so it hung more evenly. "Sadie wants to hang her own."

As if on cue, the front door opened and Sadie pressed her palms and face against the screen door. "Can we come out yet?"

Mitch chuckled, pressing a finger to her nose as it smooshed against the screen. The decorative white trim surrounding the screen provided a perfect frame for her small face. "Just you, little bit, so you can set up your present. Tell Nana to wait a few more minutes."

As she shouted his request toward the interior of the house, he laughed harder and looked back at Kristen. Her attention was firmly focused on Sadie, and the carefree grin she'd sported minutes earlier had dimmed.

"Kristen?" He waited until those gorgeous green eyes met his. "Everything okay?"

She shrugged her shoulders slightly, her grin returning full force. "Yeah. Just anxious to get Emmy's b-day started."

Mitch tensed. *B-day*, at least today, had more than one connotation. Today might be the twenty-eighth of June and Emmy's seventy-fourth birthday, but it could also be classified as a bad day—at least for Emmy.

It had started this morning. He had left early, prior to sunrise, had picked up a freshly baked batch of blueberry and cream cheese sweet rolls from the Dutch Restaurant, then had returned in what he'd thought would be plenty of time to get coffee started and greet Emmy when she woke up and made her way to the kitchen. Only, when he'd returned, Emmy had been pacing the house, wringing wet hands and frantically searching for soap. She had opened every cabinet in the kitchen, had pulled out every drawer in her bedroom dresser, and had left a trail of shoes throughout the house, having overturned every pair, apparently searching inside each one for what eluded her.

No one else had been up at the time, and he'd spent the better part of an hour calming her down and setting everything back in its rightful place. Over coffee and quiet contemplation as the sun began to rise outside the kitchen window, she'd eventually managed to regain her bearings.

Her cheeks had flushed, and she'd patted his hand awkwardly, pleading softly, "Please don't tell Kristen. All of you have worked so hard preparing for my birthday. Let's just go on as usual."

At the time, he hadn't been sure Emmy even knew the full extent of what she was asking him not to tell. And though he would've hated to burden Kristen, he'd desperately wanted to seek comfort in her arms to lighten the heavy pain that grew inside him at the confused, frightened look in Emmy's eyes.

But Emmy's wish had been too heartfelt for him to deny. Especially on her birthday.

So, he'd nodded in agreement, and they'd finished their coffee. When Kristen and the kids joined them in the kitchen shortly afterward, they'd returned to the normal morning routine.

Everything had continued as it had every day for the past month—except for the way Mitch had found his eyes returning to Emmy throughout the morning and well into early afternoon, studying her wary expression for any signs of renewed confusion or fear, until he'd finally had to drive to town to pick up the screen door.

The screen door burst open, the frame bumping into Mitch's legs, as Sadie ran out onto the porch. "Whoa there, sweet Sadie." He caught her elbow and steadied her when she stumbled. "That gourd of yours isn't going anywhere."

Bouncing with endless energy, she squeezed his forearms. "It turned out perfect, didn't it? Just like Ms. Kristen said it would."

His smile returned. "It sure did, baby."

That, he had no trouble admitting without reservation. He watched Sadie skip down the front porch steps, join Kristen and Dylan by the gourd rack, and pick up her gourd from the ground. It was purple with big, colorful daisies adorning each side.

Over the past several weeks, Kristen had spent one hour with Sadie every night after dinner, guiding her hand across blank sheets of paper, helping her sketch flowers and color them in with colored pencils Kristen had picked up in town. When Sadie had asked Kristen for a more challenging practice, they'd moved on to oil-based paint, using several small canvases Mitch had ordered online and had shipped to the house.

Emmy had admired them from afar, usually seated at Mitch's side, and had commented on how patient a teacher Kristen was. How caring and kind.

It had taken every ounce of restraint Mitch had not to divulge Kristen and Sadie's secret project and let Emmy know that all the practice was for her benefit. Or that the hours Kristen spent on the front porch each night after Emmy went to bed had been used to piece together a scrapbook of Emmy's favorite memories using photos he'd removed from her shoebox when she wasn't around. All this effort on behalf of creating the perfect birthday.

And oh, man. Just watching Kristen—the gentle way she cradled Sadie's hand in her own as she taught her to paint, and the careful, precise way she pieced together Emmy's photos, rubbing her tired eyes as she bent closer to the task at hand, her blond hair sliding over her shoulders—had melted his heart that much more.

"Can I hang mine now?" Sadie asked, stretching up on her toes and lifting her gourd toward one of the metal arms protruding from the rack.

"Of course." Kristen walked around the fourteen-foot pole that supported a large rack, placed her hands at Sadie's waist, then lifted her high enough so that she could reach the metal arm, which was lowered to half-mast. "Got it?"

Sadie giggled, wobbling in Kristen's grasp, as she slid the gourd onto the metal arm. Dylan moved swiftly and tacked it in place with a cotter pin.

"Got it," Sadie shouted, clapping her hands together.

Kristen lowered her back to the ground, and the trio stepped back and exchanged smiles as they admired their handiwork.

"Do you have your other present ready, Kristen?" Mitch asked.

She nodded. "It's in the gift bag on the porch swing."

"Dylan?" Mitch glanced at a small table on the porch. It was covered with a white tablecloth, and a chocolate cake sat on a plate in the center, sealed with plastic wrap. Surprisingly, Dylan, who'd asked for Ruth

Ann's help, had baked it himself. "You want to light the candles on that excellent cake of yours?"

A few minutes later, after Dylan had unwrapped the plastic and arranged candles on the cake, he lit the final one. "Can she come out now?"

Mitch glanced at Kristen, Sadie, and Dylan, all gathered on the porch, eyes shining with excitement and faces lit with smiles. He laughed. "Yeah. I think y'all will burst if we put it off any longer."

He went inside. Emmy sat at the kitchen table, sipping tea and staring at the table.

"They're ready, Emmy. Feel up to joining us?"

She glanced up at him, blinked a few times, then asked, "They're ready for what?"

"For you." He walked over, cupped her elbow, and leaned close. "It's your big day, Emmy."

"My big day?" A thread of uncertainty laced her tone.

Mitch's throat constricted. "Your birthday."

"Oh." She shook her head, a bit of the confusion leaving her eyes. "You know I don't like people fussing over me."

"I know. But maybe just this once? For the kids? They've worked really hard on your gifts." He smiled. "So has Kristen."

"She has?" A small smile appeared.

"Yep." He tugged gently on her elbow. "So help me out here, and let's humor them, okay?"

She patted his cheek, her smile growing. "All right. But just this once."

They walked to the screen door, Emmy limping more than usual. Then she stopped. "Look, it's . . ." She paused, reaching out and trailing a hand over the screen. "It's new. You did this, didn't you?"

He grinned. "Yes, ma'am, I did."

"Thank you, Mitch. It's beautiful."

"There's more where that came from." Smiling, he opened the door and swept out his arm. "After you, birthday girl."

A laugh escaped her, and as soon as her foot touched the floor of the front porch, the first verse of "Happy Birthday" rang out. Kristen, Sadie, and Dylan swayed from left to right, their arms around each other's waists, as they belted out the tune.

Mitch laughed along with Emmy, and dang if she didn't perk up pretty good at their display. She watched the candle flames flicker in the breeze and squeezed his hand tighter as they sang.

When they finished, Dylan beckoned her over. "Blow 'em out, Nana."

She walked over and blew the candles out, laughing the whole time.

"Dylan made the cake for you," Kristen said, nudging him forward.

"You did?" Emmy asked.

He blushed. "Yes, ma'am. Mrs. Ruth Ann helped me."

"Well, that was wonderful of you." Emmy bent and kissed his cheek. "Thank you, son."

Mitch waited, watching Dylan's expression for any signs of aggravation at the endearment. Dylan had been so put out by the term when Emmy had used it the night Mitch had returned to Hart's Hollow. But he didn't seem bothered by it today.

"You're welcome." Dylan grinned, blushing a deeper shade of red. "And happy birthday."

"I got something for you, too, Nana." Sadie grabbed Emmy's hand and pulled.

"Easy, Sadie." Mitch walked over, loosened Sadie's grip on Emmy, then helped Emmy make her way down the front porch steps to the small gourd rack.

"That's the one I made for you," Sadie said, pointing at her purple, daisy-laden gourd.

Emmy cupped it in her palm and examined it more closely. "It's gorgeous, Sadie. Absolutely gorgeous."

Mitch guided her hand over to the other gourd. "Kristen made this one."

He examined it with Emmy. Though he'd watched Kristen paint the gourd in its beginning stages, this was the first time he'd seen her finished handiwork.

She'd painted the top of the gourd a deep yellow reminiscent of sunlight; the bottom, a deep red in the form of Hart's Hollow's winding dirt driveway; and in the center, she'd painstakingly sketched and detailed Joe's original tractor.

Emmy leaned closer. Her eyes glistened as they traced the path of vibrant blue that outlined Joe's favorite machine. "Why, it's Joe's tractor. That's it, exactly."

"She's captured a memory," Mitch said, admiration filling him when he glanced at Kristen. "One of your favorites."

"And there's more." Kristen sprinted up the front porch steps, grabbed the gift bag from the swing, and brought it to Emmy. "Happy birthday, Emmy."

Emmy, still enthralled with the painting cupped in her palm, stared at Kristen, then the bag. "What is it?"

Smiling, Kristen set the bag on the ground, removed the tissue paper, and pulled out the scrapbook. The cover was made of wood and it had a black leather binding. In the center, she'd carved a large heart with Emmy's and Joe's initials entwined inside, and two large oak trees resembling those in front of the farmhouse framed the edges.

"All your favorites are inside." Kristen opened the album, then slowly turned the pages. Each one held two or three of Emmy's photos. Some were just of Joe, others were of Emmy and Joe, but all of them were arranged elegantly with a loving hand. "Here's Joe fishing in the pond." She turned another page. "And here's his tractor. This one's—"

"Where did you get those?"

The sharp bite in Emmy's voice startled them all. Sadie flinched, and Dylan stepped back.

Kristen's hand froze on the scrapbook, her fingers digging into the picture she was displaying.

"I gave them to her." Mitch moved to Kristen's side and covered her hand with his. "Kristen wanted to make something special for you and asked me to h—"

"Asked you to steal for her?" Emmy's mouth tightened, and bright red blotches formed on her neck and cheeks.

"No." Mitch swallowed hard. Tried to steady his voice. "Kristen asked me to help her put together a scrapbook for your birthday, so all your pictures could be kept safe in one pla—"

"Safe?" Emmy snatched at the scrapbook, wrenched it out of Kristen's hands, and clutched it to her chest. "She stole from me." Her eyes flashed, and she pinned Kristen with a look of hatred, which Mitch had never seen on her face. "What'd you bring, girl? What're you trying to do?" She stabbed a gnarled finger in Kristen's direction. "You said you wouldn't steal from me. Said you wouldn't lie. And here you are, doing both."

"I-I'm sorry, Emmy," Kristen whispered.

Mitch nudged Kristen's back, stepped in front of her, and spoke calmly. "Kristen didn't lie, and she didn't steal from you. She was trying to do something nice for your birthday."

"You're just like the rest of them," Emmy continued, shouting at Kristen, her face crumpling, tears streaming down her cheeks. "A thief and a liar. You came to tear down my house. To steal from me. Get off my land. You hear me, girl? This ain't your home."

Kristen's face paled, and the hurt flashing in her green eyes stabbed Mitch on the inside, making his hands shake as he guided Emmy toward the house. "Emmy, everything's all right. We'll take the pictures back out if you'd like."

"She stole from me." Emmy trembled in his hold. "I won't let someone steal from me."

"It's okay," he repeated, helping her up the steps and into the porch swing. He knelt in front of her, covered her hands with his on the scrapbook. "We'll take them all out and put them back in the shoebox if that's what you want." He waited for a few minutes, until her sobs began to subside. "Is that what you want to do, Emmy? Do you want to take them out and put them back in the shoebox?"

The panic left her eyes and her brow furrowed as she focused on the task he'd suggested, then said calmly, "Yes. I want to take them out."

"Okay." He squeezed her hands and stood. "Come with me. I'll get the shoebox, and we'll take them out, okay?"

She nodded, a strand of gray hair slipping from her topknot and falling over one eye.

He brushed it back, then helped her inside, casting a quick look over his shoulder at the front lawn. Sadie, crying, pressed her face against Kristen's middle. Kristen hugged her close, her mouth moving as she spoke softly to Dylan, who stood close by her side. The smiles they'd sported earlier were gone, a mix of shock and sadness having taken their place.

Bad day, it seemed, had been an understatement.

Thirty minutes later, Emmy sat on the edge of her bed as he carefully peeled the last photograph from the scrapbook Kristen had created. Her tears had stopped almost as abruptly as they'd begun.

"They're all back where you had them now," Mitch said, placing the picture in the shoebox with the others. He lifted the shoebox from the floor and set it on her lap. "Would you like to look through them?"

She blinked slowly, then shook her head. "I'm tired."

"Then lie back and take a nap." He stood, moved the shoebox to the nightstand, and helped ease her back against the pillows. "I'll be right outside when you wake up."

Her eyes closed and she drifted off before he reached the door, her deep breaths steady and even. He closed the door behind him quietly, then followed the soft clink of silverware into the kitchen.

Dylan and Sadie sat at the table with half-empty glasses of milk in front of them, taking bites of two large slices of birthday cake. Chocolate icing coated their lips, and crumbs clung to their chins. Sadie was no longer crying, and Dylan looked more at ease, too.

"Where's Kristen?" Mitch glanced around, an uneasy feeling knotting in his gut.

"She went to get the truck," Dylan said around a mouthful of cake. "Said she's going to check the fields while we eat. Is Nana okay?"

Mitch nodded, already heading for the front door. "She's taking a nap. Stay here with Sadie, all right? I'll be back in a sec."

He didn't wait for an answer, and by the time he reached the front lawn, Kristen was pulling Emmy's truck onto the driveway. Jogging, he caught up to the slow-moving vehicle, then rapped his knuckles against the driver's side window.

She spotted him, stopped the truck, and rolled down the window. "How is Emmy?"

"Resting." He leaned on the windowsill and studied her blank expression. It was guarded and unapproachable. So much like when they'd first met. "Thank you for taking care of Sadie and Dylan."

"I was happy to." She faced the driveway again, a tiny muscle ticking in her jaw as her hand moved toward the old-fashioned window handle. "I'll head out and take care of the field work."

"She didn't mean it." He reached inside the cab, captured her hand, and threaded his fingers through hers. "She's having a bad day. It's going to happen occasionally, and it has nothing to do with you."

Kristen nodded, giving a small smile that didn't reach her eyes.

He waited. Searched her expression. "That was her illness talking, Kristen. Not her heart. You know that, don't you?"

Eyes gentling, she lifted her hand, cupped his jaw, and smoothed her thumb across his cheek. "I know. Please don't worry about me. I'm fine. You have enough on your mind, and Emmy needs you. Besides, it's getting late, and the fields need to be checked. I think it'd help if I give her some space for a while."

Reluctantly, Mitch released her, then moved back, watching as she put the truck in gear. "That was her illness talking," he repeated. "Not her heart."

Kristen glanced at him, smiled that empty smile once more, then drove away. Red clouds of dust billowed out from the worn tires and drifted slowly across the front lawn.

The strained note in her voice left Mitch wondering if she truly understood. And the vacant, detached look in her eyes made him question when—and if—she'd return.

Kristen ran. Legs burning, she forced one foot in front of the other, propelling herself farther away from the truck, which she'd parked a mile back at a neighboring field. Farther away from the grave intensity in Mitch's eyes, and as far as she could manage to get from Emmy's angry shouts, Dylan's fear, and Sadie's desperate sobs.

Get off my land.

Her lungs constricted with each fierce stride, struggling to catch the brief air she snatched in with ragged breaths. Bits of gravel, soil, and clay stung her bare ankles and shins, and sweat slicked down her back, plastering her thin T-shirt to her skin.

This ain't your home.

Just ahead, the sun hit the horizon. The bright blaze of light pulsed more strongly just as the dusk-darkened land began to swallow it, the trees and the beaten red path starkly defined below. And in that moment—God forgive her—she'd never seen a thinner line between heaven and hell.

She broke from the dirt path and darted left into the cornfield she'd planted almost two months ago.

The ten-foot-tall stalks slapped her shoulders and neck as she sprinted past. Out of breath, she drew to a halt in the middle of the field; shoulders sagging, she dropped to her knees.

A high-pitched screech rang out and echoed across the field. She looked up, eyes drawn to the dark outline of a familiar red-tailed hawk. Wings spread wide and talons stretched, it swept across the gold-streaked sky on a strong current, then circled back, swooping low.

"You're back," she said, her breath puffing between dry lips. The bitter taste in her belly crept up her throat, and she forced a halfhearted smile, hoping to subdue it. "It's been a while. Are you looking for dinner? 'Cuz I'm not it."

Another cry, sharp dive on the current, then return glide.

"Though I will say, you're seeing me hit a new low." She pressed her palms to the ground and curled her fingers into the red soil. "Sitting in dirt, talking to some bird a hundred feet up who can't hear what I'm saying, much less care or understand."

The soaring movement of the hawk blended with the shadows, which loomed larger as the sun descended. She fixed her attention on the bird, her eyes and chest burning.

When I get better, we can go back home, can't we, Mama?

"She won't get better." Her throat closed. "Emmy won't get well. She'll only get worse, like Ruth Ann said."

Kristen squeezed her eyes shut, and hot tears rolled over her lashes. The thick leaves adorning the cornstalks rustled on the breeze, brushing her arms.

"She'll have to leave here, and so will Mitch. He'll take Sadie and Dylan with him. Then they'll build the bypass, pave Hart's Hollow over, and it'll disappear."

The wind picked up, lifting her hair from her neck in waves and drying the salty tears in tight patches on her cheeks.

"Or what's left of it," she said, mouth trembling. "There's not much out here now as it is."

Only there was. There were fertile fields stretching as far as the eye could see. Rich red soil that nourished and grew new life in places that had once been barren. There were honeysuckle breezes and enchantment in the land that birthed the healthiest berries and the sweetest dreams that could be imagined. There was the warm grip of Sadie's trusting hand and the renewed hope reflected in Dylan's smile. There was the comforting feel of Emmy's approving words from days ago.

And there was Mitch. His soft kisses, gentle touch, and strong embrace. The intense want in his eyes whenever he looked at her since their trip to Peach Grove. An unspoken urging of sorts, as though he were silently asking her to voice what she was only now being forced to face. That Hart's Hollow Farm itself had become the home and family she'd always hoped to find.

But she had to leave. And soon.

Kristen tilted her head back, watched the hawk glide away. "Because how can I love someone else I know I'm going to lose?"

CHAPTER 11

Funny how a plank of wood less than two inches thick could feel as insurmountable as a four-mile-high mountain range.

Mitch raised a balled fist and knocked on the door of the guest bedroom again. "Kristen? Are you awake?"

No answer. He shifted from one foot to the other, then pressed his ear to the door. There was no rustle of sheets or footsteps across the floor, just continued silence.

Yesterday, after Emmy had settled down for a nap and Kristen had driven off, he'd spent a few hours with Sadie and Dylan. They had eaten another slice of cake, had played a short game of baseball in the front yard, then had drunk sweet tea and chatted on the front porch before he ushered them off to bed. Emmy had got up once, had eaten what passed for a decent supper, then had retired to her bedroom for the night.

Mitch had returned to the front porch, had sat in the swing and watched the driveway, hoping for Kristen to drive back up in Emmy's truck before dark.

But the afternoon sun had come and gone, night had fallen, the stars had come out, and there had still been no sign of Kristen.

Around eleven, he'd trudged inside and taken a shower. By the time he'd made it back to the front porch, Emmy's truck was parked in its usual spot by the shed. Upstairs, there had been no light escaping from beneath the door of Kristen's room, and only the low creak of the bed had let him know she'd made it safely inside.

He'd gone to bed himself then. After hours of tossing and turning, he had gotten up at five this morning and had worked his way through a few morning chores. By six, he hadn't been able to concentrate any longer and had returned to Kristen's bedroom door.

"Kristen? I'm worried about you." He rattled the doorknob a bit. "I'm coming in. All right?"

No answer again. After opening the door, he glanced hesitantly at the bed. She was there, all right, lying on her left side, huddled beneath the sheet. Her blond hair had slid over her cheek during her sleep, and it gleamed beneath the tendrils of soft morning sunlight shining through the window at her back.

He walked quietly across the room, leaned over the bed, and brushed her hair over her shoulder with a knuckle. "Kristen."

She stirred, a sigh escaping her, then opened her eyes. Sleep faded from her expression, and a smile appeared as she focused on his face.

He smiled back. "Morning. Sorry for waking you, but I was worried."

And just like that, her happy look of greeting dissolved. She didn't move, didn't speak, but the change was apparent all the same.

Dragging one hand across the back of his neck, he motioned toward the empty space beside her. "May I?" At her slight nod, he eased into a seated position on the bed. "I waited up for you last night. Where'd you go?"

She rubbed her forehead, stifling a yawn. "I checked the fields, then took a walk. Guess I lost track of time."

"After it got dark?" He held her gaze. Watched the color in her cheeks deepen. "For over six hours?"

She frowned, lifted to an elbow, then pushed herself upright against the pillow. "Did you come in here and wake me up just to interrogate me?"

"You can't blame me for being concerned, after the way you left yesterday," he said quietly. "And if you'd open up once in a while, I wouldn't have to ask."

"What do you want me to say?"

"Whatever you're feeling. Whatever you're thinkin—"

"I'm thinking it's Sunday and I could've used another hour of sleep." The frown morphed into a scowl. Her small nose wrinkled, and there was just a hint of dimples at the corners of her pinched mouth.

He grinned. "You're damned cute when you're angry, you know that?"

She stared for a minute, and then her mouth twitched. "That might've been a smooth line about twenty years ago, but it's kinda striking you out right now."

He laughed, the gleam of humor in her eyes lifting some of the tension from his shoulders. "Really?"

"Uh-huh."

"Hmm. Guess I'm gonna have to work on my approach."

Her eyes traveled over him, lingering on his chest, arms, then thighs. "Well, you have an advantage in at least one department."

He leaned closer, his gaze tracing the gentle swell of her lower lip. "Which one would that be?"

Her chest rose on a quick breath. "You're pretty easy on a girl's eyes. Especially first thing in the morning."

"It's pretty nice waking up to you, too."

He brushed his mouth across hers and waited. When she lifted her chin in invitation, he dipped his head again, parted her lips with his, and deepened the kiss until he coaxed forth a low, contented moan.

Her warm palm slid up over his shoulder, then cupped the back of his head. Her fingers weaved through his hair and then tugged him closer. Pleasurable tingles rippled over his scalp and down his back, and the feel of her hand on him, the soft glide of her touch, conjured forth a mix of emotions he'd never experienced before. Fierce desire, gentle tenderness, and an overwhelming urge to protect.

They caught him off guard. Made it damned near impossible to lift his mouth from hers and raise his head.

"Mitch?" She gazed up at him, returning his stare, her kiss-reddened mouth slightly swollen and lids heavy. A wary look crossed her expression as she whispered, "What is it you want me to say?"

That you love me. That you need me as much as I need you. That no matter what I'm up against, you're in it with me, and you'll stay, even though I know you want to run.

The words were on his tongue, were parting his

lips and stealing his breath. But the distant pain in her eyes, which appeared so often, halted them and made him choke back the plea for fear she'd bolt.

Instead, he reached behind his head, brought her hand forward, and turned it over. He trailed a fingertip from the edge of her soft palm to the pads of her fingers.

"I want you to say that you'll get dressed, then meet me on the other side of that door with an open mind." He reached out, lifted her other hand, and squeezed them both tight. "And that you'll let me borrow these for a little while."

Her brow furrowed, and her gaze moved from his face to his hands, still holding hers, then to the door. "That's all?"

"For now."

She remained quiet for a few moments before refocusing on him. Her voice so soft he barely caught her answer, she said, "Okay."

Ten minutes later, Mitch stood in the hallway, in front of the upstairs picture window Kristen had admired weeks ago, eyeing the streaks of dirt and the cloudy glass beneath the dim overhead light. He'd arranged two step stools, a bucket of distilled water, a stack of soft cloths, and a bottle of dishwashing liquid at his feet.

"All right, I'm here. Now what?"

He turned and grinned at Kristen, who stood outside her bedroom door, dressed in jeans and a T-shirt and looking somewhat accommodating. "You can start by coming a little closer."

She did, a brief smile appearing before she lifted an eyebrow at the materials on the floor and stepped up beside him. "So you want to borrow my hands to help you clean windows?"

"Nope." Mitch looked down at her, lifted her hand, and kissed the center of her palm. "I need you to help me uncover some hidden beauty." He grabbed a cloth, applied a small amount of dishwashing liquid to it, then dipped it in the water and pressed it into her hand. After guiding her hand to the top left corner of the window, he pressed her palm to the glass and began a gentle circular motion. "Start here. Easy movements, one section at a time. When you reach the edge, dry that area off before moving to the next. I'll start on the other side."

She moved to speak but seemed to think better of it, shrugged and went to work.

Smiling, he prepped another cloth for himself, then moved to the window's right upper corner and started cleaning. They'd been working for half an hour when the sun began to rise, the tentative glow of sunlight dimming the brightness of the interior light. With each motion of her arm, Kristen leaned closer to the window, narrowing her eyes, and peered more closely at the small section of glass she'd uncovered. A thin line of deep green and a semicircle of vibrant pink were visible.

Mitch paused, his hand hovering over the glass, as she stopped scrubbing and roved her eyes over the upper expanse of the window. The surprised delight on her face alone was worth the risk he'd decided to take.

Her long blond hair rippled over her shoulders and spilled down her back as she craned her neck for a better view. "Stained glass?"

Hiding a smile, he went back to scrubbing. "Suppose we'll find out."

He felt her gaze on him, heard the small laugh

that escaped her, then grinned wider when she went back to work.

Over the next hour, the sun rose higher as they continued to wipe thick layers of grime from the glass. Sunlight cut through the gleaming panels, and bursts of color surrounded them. Various hues of pink, red, yellow, and green splashed across the walls, covered the hardwood floor and tinted the creamy complexion of Kristen's cheeks as she cleaned.

When they finished, Kristen dropped her cloth, stepped back, and studied what they'd uncovered. Mitch tossed his rag and joined her.

A green vine intertwined with delicate pink roses covered the top half of the window, the ends trailing down the outer edges. It framed the scenery outside, hugged the outer slopes of the distant fields, and curled around the clear blue sky above the oak trees in the front yard.

Kristen stared, a look of awe appearing and her eyes glistening. "You were right, Mitch. It's beautiful."

"Another gift from Joe," he said, tipping his head back for a better view. The sun was strong now, its heat beating through the glass and warming his skin. "It's been years since I've thought about it, and even more since Emmy's been able to get up here and clean it. I'd almost forgotten what was underneath those layers of grime from years of neglect."

After stepping closer, he unlocked the window, then tugged it upward. The morning breeze swept in, filling the hallway with fresh air and the scent of honeysuckle.

"Needs a little greasing up, but it still works." He glanced over his shoulder. "Come take a look."

Kristen walked to his side and looked out at the scenery below.

"Is it as good a view as the first time you stood here?" he asked.

She nodded slowly, a muscle in her jaw ticking. "Better."

He followed her gaze to the land that sprawled before them. The red dirt driveway wound gently around the tall oak trees. Thick green grass carpeted the lawn, and beyond, the fields on either side of the farm's entrance were filled to the brim with lush, healthy soybean plants. And even farther in the distance, tall cornstalks gently waved with the push of the breeze.

"Had things been different for me and Carrie," Mitch said, a pang of regret stealing through his chest, "this could've been paradise. Or at least closer to heaven than to hell." He closed his eyes and exhaled a heavy breath. "It should've been, but I don't want to dwell on that anymore." After opening his eyes, he faced Kristen, speared his fingers through her hair, cupped her cheek in his palm. "I want to forgive."

She blinked up at him, her mouth trembling. "Forgive Emmy?"

Mitch nodded. "And Carrie. My dad. The world's disappointments, the bottle, whatever tempted them to become what they did." He moved closer, lowered his forehead to hers. "And myself, for holding on to all that mean hate for so long."

A small sound escaped her. She pressed close, sliding her hands up to splay over his chest. "There's no meanness in you, Mitch. And if you asked Emmy, she'd say there was nothing for her to forgive you for."

He lifted his head, encircling her wrists with his fingers. "I'm not asking her right now. I'm asking you." He steadied his voice, met her eyes. "This place was heaven for Emmy once. Help me make it that for her again?"

And for Sadie and Dylan. For us.

Her mouth parted soundlessly as she studied his face. Then she asked, "What do you mean?"

"I want Emmy to be able to stay here for as long as she wants. That means creating an alternative to that bypass. One that's so persuasive, it'll turn the most stubborn head." Tugging her hands from his chest, he entwined his fingers with hers. "These hands of yours are magic. I need 'em a little longer than just for today." He touched her temple with his thumb. "I need this sharp, magnificent mind." Mitch placed his palm on the upper swell of her breast, felt her heartbeat thumping strong against his skin. "I need that creative passion you hide in here."

Her chest lifted rapidly against his touch, and her gaze slid away, then focused on the base of his throat.

"We have one week from Tuesday until the next county meeting," Mitch urged. "One week to make a plan that will help this place breathe again."

"And if it doesn't work?"

The uncertainty in her tone chilled his blood. "Then at least we tried."

Kristen was silent for so long, his hand shook against her skin and his mind struggled to string together a more convincing argument. But then she lifted those beautiful green eyes back to him and spoke.

"Nine days, Mitch. I'll help you for nine days."

* * *

Kristen secured a gourd to the last empty metal arm on the rack in front of her. A particularly large one, the gourd had made a perfect canvas for a bright sunflower, and the brown background made the yellow paint pop in an appealing way. The other fifteen gourds she, Sadie, Emmy, Dylan, and Mitch—and even Zach—had painted were equally as impressive in terms of creative passion, if not artistic skill.

"Man, that's a whole lotta gourds."

Kristen smiled and glanced over her shoulder toward the sound of Zach's voice. He stood several feet farther up the driveway, with Dylan and Sadie by his side. Their heads were tipped back, eyes shielded from the late afternoon sun, as they looked up, admiring the view.

And it was most definitely a view to admire.

Since Sunday's early morning project with the stained-glass window almost one week ago, she and Mitch had gone straight to work. The house had been first on his list—"Revamp from the inside out," he'd said—so they'd started upstairs. They'd swept, mopped, then shined the hardwood floors and the staircase railing in the upstairs hall until every inch of wood gleamed beneath the sun pouring through the vibrant stained-glass window.

Bedrooms and bathrooms had been next. The guest rooms upstairs had been thoroughly cleaned, dusted, then redecorated with fresh bedding, antique oil lamps, and framed art Emmy had stored away in the shed for years. New shower curtains and fluffy towels had been placed in the bathrooms downstairs, and patchwork quilts Emmy had sewn years ago had been cleaned and added to the children's beds as well as Emmy's.

Downstairs, they'd knocked spiderwebs and dust bunnies out of nooks and crannies with brooms, scrubbed the kitchen countertops, and painted faded and chipped cabinets. Colorful area rugs and runners, which Mitch had purchased in town, had been spread across the living room floor and down the hallways; a welcome mat had been placed at the front door.

And the porch lights by the door . . . Oh, that had been the final touch. Already restored beautifully by Mitch's skilled hands, the Gothic trim and immaculately crafted porch rails beckoned every passing soul to take a seat on the new outdoor furniture, smile, converse, and rest beneath the gentle yellow glow of the new lantern-style fixtures Mitch had installed.

Even from where she stood now, with half of the long, winding driveway between her and the front porch, the white house seemed to rise higher from the lush green landscape surrounding it. Wide windows sparkled in the sunlight, the red chimneys stood proud, and Mitch's painstaking renovations had brightened the façade so much, it looked as though it had lifted slightly to cast a pleased, confident eye over the long line of gourd racks adorning both sides of the winding driveway.

Mitch has the magic touch. . . .

Emmy's comment had been an understatement.

"How many is it altogether, you think?"

Kristen blinked, shook herself slightly, then faced Zach. "Gourds?"

He nodded.

"Oh, about forty maybe."

Give or take. It'd taken hours and hours after long days of field work, but they'd all pitched in, each of them painting at least five gourds and Kristen crafting several more well past two in the morning each night over the past few days.

Even Zach, who'd finished his father's assigned community service and earned his skateboard back long ago, had continued to return to the farm each summer day to hang out with Dylan, help Mitch in the fields, and play baseball in the front yard.

With the house spiffed up, the fields packed full of lush green crops, and the sound of children's laughter echoing across the landscape, Hart's Hollow Farm vibrated with renewed energy.

"And it's all because of Kristen." Mitch strode up behind the boys, placed his big palms on the top of their heads, and ruffled their hair. "She's gonna turn us all into artists, if she hasn't already managed it."

His smile, adoring and warm, stirred flutters inside her that spread. "I don't think you needed much help from me."

Tamping down a familiar surge of desire, she turned away and studied the half dozen racks filled with colorful gourds of all shapes and sizes. New patches of painted circles and lines were revealed as the lazy rays of the setting sun roved over the gourds at different angles. Cicadas rattled in the distance, and the rhythmic vibrations, coupled with the slow-moving sunlight and the breeze-ruffled soybean plants, gave the scenery around her a gentle, throbbing presence. One that could be felt as much as seen.

Kristen unwound the rope from the pole's anchor and pulled, activating the pulley and raising the racks with smooth movements to the top of the pole.

"I wish Joe were here."

Kristen tensed, and her hands faltered around the

rope for a moment at Emmy's words. The rack rattled, and Mitch's hands covered hers, then helped pull the slack from the rope. The heat radiating from his muscular frame at her back made her long to turn, lay her head on his chest, and wrap her arms around him.

Kristen took a step forward and renewed her strong pulls on the rope.

"He would've loved the view." Emmy walked from the center of the driveway to the grassy edge beside Mitch, leaning on her cane, and ran a frail, thin-veined hand along the rack. "You did a wonderful job, Kristen."

With Mitch holding the rope along the rack, Kristen began knotting the end around the pole's anchor. She focused on the coarse rub of the weathered nylon against her fingers and the musty scent it released as she worked it into a secure position. "It wasn't me. All I did was pick up some paint, cut a few holes, then give y'all some pointers. You did the rest."

"No. You and I are both wrong." Emmy's voice, hesitant and affectionate, drew closer. She reached out, her arm brushing the front of Mitch's shirt as she stretched across him, and placed her soft palm over the back of Kristen's hand, stilling her movements. "We all did it. Together."

Kristen glanced down, and the sight of Emmy's pale hand resting over her own and Mitch's towering strength positioned by her side filled her eyes with wet heat.

After the painful incident that had occurred on Emmy's birthday, she'd kept a careful distance from Emmy for a couple of days. It wasn't that she hadn't wanted to spend time with Emmy—it was, in fact, the opposite.

She'd longed to take Emmy's elbow and assist her across the front lawn, listen to her stories of Joe, Cindy Sue, and life as it had been when Emmy was younger. She had even found herself missing Emmy's quick bites of sarcastic humor when Mitch was around. She'd hoped to collect a few more pleasant moments with Emmy, which she could carry with her down lonely roads when it was time to leave.

Despite wanting those things, Kristen had taken to leaving the house especially early in the morning over the past few days. She'd worked the fields alone save for the few hours Sadie had managed to persevere through the summer heat to trail after her. Every evening at dinner, she'd eaten slowly and methodically, spoken quietly, and maintained a humble, predictable presence in hopes of creating a calm atmosphere for Emmy.

Her actions hadn't had the effect she'd hoped for. Emmy, who had no recollection of her prior outburst, had cast wounded looks in her direction across the kitchen table during dinner and on the front porch, as they'd painted gourds each night. To Emmy, things were as they'd always been between them, and though Kristen knew in her head they still were, her heart had difficulty understanding.

She never knew, at any given moment, if she was speaking to the woman who'd welcomed her into her home, admired her hard work and dedication, and encouraged her to take charge of the family farm or if she was about to be confronted by a woman who thought she was a stranger, a thief, and a liar.

All things Kristen knew were untrue, but yet . . . they weren't. Not really. Because one day, Emmy wouldn't remember her at all, and in Emmy's mind at least, that was exactly who Kristen would become.

That realization had hit her Sunday, while she and Mitch had shined up that stained-glass window. The knowledge that no matter how beautiful, strong, or vibrant someone might be, they could slowly disappear, as though they'd never been. Like Cindy Sue, Emmy's cherished sister-in-law and best friend. Like Emmy when her mind failed her for the final time. And like Anna—a young, energetic, and once healthy daughter who should have long outlived her mother.

The thought was too painful to bear.

"We should celebrate," Emmy said, squeezing her hand. "I'll call Ruth Ann, invite her over to see the gourds. Then we'll bake something sweet again. Maybe a batch of cool lemon bars this time instead of shortcake. What do you say?"

Glancing up beneath her lashes, Kristen winced at the look of excitement on Emmy's face. "I'm sorry, Emmy," she whispered, sliding her hand away. "I need to work on some plans for Mitch."

"But can't that wait for a little while?" Emmy asked, confusion clouding her eyes. "I thought you enjoyed our last visit with Ruth Ann. We don't have to cook. We could do something different, like—"

"It's not that, Emmy." Kristen moved away, putting distance between them and pulling in a much-needed lungful of air. "I've been putting off finishing this for Mitch the last day or two, and it'll take a while."

"One afternoon off won't hurt," Mitch said, stepping toward her, his mouth tightening.

"It's Friday, Mitch. Your nine-day deadline is in four days." Steeling herself against the discomfort that appeared in his eyes at the reminder, she added,

"You can't walk in there empty-handed and expect a good result."

"You mean *we*, don't you?" His intense gaze held hers. "*We* can't walk in there empty-handed."

"Walk in where?" Emmy asked.

Hesitating, Mitch continued watching Kristen for a moment, then answered Emmy. "The Citizens Advisory Committee meeting on Tuesday."

"About the bypass?" Emmy studied both of their faces. "Y'all are making a plan?"

Mitch gave a reluctant nod. "I haven't mentioned it, because we have no way of knowing how it'll turn out." He spoke gently. "It may go well, and the Department of Transportation may reconsider taking the farm. Or there's a chance it'll make no difference what we say and they'll move forward in the same manner they've planned all along."

Emmy straightened, her fingers tightening around her cane and hope lighting her features. "But what you're planning might work? There could be a chance they might change their minds?"

Mitch glanced in Kristen's direction, and the gentle urging in the depths of his blue eyes and on his handsome face made her long to reassure Emmy, even though she knew it was a long shot. He walked over to Emmy, cupped the back of her gray head, and kissed her forehead softly. "That's one thing you've taught me well, Emmy. There's always a chance."

A wistful smile appeared on Emmy's face as she reached up and patted his cheek. "There's the sweet boy I've always known."

Throat tightening, Kristen spun around and headed for the house. Each brisk step kicked up a stinging spray of red dirt against her calf muscles, but she continued on, forcing a brief smile at the children as she passed.

Moments later, the familiar tread of heavy footsteps fell in behind hers. "Kristen, wait."

She closed her eyes and stifled a groan. "I'm sorry, Mitch, but I really need to get back to work in order to have the plans ready on time."

"I know, but there's one more thing I need to ask you to do."

The throb of urgency in his tone slowed her steps. She stopped, waited until he drew close, then said softly, "I've followed your notes to the letter, and I'm finalizing the sketches now. Is there anything else you'd like me to add to the polished illustrations?"

"Yes." His hands settled on her shoulders, then slid down to curve around her upper arms. The tangy scent of his aftershave grew stronger as he dipped his head and kissed the curve of her neck softly. His lips moved against her skin, the warm puffs of his breath ruffling wisps of her hair. "I want you to envision Hart's Hollow as your own. Imagine that Peach Grove is your town. And I want you to add all the things that would make it feel like home to you."

In spite of her best effort, a soft sob escaped her. She ducked her head, reached up and squeezed Mitch's hands, then pulled out of his hold and walked away.

There would be nothing to add to the final illustrations of Mitch's plans for the property. Hart's Hollow already felt like home exactly as it was, and walking away from it and the family she'd grown to love would be one of the hardest things she'd ever done. The painful act would be second only to let-ting go of Anna when fate had denied her the option to continue holding on.

But she wasn't a Hart, and this wasn't her home. She'd lost her family years ago, and if she stayed, she'd eventually lose Emmy, then Mitch, Sadie, and Dylan. Her heart couldn't survive another loss that big. She had to remember that and, when it was time, pack up and go.

"I'm no one," Kristen reminded herself quietly. She ducked under the oak trees' low branches, crossed the front lawn, and ascended the front porch steps. "Just a hard worker who'll soon be looking for a new job and place to stay."

CHAPTER 12

There's the sweet boy I've always known.

Mitch grinned, tightened the towel around his hips, wiped the steam from the bathroom mirror, and stared at his reflection. The tan he'd acquired from weeks spent outside planting the fields, scouting for pests, and spraying weeds had shaded the small crow's-feet beside his eyes. The thin grooves framing both sides of his mouth had lightened, and the extra ten pounds he'd picked up sitting in a cushy New York office chair over the past several years had fallen off, bringing a youthful definition to his cheekbones.

But what was most noticeable of all was where he stood. Here at Hart's Hollow, in Emmy's house, without so much as a scratch on him, preparing a way to persuade a committee of fifteen Adams County residents to save his childhood home, a once abusive and painful place. Somehow, he'd grown to feel connected to the land in so many ways since he'd met and begun working with Kristen.

He dragged his thumb and forefinger across the

stubble on his jaw and smiled. "What I want you to understand is that I never thought a stretch of land in the middle of nowhere could end up mattering so much to me."

No. That wasn't quite right. There was so much more to it than that.

He shifted his stance, cleared his throat, and tried again. "Three months ago, I was as skeptical as you and believed Hart's Hollow Farm was nothing more than land that needed to be sold and paved over in the interest of progress. But now I—"

He what? Frowning, Mitch stared at the sink and rubbed his palm absently over his abs, where droplets of water from his recent shower clung to his skin.

"Now it's . . ."

Impossible to imagine feeling as though he truly belonged anywhere else. Or uncovering the kind of hidden beauty—small pieces of heaven—that he'd found here, beneath painful memories and years of regretful neglect. Things like the unwavering devotion he'd found in Emmy; the untarnished hope Sadie and Dylan still possessed, despite the hardships they'd faced; and the quiet strength and endless comfort Kristen offered, despite the pain that obviously still lived inside her.

"Need some help with your speech?"

He started, his hip banging into the corner of the sink as he faced Kristen, who stood in the bathroom doorway.

"I'm sorry," she said, her grin fading as her wide eyes drifted over his bare chest, then lingered on his right hip, where he rubbed the sore spot. "I didn't mean to intrude. I was going to freshen up before the meeting and didn't realize you were still in here." Face red, she spun on her heel. "I'll come back la—"

"No." He snagged the hem of her T-shirt and tugged. "There's plenty of room. I'll take one side of the sink, and you can have the other." Smiling, he shrugged. "Besides, I think I could use some help in the speech department. My nerves tend to get the better of me, no matter how many presentations I've given."

Blushing a deeper red—if that was even possible—she glanced over her shoulder, met his eyes, then skirted carefully around him to the other side of the sink.

"Here." Mitch reached around her and scrubbed a second steam-free circle in the mirror. "Have at it."

"Thanks." Biting her lower lip, she tugged a drawer open, grabbed a ponytail holder, and pulled her long hair back. "Emmy and Dylan are ready. They're waiting on the front porch. And I just helped Sadie fix her hair, so we should be able to head out whenever you're ready."

"Sounds good." He grabbed a toothbrush, applied toothpaste, then began brushing, pausing every so often to speak around the bristles. "I looked over your illustrations last night. They're perfect. Thank you."

It was amazing what she'd accomplished in such a small amount of time. His bland black-and-white architectural sketches had been re-created on large canvases and given life with splashes of color and delicate details. But there'd been plenty of extra time for her to concentrate, considering she'd distanced herself from him, Emmy, and the kids more and more over the past four days.

"You're welcome." She twisted the top off a jar of moisturizer, dipped her fingers in the white cream, then smoothed it into her cheeks with slow circular movements. "If you need something else, just let me know."

Finished brushing his teeth, he rinsed his toothbrush, then his mouth, all while watching her graceful fingers travel over her pink cheeks in the mirror. "You're going to present the plan with me, aren't you?"

Her fingers stilled as she met his eyes in the mirror, then resumed their task with greater speed. "If you'd like me to. I don't know what I'd bring to the table that you haven't already covered. They're lucky to have you in New York. You're excellent at what you do."

"You had as much input as I did, if not more. I couldn't have done it without you."

Holding his gaze in the mirror, she lowered her hands, her chest lifting on quick breaths. After a moment, she looked away, and her eyes focused on the other side of the sink.

"Could you pass me that—"

"Do you mind handing me—"

Their outstretched arms bumped as they each reached for something on the opposite side of the vanity.

Mitch stilled, savoring the sensation of her warm skin pressing against his. Her forearm slid away as she pulled back, and he followed, curling his palm loosely beneath her elbow and stepping closer. "You asked me if I needed anything else," he said softly.

She glanced down at his hand, then focused on his bare chest, her eyes darkening. "Yes?"

He grinned. "I'm not above a good luck kiss if it'll help us pull this off."

Us. Man, that felt good on his tongue and sounded even better out loud. If only he could make it feel and sound as good to her.

Kristen looked up at him, a small smile forcing its way to her lips and a gleam of humor entering her eyes. "All right." Her attention drifted down to his chest, and she jerked her eyes back up to his, her smile fading. "But just one."

"Just one," he promised.

Nodding, she lowered her arms to her sides, closed her eyes, then lifted her chin and pursed her mouth just a tad.

A chuckle rose in his throat, but he stifled it, stepped closer, and cupped her jaw. *Just one*, he reminded himself, his laughter trailing away. Though he sensed she was pulling away from him, this was one of the few times she'd offered to let him in. He'd be damned if he wouldn't make it a good one.

He lowered his head and touched his mouth to hers. Nudging her lips apart, he swept the tip of his tongue across her bottom lip, savoring the taste of her and absorbing her soft cry of pleasure.

Her arms encircled his waist, and her small hands slid over his bare back, her fingers trailing along each dip and rise of his muscles, until they reached the towel. Curving inward, they tugged him closer. Then she went on her toes, pressed tighter against him, and urged him to deepen the kiss.

He complied, angling his head, touching his tongue to hers and sliding his hand around to cradle the back of her head. He walked her toward the wall slowly until the back of his hand and her bottom bumped it, and then he slid one leg between hers.

She moaned and squeezed his lower back with her fingertips. The gentle pressure of her touch, the sensual movement of her mouth, and the soft press of her breasts against the hardness of his chest were incredible.

His stubbled jaw rasped against her smooth, moisturized cheek, and the light scent of lotion mixed with the sweet smell of her shampoo as she hugged him closer.

Lord, he wanted her. Wanted to touch her, hold her . . . make love to her. Show her how much he needed her. But this wasn't the right time or place.

Every inch of his body hardening, he groaned, then forced himself to pull his mouth from hers, lift his head, then step back. And there she stood, gazing back at him with heavy eyes, flushed cheeks, and plump, thoroughly kissed lips, every bit of which intensified the waves of pleasure moving through him.

"I think that did the job," he rasped.

For now, but he wanted forever with her. He wanted the chance to wake up to her sleepy smile every morning, hear her throaty laugh in the fields while they worked every afternoon, and caress her soft, warm body every night, giving her pleasure, showing her love and proving every damn day what a rare gift this feeling was that she inspired in him—this unconditional, unwavering devotion to love her despite whatever challenges came their way.

She touched her mouth, her fingertips lingering on the moist curve of her lower lip. "Yes." Clearing her throat, she blinked rapidly, dropped her arm back to her side, and straightened. The eager, welcoming light left her eyes, and a blank, empty look took its place. "We should finish getting ready. It'll be time to leave soon."

Thirty minutes later, they did. Mitch drove, and Emmy sat in the passenger seat, her hands twisting nervously in her lap. Sadie and Dylan sat in the back of the cab, with Kristen in between. Every couple of miles, her eyes would meet his in the rearview mirror for a moment before she looked away, and he'd voice a silent plea for fate to tip the scales in his favor for once.

The fifteen members of the committee were already seated at the large table in the conference room of the community center when they arrived. Charles, Zach, and Iris smiled at them in greeting, as did fellow farm owners Al and Stephanie Jenkins and Jenny Yarrow, who sat in their usual places. Local mechanic Terrance Smith and teacher Elena Martinez had taken their seats beside the mayor, Bud Watson, and they gave a brief hello, as well. A few new faces were present, too. Two men and a woman Mitch didn't recognize watched the group from their seated positions on chairs lining the wall.

Dana Markham left the podium at the front of the room, walked over, and put out her hand. "Good evening, Mr. and Mrs. Hart."

A strong pleasant sensation unfurled inside Mitch at the greeting, and he smiled at Kristen as he shook Dana's hand. His smile fell a little when Dana moved from him to Emmy and shook her hand, too.

"Good to see you again," Emmy said, laughing, "even though I wish we'd met you somewheres else."

Dana's smile was full of kind regret. "I feel the same way, Mrs. Hart. But I'm very glad you've all joined us again tonight. I've been looking forward to this." She glanced at Mitch. "Did the reports and aerial views you asked me to email help you?"

"They did. Thank you," Mitch said, lifting the bags he held and exchanging a glance with Kristen.

After nodding, Dana stepped back, glanced at the group seated at the table, then rubbed her hands together briskly. "Let's get started, shall we?"

Over the next half hour, Dana introduced the new

guests who had joined them—all three were project manager consultants for the Department of Transportation—then walked the committee through a slideshow presentation on the wide screen at the head of the room. Each slide presented detailed data regarding traffic patterns and survey results. When the slideshow ended, Dana picked up two rolled posters, slid the rubber bands off, and spread the posters across the center of the table.

"These are the proposed plans for the bypass." She leaned across the table and pointed to the upper right section of one plan as everyone leaned in for a better look. "Construction would begin just north of the outskirts of Peach Grove on Highway 1, would extend several miles outside the city limits, then would reconnect with Highway 1 well beyond the southern outskirts of town."

Bud sat back in his chair, rubbing his chin and nodding. "That's exactly as we discussed. Looks good."

The room grew quiet as everyone studied the plans silently; then Elena scooted closer to the table. "And this?" Her finger touched a large area toward the center of the proposed bypass. "Whose land would the road be next to here?"

Dana shook her head. "Not next to but through." She cast a sad smile at Emmy. "That's where the bypass would cut through the center of Hart's Hollow, a farm I believe belongs to Mrs. Hart."

Mitch tensed as Emmy stared down at the plan, her chin trembling. "It's one thing to hear it," she said, her voice breaking, "but it's another to see it."

"What are they talking about, Nana?" Sadie, who'd left her seat beside Dylan and Zach, placed her hand on Emmy's forearm and lifted to her tiptoes, straining for a glimpse of the papers on the table.

"They're talking about taking our house," Dylan said, joining her, with Zach at his side. He frowned over Emmy's head. "You're not gonna let them, are you, Uncle Mitch?"

Mitch hesitated, glancing at the faces around the table. The pleased look on Bud's face had slowly receded, and Elena's eyes glistened as she stared at Emmy.

"That's not my decision," he said, standing and facing the DOT project managers. "But I'm hoping all of you will be willing to hear and consider an alternative."

The room fell silent. Al handed Stephanie two tissues from his shirt pocket. One she kept for herself; the other she handed to Jenny. Tears rolled down their cheeks.

Sniffing, Emmy turned her head and looked up at Mitch, her eyes welling. "My Mitch has a plan. A great one."

Mitch's lungs stalled. Oh, man. If this plan failed—if *he* failed—to save Hart's Hollow Farm, Emmy's heart would break, and every reason she had for getting out of bed each morning would be lost. Every ounce of hope she had would leave her, and there would be nothing left to hold on to. There would be only the slow decline of her health in a strange place. And that was all any place other than Hart's Hollow could be for her now.

A hand slipped inside his and squeezed. "Mitch has spent hours reviewing the needs and wants all of you expressed at the previous meeting and in subsequent surveys, and I think you'll be pleased with what he's proposing, if you'll allow us to proceed."

Mitch looked to his right. There was Kristen, holding his hand and smiling at him, as though he was the only man in the world, and in that moment, that was exactly how he felt. *Us* had sounded as good on her lips as he'd imagined.

"Please go ahead," said one of the men seated by the wall. "We'd like to hear you out."

Kristen squeezed Mitch's hand once more and gave him an encouraging smile. Not much was different at this meeting compared to the last one, except for the three project managers, who watched them from afar with polite but otherwise blank expressions.

It was nerve-racking, to say the least, but Mitch had created a solid plan that posed a good chance of persuading them all.

"Mitch?" Kristen prompted, nudging him with her elbow. "You want me to grab the plans?"

He straightened his tie and smiled. "Please."

Kristen bent, sifted through one of the bags they'd set beside the table, then withdrew a plastic tube housing a rolled canvas. Mitch took one end of it, and they placed it on the table.

"I took the liberty of contacting Mrs. Markham over a week ago and asked her to send me as much data as she could release regarding the plans proposed for the bypass." Mitch pulled several packets from another bag at their feet, then passed them around the table. "In these handouts, you'll see the Department of Transportation's plan laid out in detail, with the relevant data supporting each potential change notated in the margins," he continued. "The most prevalent concerns center around congestion and noise in downtown Peach Grove, the safety of pedestrians and the impacts any proposed change might have on our environment, businesses, and community."

Mitch placed a hand on Emmy's shoulder and leveled his blue eyes at the group in front of him. "At our last meeting, Emmy brought up the point that dismantling Adams County farms will break the backbone of our families and community." He glanced at Kristen, and the appreciation and admiration in his expression warmed her chest. "The new plan that Kristen and I are proposing directly addresses all the aforementioned concerns—and integrates elements that are specifically designed to strengthen our families, businesses, and communities—while staying within the budget allotted for a potential bypass."

He lifted his chin at Kristen, and hands trembling, she unsealed the plastic tube, slid out the rolled canvas, then peeled off the small piece of tape that held it together. The canvas loosened, and Mitch's big hand joined hers in unrolling it across the table.

Audible gasps escaped Iris and Elena as the canvas settled into a flat position, revealing an appealing mix of color. One of the aerial photos Dana had provided had been enlarged and enhanced for detail, and it formed the foundation of the plan. A printout of the final draft of one of Mitch's architectural sketches overlaid it, and the amenities, streetlighting, and landscaping in each individual section had been hand-painted by Kristen.

"Oh, it's gorgeous," Iris said, leaning closer for a better look.

"And functional." Mitch smiled and tapped the far right and left sections of the plan. "This plan incorporates a third lane into downtown Peach Grove, which will be designated for turning, and the two roundabouts Mrs. Markham mentioned at our last meeting—one at each end of the city."

Stephanie stood up, put on a pair of reading glasses,

and bent closer. "Is that a fountain in the middle there?"

"Yes," Kristen said. "There would be one in the center of each roundabout, and it could be dedicated to anyone we, as a community, choose—such as veterans or current service members. And there'd be no limit to the landscaping designs we could create around them. And if you look here"—she directed their attention to the large green areas framing the roads connecting to the circular roundabout—"you'll see we've integrated additional landscaping areas. Those are big enough to plant trees in a loved one's memory. It would be an excellent way to involve lifelong members of the community and make them feel as though they are an essential part of Peach Grove and Adams County."

"We've also included additional streetscaping that holds great aesthetic appeal," Mitch said. "One of the things I believe we all feel passionately about is providing a safe, welcoming downtown for everyone. It was with that in mind that we included a bike lane, pedestrian walkways, and attractive lighting. We also made room for HAWK lights at regular intervals."

"What are those?" Jenny asked.

"They're devices used to control traffic lights and allow pedestrians to cross more safely and conveniently. When you push a button, the traffic light will change, and you'll be able to cross the road with ease."

"That would help our students in the mornings and afternoons." Elena smiled. "And I wouldn't mind having a bike lane." She laughed. "It's been years since I've dusted off my ten-speed and taken a ride. If this plan looks as good in real life, I think I'd be tempted to do it more often."

"Which is part of the reason why we feel it's so important to include as many aesthetically pleasing elements as possible." Kristen looked at Terrance. "The more people we can entice out of their homes and cars to mill about downtown and socialize, the more—"

"Customers we'll have," Terrance said, finishing for her, flashing a smile. "Now I can go for that right there. The more feet on the street, the more change in my pocket."

"But the trucks," Bud said, standing. "What will this do to help with the speed of those semis, the congestion, and the noise?"

"Roundabouts are designed to slow through traffic without forcing vehicles to stop. They should take care of the speed and congestion issues," Kristen said. "The noise, I'm afraid, will still be there, which is why we're proposing one more significant change."

She stepped back and glanced at Mitch. He retrieved another rolled canvas from the bag at his feet, placed it on the table, and unrolled it.

A small cry escaped Emmy, and bracing her hands on the table, she pushed to a standing position. Her frail arms shook slightly as she leaned over the canvas.

In the center of this second hand-painted architectural plan, two large oaks with low, thick branches framed a white house, complete with two red brick chimneys, a front porch with Gothic trim, and a stained-glass window, which glinted beneath the bright flashes of fireworks above in a starry night sky. Wide fields full of lush green soybean plants, strawberry patches, and cornstalks surrounded the house, and a red dirt driveway wound through the picturesque landscape, with brightly painted gourds hanging from racks on both sides. Cars, trucks, and SUVs were parked head to tail all the way to the road, and the aerial depiction showed dozens and dozens of groups of people sitting on blankets or on the lowered tail-gates of pick-up trucks, admiring the pyrotechnic display above.

"It's my house," Emmy said. Her eyes brightened and a pleased look appeared on her face as she pointed at the line of cars. "What's happening here?"

"Look at the end of the driveway." Grinning, Mitch pointed at a rustic white sign with red lettering. "What does it say?"

Emmy peered closer, clucked her tongue, and shook her head. "Lord, have mercy. Ain't nothing more aggravating than a pair of tired eyes."

"Here, Emmy." Laughing, Stephanie took off her reading glasses and held them out.

"Thanks." Emmy took them, put them on, then looked again and read out loud, "Hart's Hollow Farm. Family owned and operated. All welcome!" Her smile grew as she touched the small, elegant script with her forefinger and traced the delicate vine and strawberries surrounding the wording. She turned to Kristen, tears spilling over her lashes. "You did this?"

Kristen swallowed hard past the thick lump in her throat, the grateful adoration in Emmy's gaze flooding her own eyes with tears. "Yes. The new sign is finished and in the shed, ready to hang."

"But the fireworks . . ." Emmy spread her hands. "And the cars?"

"You have so much to offer, Emmy." Kristen returned her gaze to the table and gestured toward different areas of the hand-painted architectural plan. "The farm would become the hub of community events. Corn mazes, apple bobbing, and hayrides could be offered in the fall. A tour of Christmas lights, caroling, and your homemade treats in the winter. Spring would be a perfect time for strawberry picking, eating contests, and pie walks. And summer—"

Her throat tightened at the surge of pleasant memories that flooded her: driving the tractor and planting the fields with Mitch, renovating the porch and laughing as Dylan and Zach played makeshift hockey across the floor, running through cornfields with Sadie and making strawberry shortcakes with Emmy and Ruth Ann.

All wonderful things she'd soon leave behind.

Kristen collected herself and tried again. "Summer would be a time for fishing, stargazing, and fireworks in July. We've already planned Hart's Hollow Farm's first event." She faced the committee members. "We'd like to invite all of you to Emmy's first Fourth of July celebration this Friday. She'll have food, games, and fireworks."

"We ask only that you hold off on making a decision regarding the bypass until you've attended the event," Mitch added. "I'll pass around details in a moment, and you're welcome to contribute in whatever way you'd like—be it a booth to promote your business, a stand to display your crafts, or a table to share your own homemade dishes for others to enjoy. We want you to see the sense of community and collaboration this type of operation can bring. How a small local farm can attract local residents and tourists, while strengthening our community and downtown businesses."

"Like the day we picked strawberries," Elena said softly. "That was a lovely afternoon, Emmy. Your home is beautiful, and you made us all feel so valued and welcome."

Emmy ducked her head, her mouth trembling around a smile.

"Friday. Don't forget," Mitch reminded them, glancing at the project managers. "We look forward to having you all as our guests for the day. After that, we'll accept whatever decision is made."

Soon after, Dana adjourned the meeting. There was a bustle of movement as everyone took a last look at each of the plans, asked questions about Friday's event, said their good-byes, then left.

Kristen stood to the side with Sadie and Dylan as Mitch answered questions from Charles and Iris. Emmy, drying her eyes with a tissue Al had offered her, walked over and opened her arms.

"Kristen." Her voice shook, and happiness shined in her eyes. "You dear girl."

Before she knew it, Kristen was gathered up in a hug so strong, it stole her breath. Emmy's arms were warm and comforting, and her whispered bittersweet words coaxed Kristen into sinking deeper into Emmy's embrace and broke her heart all at once.

"I couldn't be more proud of you if you were my own daughter."

CHAPTER 13

Kristen cut the stem of a white hydrangea bloom and placed it in a red vase on a picnic table. She had finally finished decorating each of the twenty tables Mitch had arranged on Hart's Hollow Farm's front lawn with red, white, and blue vases filled with hydrangea blooms.

Essie Templeton, owner of Essie's Odds and Ends, had been extremely generous in renting the picnic tables, chairs, and vases for Hart's Hollow Farm's July Fourth event at a very low rate. Her only stipulation had been that customized signage advertising her party supply service be affixed to each table for the duration of the event.

"I found the big one," Sadie shouted from the front porch steps, holding up a large white vase with red and blue stars on it. "Want me to put it on one of those tables?"

"No, that one's extra special. We're going to make a much bigger setting for the front porch. That way Emmy will have something beautiful to admire when she gets tired and needs to rest on the porch swing."

Smiling, Kristen grabbed a bag of supplies, weaved her way through the picnic tables, and motioned for Sadie to join her at one of them. "What do you say we both put that one together?"

"Yeah," Sadie piped, joining her on the bench.

Kristen dug around in the plastic bag for a pair of scissors, bows, and packets of flower food. "There's a white basket on the front porch with more flowers. Would you mind grabbing that for me and bringing it down here?"

"Yes, ma'am." Sadie spun around on the bench, hopped down, then ran toward the porch. Her long brown braids bounced across her back with every step.

Ever since Kristen and Mitch had rolled out the new plans for downtown Peach Grove and Hart's Hollow Farm's first July Fourth celebration at the county meeting three days ago, Sadie and Dylan had been balls of energy. Dylan had even taken it upon himself to borrow an alarm clock from Emmy and had gotten up early each morning to wake Sadie. While Mitch and Kristen had tended to the crops, Sadie and Dylan had stayed at the house with Emmy, making plans, collecting decorations, and hanging streamers and banners in places Emmy couldn't quite reach on her own. And they'd done a dang good job of it.

Kristen tipped her head back, shaded her eyes from the late morning sun, and admired their handiwork. Thin red, white, and blue bunting had been knotted and draped elegantly along the porch rails. A patriotic-themed wreath adorned the wide front door, and colorful cushions with celebratory designs had been fluffed and placed in each rocking chair and on the porch swing. A flag had been affixed to a pole on the front porch, and now it rippled slowly in the humid breeze.

"They did a great job, didn't they?" Big hands settled on Kristen's shoulders from behind, and warm lips nuzzled her temple. "Never imagined they'd sacrifice TV and lounge time to set up decorations."

Before she could talk herself out of it, Kristen eased back, nestling farther into Mitch's embrace. "They know how excited Emmy is about it." Oh, he smelled wonderful—like freshly tilled earth, clean air, and man. She inhaled, her eyes closing. "They wanted to please her."

"And you," he murmured, his mouth moving against her skin. "They wanted to make you happy, too."

She tensed. "I know."

And she did. The kids had done everything she'd asked to help prepare for today's celebration, and they'd even taken the initiative to tackle things she hadn't asked of them. Like when Dylan had cut the grass after she'd mentioned she didn't think she would have time to finish the field work before dark and wouldn't be able to get to the grass until the next day. And the time Sadie had removed the dirty dinner dishes from the table and washed them on her own when Kristen had limped into the house and over to the dinner table with a sore calf muscle.

It was amazing how they'd all pulled together to make today a perfect day for Emmy.

"They've been wonderful," Kristen whispered, opening her eyes and watching Sadie bound back down the front porch steps, flower basket in hand.

"Uncle Mitch, I'm gonna help Ms. Kristen make an extra-special flower 'rangement for Nana." She grinned and held up the basket.

Mitch's gentle touch trailed away as he straightened, and then he hugged Sadie to his side. "Thank you for helping, sweetheart. I know Emmy will love it." Releasing Sadie, he glanced up at the sky. "The fireworks are set up, Charles and Zach are putting the finishing touches on the decorations along the driveway, Lee's heating up the grill, and Ruth Ann and Emmy are making hamburger patties. Everything's set and ready for guests. It'll be a perfect day if those clouds will just hold off until morning."

Kristen followed his line of sight and frowned at the distant dark masses lingering on the horizon and marring the blue sky. "What time are we shooting off the fireworks?"

"Around nine, after it gets good and dark. Lee and Charles offered to take on that job so I could stay with Emmy."

"Then we should be okay." Kristen studied the lawn, full of picnic tables and games, and the driveway, adorned with festive welcome signs and arrows to direct cars for parking. "The weather report said the worst of it isn't supposed to blow in until after midnight."

"Yeah, but they're not always right." Mitch stared back up at the sky. "When it comes to weather, nothing's ever certain."

Kristen looked down and reached for the basket Sadie held, her stomach turning. "No. It never is."

Speaking low, he leaned on the table next to her. "Emmy's had a really great week so far, and today's gone well, but I'm planning on staying with her most of the night, just to help her stay comfortable if the crowds and unfamiliar noises agitate her. Would you mind taking my place with her once or twice tonight if I need to check on things?"

"Of course."

"I thought we could sit with her on the front porch when Charles and Lee start the fireworks. Just so I can help her inside if she doesn't like them."

She nodded, keeping her eyes focused on the basket.

"Kristen?" There was a familiar tone in Mitch's voice. The same one she'd heard several times since the county meeting—heavy, concerned.

Hesitating, she glanced up at him from beneath her lashes.

"Are you . . . ?" He stopped, looked at Sadie, then raked a hand through his hair. "If you have time, Emmy wants to speak with you before the guests start getting here. I told her I'd let you know."

"I'll go in as soon as Sadie and I finish this." After turning to the side, she sifted through the flowers and snagged several silk ribbons from the bottom of the basket. "We'll need three different colors of bows. Would you like to pick them, Sadie?"

Mitch watched them for a few moments, a strained smile appearing as Sadie chatted about which bows to use with which flowers. "I'm gonna take a shower and change. Then I'll help Charles direct everyone in to park. You okay with things here?"

Kristen nodded, then glanced up to smile at him once before he walked away. Her eyes followed his movements toward the house, and her belly fluttered at the strong line of his shoulders, lean waist, and slim hips. And the thought of his quiet intelligence, unending patience, and tender touch made it even more difficult to pull away from him. Mitch was as magnificent on the inside as he was on the outside, and it had become increasingly harder for her to dodge his intense gaze and searching questions.

But it wouldn't be fair to him for her to open up and take their relationship to a deeper level when she knew she'd be leaving soon. Only how in the world was she going to look him in the eyes and tell him?

"How 'bout this, Ms. Kristen?"

She blinked, then focused on Sadie's small hands, which clutched a crooked arrangement of hydrangeas tied with a lopsided bow. "I think . . ." Her attention drifted up to Sadie's big, happy smile, and a rush of affection swept through her. "I think it's perfect," she whispered. "Just perfect."

If possible, Sadie's smile grew bigger, and she leaned across the table and kissed Kristen's cheek. The peck of Sadie's lips, the sweet chime of her laughter, and the sharp scent of freshly cut flower stems brought tears to Kristen's eyes.

Choking back a sob, she wrapped her arms around Sadie and hugged her close, wondering how she'd manage to walk away from Sadie and Dylan. And if she'd be able to find a way in her heart to ever truly let go of them.

Twenty minutes later, after the final bows had been tied and the floral arrangement had been set up on a small porch table by the swing, Kristen and Sadie joined Emmy and Ruth Ann in the kitchen.

"Something smells wonderful," Kristen said, standing on the threshold of the kitchen and watching the two women work.

Ruth Ann patted hamburger meat between her hands and smiled. "Garlic, oregano, and oni—"

"Onion powder," Emmy chimed in, smacking an even hamburger patty on a tray covered in wax paper and full of dozens more like it. "The secret to anything on a grill is onion powder."

Kristen laughed. "I'll have to remember that."

Emmy's expression dimmed, and she muttered, "Won't we all."

Wincing, Kristen smoothed a hand over Sadie's hair. "Sadie did an excellent job setting up the floral arrangements. If you have anything you need taken outside to the grill, I'm sure she'd be happy to help."

"Now, that's a plan." Ruth Ann clapped her hands together and waved Sadie over. "Come here, hon, and we'll get this first round of hamburgers and buns out to the gentleman manning the grill."

Emmy held up a hand. "And I'd like you to come with me, Kristen, if you have a moment?"

After washing her hands in the kitchen sink, Emmy led the way down the hall to her bedroom, opened the door, and went into the walk-in closet. Kristen hovered nearby, admiring the blue handwoven afghan folded on the foot of Emmy's bed.

"This afghan is beautiful, Emmy."

"Keeps my feet warm at night," Emmy called out from inside the closet.

Kristen fingered the soft edges. "Did you make it?"

"Nope. Ruth Ann did. She brought it by yesterday. These hands of mine haven't touched a needle and yarn in years. As a matter of fact, I can't do most things I did years ago, but there is one thing I can still manage to do, and that's shop. When Ruth Ann took me into town yesterday to pick up food for the party, we stopped by the dress shop." Emmy reemerged from the closet, holding a pretty off-the-shoulder denim shift dress. "What do you think?"

Kristen moved closer, ran a hand over the soft fabric, and inspected the elegant neckline. "It's beautiful."

"It's yours."

"What?"

"I bought it for you to wear today, if you'd like." Emmy flipped the dress around, pressed it against Kristen's shoulders, then smoothed it across her middle. "It's not real fancy, but it's a good style for a Fourth of July party, and you've done nothing else but work for months now, so I thought it was high time you had something nice to enjoy. I had to guess your size, but it looks like it'll be a perfect fit. And I could curl your hair. All that blond will look just gorgeous against this deep blue. That is"—she shrugged meekly—"if you want to wear it."

"If I want to . . . ?" Throat thickening, Kristen shook her head and smiled. "I'd love to wear it. Thank you, Emmy."

Emmy smiled back, her face flushing. Then she crossed to the window, pushed the curtain to one side, and peered out at the sky. "Looks like rain's a-coming. It'll do the corn good. Just hope Joe doesn't get stuck in it."

Kristen's hands stilled on the dress hem as she smoothed it against her thighs. She studied the rigid line of Emmy's back. The way her hands twisted tight against her middle.

"The truck gets trapped in the mud a lot on account of the rain soaking the clay roads between the fields," she continued. "If those clouds will just hold off for a while. At least until the morning. Give him time to get back home."

Kristen's hands clenched around the soft denim, the warm, pleasing glow of moments before fading.

"I have to hand it to you, Mitch. You sure know how to throw a party."

Mitch eased onto the porch swing next to Emmy and smiled at Charles. "Can't take all the credit. Everyone's chipped in, and Kristen has been a godsend. None of this would've been possible without her."

He glanced to his right, where Kristen sat in a rocking chair, Sadie perched on her lap and Dylan seated in the chair beside her. The soft glow of the porch light highlighted her blond curls, caressed her flushed cheeks, and bathed her bare shoulders above her flirty neckline. Heaven help him, he'd had no idea denim could be so damned sexy.

"It took all of us," she said softly.

Us. There was that word again—the sweetest syllable he'd ever heard when it was on Kristen's tongue.

"When are the fireworks starting?" Sadie licked the ice cream cone she held, then rubbed her eyes with a grubby hand, smearing dirt across her forehead. "Is it dark enough now?"

Mitch chuckled. "Yeah, sweetheart. Though I'm beginning to think you might not manage to stay awake through 'em."

Or Dylan, either, for that matter. They both blinked heavy eyelids, sported ruddy cheeks and tousled hair, and slouched in their seats with a general look of summer-fun exhaustion. And Emmy looked equally exhausted, despite the fact that she'd refused to call it a night and insisted on staying outside with them for the fireworks. She kept nodding off beside Mitch as he nudged the swing slowly back and forth, her chin bumping her chest occasionally.

None of that was surprising considering the way the afternoon had worked out. After showering and dressing hours ago, he had returned outside and had been greeted by a line of cars already forming at the end of the driveway. Guests had arrived in a steady stream from one o'clock to three, and by that time, the empty fields Mitch and Lee had quartered off for parking and fireworks watching had been busting at the seams with cars, pick-up trucks, and SUVs.

Over the next five and a half hours, a constant hum of exuberant conversation, sporadic laughter, and the low beat of country music had pulsed on the humid summer breeze. Lee had done a jam-up job on the grill, having chosen good ole charcoal instead of gas to cook seasoned hamburger meat and hot dogs, and he'd even thrown about five pounds of sliced Vidalia onions on the rack, too. The mouth-watering scents had traveled for what seemed like miles, had hovered over the children's games of tag, water balloons, and baseball on the front lawn, and had wafted over the strawberry fields, where guests picked the last of the strawberries still hanging on the vine, begging to be eaten.

The sun had beaten down on the milling crowd the hardest between five and seven, which had lured several groups to the front porch to lounge on the steps, rock in the chairs, or fan themselves on the swing. As night approached, tall tales, humorous gossip, and a wealth of treasured stories birthed during the early days of Peach Grove's establishment had peppered the air, echoing against the walls of the farmhouse, mingling with the rattle of cicadas and passing from one group catching their breath to the next.

And even now, the distant bursts of small orange flames in the dark, the subsequent sweet smell of tobacco, and the deep chuckles mingling with the curls of smoke conjured up one of the few pleasant memories Mitch had of his dad. The one night Mitch could recall his being sober, holding a poker game with the boys and inviting Mitch to sit by his side as he smoked Joe's old pipe.

Strange that this was the most comforting memory he had of his father, but the fact that he'd managed to recall one at all was worth the discovery.

"I think Dylan and Sadie can find another ten minutes of energy if it involves fireworks." Kristen reached over and ruffled Dylan's hair. "Whatcha think, little man?"

The boy grinned. "Definitely."

Charles checked his watch. "Lee and Zach should be finished packing up the grill by now. I'll let him know we're ready for the big show."

"Y'all need some help?" Mitch made to rise.

"No, no." Charles held up a hand and headed down the steps, calling over his shoulder, "Put your feet up and spend some time with your family. We'll take it from here."

Mitch sat back in the swing and met Kristen's eyes. A small spark of pleasure and want moved through her gaze; then she looked away, shuttering her expression.

"Mr. and Mrs. Hart are?"

Catching the tail end of the question over the distant murmur of the crowd, Mitch peered through the dark toward the bottom of the porch steps. Footsteps ascended, and then Dana Markham entered the circle of the porch light.

"Oh, there you are," she said, smiling widely. "I was hoping I'd catch you at a good time."

Mitch rose, keeping a careful hand on Emmy's forearm to steady her as the swing rocked. "Glad you made it, Mrs. Markham."

"Oh, I made it quite some time ago, but I've been

so caught up in the celebrations, I haven't had a chance to stop by your way." She laughed and rubbed her belly. "I think the good food and great company slowed me down."

Mitch smiled. "That I can understand."

Bending, Dana held out her hand to Emmy. "I wanted to thank you for the pleasant afternoon, Mrs. Hart. I really enjoyed myself, as did a whole lot of other people."

"You're very welcome." Emmy squeezed Dana's hand, then patted it, her eyes tired. "I'm glad you joined us."

Dana straightened. "I wanted to share some good news with all of you, if I might?"

"Of course." Mitch waved a hand toward the empty cushion beside Emmy.

"Oh, no thank you. This won't take but a second." She flashed an excited smile in Kristen's direction. "All three project managers stopped by earlier this afternoon. I bumped into them when I arrived. They were on their way out."

Dylan stomped his feet on the porch floor, halting his rocking chair with a thump. "What'd they say? They still gonna take our house?"

Emmy sat up, a small cry escaping her as she eyed Dana.

"Dylan." Wincing at the worried look on Emmy's face, Mitch leveled a look at him. "Give Mrs. Markham a chance to speak, please."

Dylan frowned. "Sorry. But are they?"

"Well, the official word won't be released publicly until late next week, but . . ." Dana shook her head and smiled wider at Mitch. "They loved the alternate plans you and Kristen presented at the meeting and were even more impressed with today's turnout and activities. They saw so much potential." She reached out and squeezed Emmy's hand again. "Hart's Hollow Farm is going to stay right where it belongs. With you, Mrs. Hart."

Emmy closed her eyes and released a heavy breath, a soft smile appearing. "Thank you, Dana. Thank you so much."

Dana shook her head again. "The real thanks goes to all of you. The Hart family saved Hart's Hollow Farm, not me."

The sheer look of happiness on Emmy's face and the shouts of joy from Sadie and Dylan were worth every backbreaking hour of work.

Mitch slipped his hand along Kristen's forearm that rested on the chair's armrest, and wound his fingers with hers. She looked up at him and smiled, but there was a heaviness behind her look of pleasure. An emotion he couldn't pin down and identify.

"I hate to run, but I need to head out," Dana said. "There's a lot of work to be done to prep for the new project." She paused on her way back down the steps and glanced over her shoulder. "It was a wonderful day."

"The best," Mitch said. When she left, he returned to Emmy's side on the porch swing, his heart turning over at the happy tears in her eyes. "You don't have to worry anymore, Emmy. You're home for good."

She dabbed her wet cheeks with her fingertips. "We have to tell Joe. He'll be so happy."

Mitch froze, the exhilarating joy lifting his spirits moments before now faltering.

"Kristen"—Emmy craned her neck, looking past Mitch—"I want you with me when we tell him, okay?" Her hands moved restlessly in her lap, plucking at the seam of her skirt. "We'll have to catch him as soon as he comes in tonight. He'll be tired, but it'll be worth keeping him up awhile to tell him."

The helpless look on Kristen's face made Mitch's hands tense against his knees. "Emmy." He eased closer on the swing, sifting through words in his mind, weighing the options. "Joe won't be with us tonight."

A flash of panic appeared in her eyes; then she firmed her mouth. "Of course he will. He's just late, is all. Stays out too long lately, if you ask me." She turned her head, brow creasing, and stared at the porch rail. "Probably just got held up in one of the fields, or he might be at his thinking place, you know?" A faint smile appeared. "He likes to mull things over. Joe's always been careful about making decisions."

"Em—"

Several loud pops reverberated across the grounds, and a collective whoop rose up from the crowds gathered on the front lawn and several yards out in the empty stretch of field. Bright bursts of color streaked the night sky, and thick trails of smoke curled up behind them.

Emmy jumped, her hands clutching around his arms and her nails digging into his skin. "Mitch! The thunder . . . Joe won't make it back."

"It's okay," he said softly, leaning close and cupping her elbows. "There's no thunder. The fireworks have started, that's all."

The sharp pops continued, then transitioned into slow booms as the larger pyrotechnics exploded high above the fields, the dazzling sparkles cascading downward in a glittery array of light. Emmy shook in his hold, her fingers curling tighter around his flesh.

"Is she okay?" Dylan left his chair and walked over, his chin trembling.

"Come with me, Emmy." Mitch stood slowly, helping her rise with him. "It's getting late, and I could use some rest. I'd really like it if you'd keep me company. Dylan, head inside and get the lights on in Emmy's room, okay?"

"Yes, sir." Brow creased with worry, Dylan turned and went inside.

Mitch walked with Emmy across the porch, cradling her closer to his chest each time a firework exploded overhead.

Kristen set Sadie on her feet, got up and opened the front door, watching as they approached. "What can I do to help?"

Mitch forced a smile, the frightened whimpers escaping Emmy sending waves of pain through him. "Could you wrap things up here and get Sadie and Dylan in bed for the night? I'm going to stay with Emmy until she falls asleep."

"I'd be happy to." Kristen hesitated as they passed, then touched Emmy's arm. "Good night, Emmy."

She didn't respond, just huddled closer into Mitch's supportive embrace.

"Stop by her room and sit with us for a while when you finish here," he said, meeting Kristen's eyes over Emmy's head. "She'll be settled then."

Kristen shook her head and looked away, the bright flashes of color in the sky glinting over the wet sheen of tears hovering on her lashes. "Thank you, but it's probably better I don't disturb her."

Mitch helped Emmy across the threshold, then glanced over his shoulder at Kristen as she closed the door behind them, muffling the sound of the festive explosions outside. The party was ending, Hart's Hollow Farm was safe, and Emmy could sleep soundly in her own bed every night without fear she'd lose her home.

Those thoughts alone should bring him comfort. Only, after settling in a lounge chair by Emmy's bed, his mind kept returning to Emmy's rapid decline over the past few days. She was becoming more and more confused and afraid, and every day of memory loss would continue to be a struggle for her. But it was the distant look in Kristen's eyes that stayed with him long after Emmy had settled for the night.

CHAPTER 14

Kristen slipped a thin nightshirt over her head, smoothed it over her thighs, then picked up the denim dress Emmy had given her hours earlier. She held it out, tilted it from one side to the other beneath the soft light spilling from the old-fashioned oil lamp on the nightstand.

It was plain but beautiful. Much like Hart's Hollow and Emmy.

She hugged the dress to her chest and slowly looked around the room. The hours and hours of hard work she and Mitch had put into renovating the house, including this room, had more than paid off. The room was a far cry from what it had been when she'd first arrived.

Worn wallpaper, peeling at the edges, had been stripped from the walls, and in its place, Mitch had painted the walls eggshell white. The hardwood floor had been scrubbed gently with water and vinegar until the dark natural grain gleamed. Framed photos of the fields and streams had been hung on each side of the room, and the long lace curtains covering the open wide window had been carefully cleaned, dried, and reinstalled, allowing the trailing ends to billow out as the summer night breeze blew in from outside. And Mitch had painstakingly restored the overhead light, a circular farmhouse-style chandelier crafted out of wood and iron, so that it gave off an aesthetically pleasing glow when lit.

The room was gorgeous, as was the rest of the house. It was this bedroom she and Mitch had spent hours in, stretched out on the floor, poring over plans and sketches, analyzing and examining, reassessing and improving. It was as though Mitch's hands had breathed new life into the heart of the home, then had guided hers into coaxing it to beat again.

All the hard work and exhaustion had been worth the smile on Emmy's face that night at the meeting, when she'd seen the plans for Hart's Hollow Farm for the first time. And the words she'd spoken had stayed with Kristen every night since, whispering through her mind as she fell asleep and tugging bittersweet tears from her eyes onto the pillow every morning.

I couldn't be more proud of you if you were my own daughter.

Kristen squeezed her eyes shut, her hands tightening on the dress pressed against her chest. She had wanted to hug Emmy so tight earlier this evening. Had wanted to whisper how grateful she was to have seen Emmy's ad and come to Hart's Hollow. To have met Emmy, worked with her, learned from her . . . and loved her as she imagined a daughter would love her mother. As Anna had loved *her.*

She bit her lip, the sharp pinch of her teeth digging into tender flesh momentarily distracting her from the pain spreading inside her.

"Kristen?"

She started, her eyes springing open and focusing toward the low rumble of Mitch's voice.

He stood on the threshold of the guest bedroom, one broad hand nudging the half-opened door farther aside, his brow creased with concern as he studied her face. "Are you all right?"

Lowering her hands, she clutched the dress at her side, then forced a weak smile. "I was just . . ." Her throat tightened. She cleared it and tried again. "I was getting ready for bed." She walked to the small dresser on the opposite wall, placed the dress on its smooth surface, and began folding it with slow, methodical motions. "How's Emmy?"

"Better," he said softly. "She fell asleep a couple of hours ago."

Kristen nodded, pressing the dress flat and paying particular attention to smoothing out a crease. "That's good. I was worried all the noise of packing up the picnic tables outside and the cars leaving would wake her."

It was silent for a few moments. Then the door clicked shut and Mitch's heavy tread moved slowly across the floor, the sporadic squeak of the floorboards mingling with the distant low rumble of thunder outside.

"Did you have any trouble getting Sadie and Dylan in bed for the night?" He was so close, his soft breaths ruffled her hair against the back of her neck.

"Not at all. They helped clean up after the fireworks and were so tired by the time they came inside, they fell asleep almost before their heads hit the pillow."

Another roll of thunder, closer this time, echoed outside, momentarily drowning out the rattle of cicadas and the chirps of crickets.

"They got it right this time," Kristen whispered, her chin trembling. "It's almost midnight. The afternoon forecast said there'd be a storm right about now."

Big hands covered her fingers, which still fidgeted with the dress, the gentle pressure stilling their movements. "Yeah. I guess sometimes things do work out as predicted." His palms left her hands, drifted up her forearms, then gently tugged her around. "I should've recognized it the second I saw you. The moment I touched you. But I couldn't see it then."

His thumb and forefinger nudged her chin, and as she lifted her head, her eyes met his.

"I don't know how a feeling this big could hide the way it did, but it managed to." His hand slid around and cupped the back of her head, and the pad of his thumb swept gently over her jaw. "You asked me once if I'd ever fallen in love. I can say with absolute certainty I have now."

Her breath caught as the intensity of his gaze and his warm, adoring expression sent a wave of pleasure through her.

He moved closer and dipped his head. The heat of his broad chest and sculpted frame beckoned her to lean against him as he brushed his mouth softly across hers, whispering, "I love you, Kristen. More than I ever thought it was possible to love someone."

A sob broke past her lips, and she rose to her tiptoes, wound her arms around his muscular back and kissed him with every bit of love she wanted to confess out loud but couldn't.

He kissed her back, his tongue parting her lips, his

familiar taste and masculine scent enveloping her. Then he raised his head and examined her expression. "Ever since Emmy's birthday, you've been pulling away. You're thinking about leaving, aren't you?"

The curtains billowed on a strong gust of wind, and it swept over them, chilling her skin and making her shudder against him. She looked past him to the darkness that lay outside the window. A faint pulse of heat lightning flashed above the winding dirt driveway, illuminating the fields beyond.

For the past three years, roads had never looked cold or lonely. Instead, they'd been a welcome relief from the grief and loss she'd left behind. But now the thought of leaving the comforting strength of Mitch's embrace and putting her feet on another impersonal, neglected road made her tighten her grip on his solid warmth.

"I don't want to," she forced out past stiff lips. "But I can't go ba—"

When I get better, we can go back home, can't we, Mama?

Kristen pressed her face against the warm skin at the base of his throat, tears seeping from her eyes onto her lashes. How could she make a home here, have a new family, when Anna never could? And how could she stay and watch Emmy fade more each day, with no hope of her recovering?

She swallowed hard and tried to steady her voice. "I'm afraid."

His hands moved in slow circles over her back. "Afraid of what?"

Losing Emmy, Sadie, and Dylan. Losing you.

At her silence, he released a heavy breath. "I understand if you're not ready to tell me, and I'll wait however long it takes." His deep tone vibrated in his chest beneath her cheek. "But I want you to know

I've decided to stay. I want to make Hart's Hollow my home again—a real one. And I want to be close to Emmy, the kids and, hopefully, you. You're a Hart, Kristen—in every way that counts. This is your home, too, and whenever you're ready to return, I'll be waiting."

She hugged him harder, then pulled back and looked up, winced at the pain in his eyes and the strain on his face. Oh, God, she wanted to stay and support him the way he supported her. Wished she were as strong and certain as he. Wished she could lay this guilt and grief down for good and not be afraid of loving and losing again. But if she left now, the good memories would outweigh the bad, and her heart couldn't carry any more pain.

"I'm sorry, Mitch."

His eyes darkened, and he cupped her face. "I'm sorry, too. Because the truth is, I love you so damned much, I'll take whatever you're willing to give. Even if it's just good-bye."

Heart breaking, she reached up and tugged his mouth back down to hers, wanting to show him what she couldn't manage to voice in words.

He groaned, his arms wrapping tight around her, his hands sweeping over her back, cupping her buttocks, then traveling up to tangle gently in her hair. She kissed him more deeply, absorbing the heat of his hard frame and splaying her palms across the solid wall of his chest, before he trailed kisses down the sensitive curve of her neck.

"Love me," she whispered.

With a low moan, he complied, sliding his calloused palms along her smooth thighs and lifting the hem of her shirt above her head. The tender caresses of his mouth and hands traveled everywhere—the curve of her breasts, the gentle swell of her hips, even the sensitive skin behind her knees—leaving a trail of pulsing desire in their wake.

He removed his clothes, and she explored the hard swells of his toned chest, biceps, and thighs, the flat plane of his abs until, breathless, he eased her onto the bed, settled into her welcoming embrace, and made them one.

Outside, the storm intensified, but the flashes of lightning and the cracks of thunder faded beneath the heavy beat of his heart against hers, the urgent need in his sensual movements and the powerful emotion in his kiss, which eventually overtook them both.

Afterward, he rolled onto his back, tugging her with him, and cradled her close. His chest rose, deep and even, and eventually, he drifted off, his soft breaths stirring her hair.

Pleasure pulsed steady and slow within her, and the feeling spread through her limbs and swelled within her. She'd never felt this supported and loved . . . or more afraid.

Throat aching, Kristen rolled her head to the side and kissed his shoulder. Then her lips moved against his warm skin in a barely audible whisper. "I love you, Mitch."

She waited awhile, listening to the steady fall of rain outside the window and half hoping that he'd wake up and that she'd give in and allow him to persuade her to stay. But he didn't stir, and eventually, she slipped out of his hold.

It took ten minutes for her to gather her things quietly in the low light of the oil lamp. She pushed her jeans, T-shirts, underwear, and what few toiletries she'd arrived with into her bags. Hoisting one bag over each shoulder, she cast one last look at his sleeping form—his strong, tanned limbs sprawled across the white sheets, the strand of chestnut hair tousled over his forehead, and the relaxed, sensual curve of his mouth—before forcing herself to walk away.

Downstairs, she hovered in the hallway, right outside Sadie's and Dylan's closed doors. She wanted to slip inside the rooms, kiss their cheeks, and say goodbye, but she couldn't bring herself to follow through.

Shoulders sagging, she shook as her bags slid down her arms and dropped onto the floor. Steady rain drummed on the roof, and she looked behind her toward the staircase leading to the upper floor, recalling Mitch's strong, quiet love, then clenched her jaw.

"I'm not a coward," she said out loud, holding on to the words and drawing strength from them. "Never have been."

And she didn't want to leave Hart's Hollow or Mitch. She wanted to stay right here with Sadie, Dylan, and Emmy . . . even if it broke her heart.

Straightening, Kristen walked farther down the hall to Emmy's room, but the lamplight slipping through the half-open door slowed her steps, and her heart tripped after a quick scan of the room revealed that Emmy was gone.

"Mitch."

A hand shook his shoulder, and the sweet sound of Kristen's voice came again.

"Mitch, wake up."

He opened his eyes, and the sated sensation that had lingered in his limbs after making love to Kristen dissolved when he saw the panicked look on her face.

"Emmy's gone," she said, tugging on his biceps.

He sat up, slid his hands over her arms, then squeezed in an attempt to still her restless movements. "Wait, what do you mean? She was asleep in her room when I lef—"

"She's not there. I just checked." Voice shaking, she looked past him toward the window, her cheeks pale. "She was so confused during the party. Do you think she could've gone looking for Joe?"

The brief flash of lightning that lit up the room made him freeze. He shook off the clinging remains of sleep, nudged Kristen aside, and stood. "Did you check the bathroom?"

"Yes."

He snatched his jeans off the floor, jerked them on and zipped them up. "The kids' bedrooms?"

She nodded.

"The kitch—"

"Yes, I checked everywhere—even the porch and front yard." She grabbed his shirt from the end of the bed, tossed it to him, then headed toward the door. "I'm going to walk the driveway, see if she wandered out there."

"I'll call Ruth Ann, ask her to come stay with the kids. I'll be right behind you." He slipped his shirt over his head. "Kristen?"

She paused on the threshold, expression anxious.

"Grab a raincoat out of the hall closet. There's a flashlight on the top shelf."

Thunder boomed, rattling the windowpanes and vibrating through the floor as he jogged down the stairs. He called Ruth Ann, who assured him she was on the way, and then he rummaged through several drawers in the kitchen for another flashlight. After finding one, he headed outside, grabbing the truck keys from the key rack by the front door on his way out.

The sharp scent of rain hit his nostrils, and the downpour pummeled the porch roof and the surrounding landscape. The thick branches on the oak trees on the front lawn clacked together with fierce intensity. He ran down the front steps to the sludgy driveway, his shoes slipping and the sheets of rain so heavy he could barely see farther than five feet in front of him.

Pausing to regain his balance, he stiffened as a bolt of lightning streaked across the sky in a jagged arc, striking the dark field below with a vicious hiss.

"Dear God, Emmy." His chest burned. "Please don't be out here."

His thighs clenched, then surged forward, propelling him up the slippery clay driveway. The flashlight's glow barely cut through the thick downpour, and the shaky illumination didn't help much.

"Emmy!" Fat drops of rain spat against his face, stinging his eyes and drowning his voice.

Mitch pressed on. Dense red mud sucked at his heels, and the wind picked up, the powerful bursts knocking into his chest and shoving him backward. He reached the first curve of the driveway with no sign of Emmy and shouted once more, hoping for a faint call in response.

Instead, there was nothing but the steady pound of rain, the deep boom of thunder, and fierce flashes of lightning.

Gritting his teeth, he glared up at the storm clouds looming above. "Don't take her from me." He licked the tangy raindrops from his lips. "Not now, and not like this."

A small orb of light bounced sporadically in the

distance, fading behind the thick curtain of rain, then reappearing. Moments later, Kristen emerged from the darkness, her flashlight jerking as she jogged toward him.

He strained for a glimpse of Emmy behind her, though he knew there was no one there. "Did you find her?"

Breathing heavily, Kristen stopped by his side and shook her head. "I went all the way to the end of the driveway and back. I didn't see her in the front fields, either."

He reached out and pushed her wet hair out of her eyes, leaned close and spoke loud enough to be heard over the rain. "She must've wandered farther off. We'll take the truck." After grabbing her hand, he pulled her with him as he jogged toward the front lawn. "Ruth Ann should be here soon. We can't wait for her. If Emmy's out here, we need to find her now. And I'll need your eyes on the other side of the cab, looking for her, too."

Minutes later, they were in the truck, heading down the dirt track behind the house, the bright headlights cutting through the downpour and illuminating the edges of the fields. Kristen drove at a slow pace, and Mitch shined his flashlight outside.

There was still no sign of Emmy.

"Half a mile," Kristen said, eyeing the odometer on the dashboard.

Mitch leaned closer to the window and peered harder into the dimly lit darkness beyond. Could Emmy have made it this far? On foot in the rain?

"Maybe we missed her." Kristen's voice shook. "Should we turn around and go back? Or should I keep going?"

Gut churning, he blinked hard and continued

sweeping the flashlight across the landscape as it slowly passed.

"Mitch? What should I do?"

"Keep driving." *Keep looking. Keep trying.* God help him, what else could they do? Any other alternative was unthinkable. "She's out here somewhere. I know it." He pressed the flashlight closer to the passenger-side window. "Emmy, where the hell are you?"

His throat thickened and his lungs stalled, a pain he'd never felt before ripping through his chest. What if this was the hand fate had decided to deal? What if Emmy stood by the road fifty yards back, waiting for them in plain sight, and they'd failed to see her? Failed to save her?

He'd never forgive himself.

"Just keep looking," he rasped. "We're not giving up."

Kristen kept driving. He kept moving his flashlight through the darkness.

"One mile." She glanced at him, her green eyes dark with fear.

"She's strong," he forced out. "She may have made it this fa—"

"There!" Kristen slammed on the brakes, jerking them forward in the cab. "In the field."

And there Emmy was, huddled low into a ball between two rows of tall cornstalks that rippled and waved in the wind like wide green hands, sheltering her gray head and embracing her shivering form.

He thrust the door open, jumped out, and ran over. After squatting beside her, he ran his hands over her soaked shoulders. "Emmy."

She looked up, rain pouring in streams down her face, collecting on her chin and dripping down her chest. Her eyes gazed around blankly for a moment, then narrowed on his face. A wave of relief passed over her expression. "Mitch? I can't find Joe."

Chest clenching, he leaned closer and sheltered her the best he could from the rain. "Come with me, Emmy. Let's get out of this."

Her face crumpled, and her gnarled fingers shook as they reached for her leg. "I—I can't. My knee . . ."

"Hold on to me."

Mitch slid one arm behind her knees and the other behind her back, waited for her to grasp his neck weakly, then lifted her in his arms. Even soaked to the bone, she was so light he barely felt her weight in his hold.

She pressed her cheek to his, her fingers pressing against the back of his neck and her weak sobs in his ear. "I-I'm sorry. I didn't mean to . . ." Her tone was lost, disoriented. "I hurt, but I don't know why."

Voice strained, Mitch whispered, "It's okay, Emmy. If you want to, go ahead and cry."

And she did. Her soft cries continued as Kristen helped him get her in the truck. Tears poured down her creased cheeks the entire drive back up the muddy track to the house.

A sedan and a truck were parked in front of the house when they arrived. Ruth Ann and Lee rushed down the front porch steps to greet them as they pulled up.

"Is she okay?" Ruth Ann asked, holding an umbrella over Mitch's head as he lifted Emmy down from the cab.

"She's soaked clean through." He cradled Emmy closer to his chest, wincing as she shivered against him. "I need a blanket and dry towels. Once we get her warm, I want to take her straight to the hospital, just to be safe."

"I'll help, then drive you," Ruth Ann said, walking with him toward the house.

"Kristen?" Mitch glanced over his shoulder. An almost palpable relief poured through him when she fell in step beside him and her hand covered his on Emmy's shoulder. "Will you follow us with—?"

"Don't worry." Her hand tightened over his. "I'll wake Sadie and Dylan, and we'll meet you there."

She hurried ahead and disappeared inside the house.

After helping Emmy change clothes and wrapping a thick blanket around her, Mitch settled into the backseat of Ruth Ann's car with Emmy at his side. As they traveled down the driveway, he hugged her closer and rubbed her arms briskly, glancing back anxiously, hoping for a glimpse of Kristen close behind.

Sure enough, it wasn't long before Emmy's truck appeared and followed at a close pace.

Emmy whimpered, and Mitch smoothed a hand over her wet hair, smiling sadly. "I'm sorry about this, Ruth Ann. Thank you for watching the kids and for driving us."

She glanced back at him from the driver's seat. "No need to thank me. I'm here for Emmy whenever and however she needs me."

"In a way, I'm hoping this is one event she won't remember," he whispered as Emmy drifted off, breathing deeply against his chest. "She'd hate this. She'd feel awful about your being dragged out at this hour and Kristen searching on foot for her in a storm. Emmy never did like to put people out, and she never cared for charity."

The rhythmic squeak of the windshield wipers slowed as the storm weakened. Ruth Ann looked in the rearview mirror at the headlights following them, then met his eyes. "I know I'm speaking for me and Kristen when I say this isn't charity," she said softly. "This is love."

CHAPTER 15

Kristen slid her clay-covered sneakers beneath her chair and shifted to a more comfortable position. Or at least as comfortable as it could get in a hospital waiting room.

She fixed her attention on the wide double doors on the other side of the room. One door opened, the sunlight streaming through the windows at her back glinting across the metal handle as it swung outward.

"Mr. Pittman?" A nurse, bright eyed, with a warm smile, nodded as a man rose from one of the seats lining the back wall. "You can come back now."

A woman seated beside him stood, too.

The nurse held up a hand. "I'm sorry. Only immediate family is being allowed at the moment."

Smothering a sigh, Kristen sank farther back into the stiff chair. She'd spent the early hours of the morning in the emergency room waiting area after Emmy had been checked in, hoping for good news or, at the very least, some kind of reassurance that she was okay.

But hour after hour had passed with no news. She

hadn't seen Mitch since moments after she arrived with Sadie and Dylan. He'd come out briefly to tell her that they'd taken Emmy to a back room and that he'd return with news as soon as he could.

That had been around two in the morning. It was almost eight now.

"Is Nana gonna be okay?"

Kristen glanced to her left, where Sadie sat, blinking up at her with sleepy eyes and a fearful expression. Dylan was slumped in a chair on the other side of his sister, his eyes closed, snoring softly. Both of them had to be exhausted. After the full day they'd had yesterday, they'd barely managed to fall asleep before she'd had to wake them, load them in the truck, and drive to town to sit and wait for hours on end.

"Don't worry, Sadie." She brushed the little girl's bangs back and tapped her chin. "Your nana's tough. She's going to pull through this just fine."

The words were hard to say and even more difficult to emphasize with a hopeful smile.

Kristen turned away and focused on the double doors again. *Please, please let her be okay.*

"Ms. Kristen?"

Biting her lip, she faced Sadie again. "Hmm?"

"What if she's not?" Sadie's chin trembled. "What if she got too cold, like Uncle Mitch said?"

Kristen's heels tapped to a nervous rhythm on the linoleum floor, her knees bouncing with each movement. "She was cold," she said gently, "but Mitch got her here quickly, and I'm sure they're taking good care of her. We just have to be patient, and we have to . . ." She swallowed hard. "We have to hope for the best and be strong for your uncle Mitch."

Because he was worried—incredibly so. Kristen

cringed, recalling the ashen pallor of his skin when he'd greeted them after they first arrived. His arms had trembled around her as he embraced her, and a pained look had appeared in his eyes as he struggled to smile down at Sadie and Dylan.

"I can do that," Sadie said, leaning her head against Kristen's shoulder.

Heart aching, Kristen hugged her close and managed a smile. "I know you can. You're a strong young lady. Your uncle Mitch and I are proud of you."

"Ms. Kristen?" Sadie's head shifted against her as she glanced up. Her small mouth moved to speak; then she hesitated. Finally, she stretched up toward Kristen, cupped her hand around Kristen's ear and whispered, "I love you."

Her vision blurred, and blinking rapidly, Kristen kissed her forehead, then whispered back, "I love you, too, Sadie."

It was a strange mix of pain and joy—saying "I love you" to a little girl who wasn't Anna. Holding Sadie in her arms, as if she were her own daughter. Kristen had no idea if the pain would ever completely disappear, but for the moment, it had faded.

The double doors swept open, and the nurse reentered. "Mrs. Hart?" She scanned the room, and her eyes came to rest on Kristen's face. "Mrs. Kristen Hart?"

"I . . ." Kristen rose slowly, a warm sensation unfurling in her veins. "I'm Kristen."

The nurse smiled. "You can come back now. Mrs. Emmy's anxious to see you."

Kristen hesitated then smiled at Sadie as she said, "Wait here with Dylan, please. I'll be back soon, okay?"

Sadie nodded.

Pulling in a deep breath, Kristen followed the nurse down the long, winding corridor. They turned left, then right, then left again before coming to a stop in front of a patient's room labeled thirty-nine. The nurse knocked, and after Mitch, his tone deep, issued an invitation, she opened the door and stepped back, motioning for Kristen to enter.

As hospital rooms went, this one was roomy. There were two lounge chairs positioned on the right side of the room, and a wide set of windows lined the opposite wall. Sunlight streamed through the open blinds and pooled on the white sheets covering the bed.

"Kristen." A frail hand lifted, and heavily veined fingers splayed toward her, beckoning her closer.

Emmy lay beneath the sheet, her frame slight and gray hair curling at her temples. But her eyes were clear and focused on Kristen's face with recognition.

Legs shaking, Kristen took one step forward, then another, heavy shivers racking her body until her composure cracked and heaving sobs escaped her.

Mitch moved away from his position beside the bed, and his arm wound around her waist before he led her to a chair next to Emmy. "She's okay." He spoke gently, his lips brushing her cheek. "She's been asking for you for a while now."

After easing into the chair, Kristen reached out and slipped her hand into Emmy's. Her sobs increased when Emmy's soft palm smoothed over her hair in a gentle repetitive motion. A door clicked softly behind her as Mitch exited.

Minutes later, after she'd caught her breath and her crying had calmed, Kristen raised her head.

Emmy smiled, despite the tears shining in her eyes. "We're a pitiful pair, aren't we? Me with my weak, obstinate mind. And you with your hidden secret." Her smile widened. "Guess that's just how us Harts are."

Kristen wiped her cheek with the back of her palm, then looked down and studied Emmy's hand clutching hers. "How do you know about that?"

"I've seen and felt pain before," she said. "It's in your eyes. Noticed it the moment I first met you. Reminds me of when I lost my Joe." Her tone softened. "What have you lost, Kristen?"

Kristen closed her eyes. Saw the sweep of Anna's brown hair across her back as she smiled at her over her shoulder. Recalled the joyful sound of her laugh when they sat up in the hospital bed late at night, reading funny stories. Revisited one of Anna's most precious last moments—the one when she smiled bravely, squeezed Kristen's hand and said, "Don't cry, Mama."

"My daughter," Kristen said brokenly. "I lost Anna."

"How old was she?" Emmy asked gently.

"Five." A fresh surge of tears streamed down her cheeks. "She had cancer. We tried everything, but—" She shook her head. "I didn't want to let her go, and at first, I didn't. I carried her memory with me for so long, but then it hurt too much to remember—to realize how good life was with her and how empty it is now without her. But then I met you and . . . Mitch and Sadie and Dylan."

"And you wanted to do more than remember?" Emmy asked. "You wanted to feel alive again?"

Kristen nodded. "But it feels like a betrayal. Like I've left Anna behind. And it hurts too much to remember. It hurts too much to move on."

Emmy shook her head, tears spilling over her lashes, as she pulled Kristen into a close embrace. "Oh, Kristen, it hurts just as much to forget. And I'm afraid to stop loving and living each day to the fullest for as long as I have left." Her hand moved over Kristen's hair again. "Don't you know you're my miracle? The one I've been waiting for? I'm not willing to let you go just yet." She rocked slowly back and forth as their quiet cries whispered across the room. "So what will we do, my dear girl? Oh, what will we do?"

Kristen nuzzled her face closer against the silky skin at the base of Emmy's throat, drawing comfort, strength, and new life from her firm embrace. "We'll just do what a family should," she whispered. "We'll hurt—and heal—together."

Mitch lowered the shade over Emmy's bedroom window, but the late afternoon sun still glowed brightly through the thin covering, casting an orange light over her face. She still smiled slightly, even in her sleep, and held Sadie, who napped next to her in a loose embrace.

After being released from the hospital not long after her visit with Kristen, Emmy had been anxious to return home. She'd walked slower than usual when leaving the patient's room and making her way to the truck, but she had managed it on her own and had almost vibrated with joy when he turned the truck back onto Hart's Hollow Farm's driveway.

Emmy's face had lit up at the sight of the new sign Kristen had made, and she'd glanced into the backseat and shared a warm look with Kristen. She'd barely made it into the house, though, before the eventful day caught up with her, and she'd yawned repeatedly as he and Kristen helped her change and get settled for a nap.

Sadie, excited her nana was home, had piled into the bed with her, tucked her hands under her cheek, and promptly drifted off, as well.

Mitch grinned. They were a gorgeous sight. He bent, kissed their cheeks, then left quietly and closed the door behind him.

"Are they asleep?" Kristen stood at the other end of the hall, her hands twisting nervously at her middle. Her T-shirt and jeans were rumpled from sitting in a waiting-room chair all night, her blond hair was disheveled and there wasn't a speck of makeup on her face.

She was the most gorgeous woman Mitch had ever seen.

He nodded, his eyes tracing the curve of her mouth, her cute nose and the peaceful look in her eyes. "Dylan?"

"He's out like a light." She swept a hand through her hair and sighed. "They've all earned a decent nap. And now that they're home . . ." Her voice trailed away, and a glimmer of hope lit her expression as she studied his face.

"I put your bags back in the guest room."

Her smile faded. "My bags?"

He gestured toward the floor near Dylan's closed bedroom door. "The ones you left right there early this morning."

"Oh." Her chest lifted on a deep breath. "I wanted to talk to you about that. I need to apologize to you for—"

"That can wait." He strode to her, took her soft

hand in his, and tugged her toward the front door. "I have something to show you."

"But I need to—"

"Hey." He stopped and faced her, cradled her face in his hands and brushed a soft kiss across her lush mouth. "I don't need an apology right now. I just need you, if you're willing." He grinned. "Will you humor me, please?"

Her attention drifted to his mouth, and she smiled. "Okay."

He continued, leading her outside onto the porch, down the front steps, and across the lawn.

The sun shined bright, its rays slipping between the thick low branches of the oaks and heating his skin. A light breeze rustled the leaves on the trees and the grass at their feet. He stepped softly until they reached the wide trunk of one of the oaks, then released Kristen's hand, cupped his together, and lowered them by her knees.

She looked down and laughed. "What are you doing?"

"Giving you one of the best views around." He grinned wider and beckoned with his hands. "Come on. We've got a few moments to ourselves, and that big branch over there has our names written all over it."

Smiling, she held on to his shoulder, placed her foot in his cupped palms, then shoved off and lifted herself onto the lowest branch. He waited until she had settled, then joined her, hoisting himself onto the same branch and scooting his way over beside her.

"You're right," she said, gazing at the landscape in front of them. "It is one of the best views."

He followed her line of sight, taking in the lush

green lawn, the long winding red driveway, lined on both sides with colorful gourds, and the fields full of thick, healthy soybean plants and tall cornstalks. The blue sky was flawless—there wasn't a cloud to be found—and golden sunlight streamed in every direction.

He turned back to Kristen, took in the pink flush of her cheeks beneath the sun's warmth, the graceful fall of her hair along her back, and the soft, welcoming curves of her lips.

"Yeah," he murmured. "The most gorgeous sight in the world."

She turned to face him, and her green eyes lingered on his smile. "You're not even looking."

"Yeah, I am." Leaning forward, he cupped her face and dipped his head, then pressed soft kisses to her forehead, nose, cheeks, and chin. He smoothed his thumb over her lower lip, his arms straining to wrap around her and pull her close. "You know how I told you once before what I missed most about my childhood?"

She nodded.

"It's this feeling you give me." His hand slid down, took hers, and placed it on the upper left side of his chest, where his heartbeat was strong against her palm. "This love I've never felt before. I want that feeling forever. I want *you* forever."

Her mouth parted, and a soft gasp of pleasure escaped her.

"And I want us to give Emmy, Sadie, Dylan, and the child I hope we'll have someday the same kind of love. Limitless, unconditional." He glanced at the house. "The same kind of love Emmy had for Joe, for my father, for Carrie, and for me. The same kind of love you had for Anna."

A brief flicker of sadness crossed her face. "You heard?"

"Yes." He pressed his forehead to hers. "I want to know everything about her and about you. And I want you to know me. Do you want the same? Do you want to make a life with me?"

Her smile returned. "I love you, Mitch." She reached up, cradled his face in her hands, and whispered against his lips, "There's nothing I want more."

EPILOGUE

"Emmy! Get down from there."

Kristen shaded her eyes, tilted her head back and looked up, smiling at the cute face laughing back at her from the oak tree. At five years old, Emmy was full of mischievous energy and could charm the hardest of hearts—just like her father.

"Aw, she's just having fun," Mitch said, ducking under the low branch and glancing up. "Aren't you, baby?"

Emmy, hanging upside down, with her legs hooked over the branch, nodded, her long brown hair trailing over Mitch's shoulder. "Just having fun, Mama," she chimed, swinging back and forth and dangling her arms.

"Well, how about having fun down here, safe on the ground? Our first customers should be arriving soon, and I'll need your help today." Kristen tapped her toe, her mouth twitching, as Emmy made a face, then held her arms out for Mitch to help her down.

His broad hands gripped Emmy's waist, lifted her from the limb, then lowered her safely to the ground.

"Can I help Dylan and Sadie?" Emmy asked, hopping from one foot to the other and watching her cousins wash strawberry buckets by the front porch.

"Yes, please," Kristen said. "That'd be very nice of you, and I'm sure they'd appreciate your help."

At eleven, Sadie had grown into a tall, intelligent, and pretty young lady with a reserved disposition. Dylan, on the other hand, couldn't be more outspoken, flirtatious, and adventurous as a sixteen-year-old teenager. Both of them continued to do well inside and outside of school, Sadie having already mastered the piano and Dylan continuing to impress at every game the high school baseball team played.

Emmy—or Nana, as they'd always called her—would've been proud of them both. She would've been proud of Mitch, too.

Kristen's belly warmed as he strode over, the sun at his back emphasizing the broad span of his shoulders, the lithe strength of his sinewy frame. It was a beautiful afternoon—one of Hart's Hollow's finest—and a perfect day to open the strawberry fields for the first day of picking.

Under Mitch's magic touch, the farm had flourished. Emmy's corn had grown sweeter each year, her early production soybeans had continued to break harvest records, and the strawberries . . . Oh, Hart's Hollow Farm's customers loved them best of all.

"It's a beautiful day," Mitch said, bending his head and nuzzling her neck. "What do you say we sneak back out here after the kids go to bed and watch the stars come out?"

She smiled, wove her fingers through his hair, and lifted her mouth for his kiss. "I think that's a perfect plan."

He hugged her close, the brush of his hard thighs against her belly reminding her of the surprise she had to share. Tonight was as good a night as any to tell him that the Hart family would be growing. In eight months, Emmy would have a new baby brother or sister to love.

"I swear, I love you more and more every day," Mitch whispered before kissing her again, slow and sweet. "There's no place in the world I'd rather be."

"Same here," Kristen said, smiling.

Hart's Hollow Farm was perfect in every way. More than that—it was home.

If you love Janet Dailey,

you won't want to miss TEXAS FOREVER,

coming soon in paperback!

[illegible]

[illegible] On the broad front porch, two [illegible] rocking chairs, placed close together [illegible] each [illegible] and [illegible] sleep [illegible]

August, the present

The brutal August sun sank behind the Caprock Escarpment, streaking the cliffs with hues of gold, bronze, and deep blood red. Like silken draperies set afire, the tattered clouds blazed, then slowly melted into twilight. Shadows deepened, flowing down the narrow canyons to flood the parched foothills with the black of a moonless night.

A gray fox slipped out of its den, ears alert for the sound of a scurrying mouse or lizard. Bats darted on silent wings, catching insects in flight. A golden eagle glided to the rocky edge of a high precipice, folded its powerful wings, and settled for the night.

On the dust-swept plain below the escarpment, the sprawling heart of the Rimrock Ranch lay shrouded in unaccustomed silence. Cigarettes, dots of red in the darkness, glowed outside the bunkhouse, but the usual banter of the cowhands was absent. Even the horses and cattle seemed subdued.

The windows were dark in the imposing stone and timber house that Bull Tyler had finished for his bride fifty years ago. On the broad front porch, two figures sat in rustic log chairs, placed close together.

Will Tyler, the ranch boss and head of the family, was nursing a can of cheap Mexican beer. He stared into the darkness beyond the porch rail, saying nothing.

His daughter Erin, now nineteen, sat watching him. Her father was far from old—not yet fifty. But time and grief had aged him beyond his years. Already mourning his wife, he'd been crushed today by the sudden loss of his oldest friend. Not that he'd shown it. Even after the sheriff and his deputy had driven off, he'd expressed no flicker of emotion nor shed so much as a tear. All the more reason for Erin to be worried about him.

"I still can't believe Jasper is gone," she said, hoping her father would open up and talk. Keeping his grief bottled inside was only going to make him feel worse.

After what seemed like a long silence, Will cleared his throat. "I just wish the end had been different for him. Even at ninety-three, crashing an ATV into a gulley isn't the way you want to go." He took a swallow of the Mexican beer Jasper had always liked, as if he were drinking it as a sort of tribute. But even that did nothing to ease his inner pain. With a muttered curse, he crushed the unfinished can in his fist and flung it over the porch railing, where it would be picked up by a stable hand in the morning. "I never could understand why Jasper fancied this god-awful two-bit beer. It always tasted like horse piss to me. Still does."

Erin smiled at the feeble joke, sensing the anguish behind it. For as long as anyone in the Tyler family could remember, Jasper Platt had been the heart and soul of the Rimrock Ranch. He had worked for Will's grandfather, Williston Tyler, and for Will's father, the legendary Bull Tyler. To Will and his brother Beau, Jasper had been like a second father, watching over them as they grew to manhood, and teaching them all the skills they'd need to be good cowboys.

Even in his old age, when arthritis would no longer allow him to sit a horse, Jasper had served as honorary foreman to the ranch as well as friend and confidant to three generations of Tyler men.

Erin had adored him. To her, Jasper had been like a loving grandfather. She couldn't imagine the Rimrock—or her own life—without his wise, crusty presence. She'd been in denial about Jasper's age and the certainty that he wouldn't last much longer. But when he'd failed to show up for breakfast that morning and when circling vultures had led searchers to his body, barely a mile from the heart of the ranch, the shock had been unimaginable. It was still sinking in that the old man was gone.

After examining the scene, Sheriff Cyrus Harger had declared his death a tragic accident. What else could it be? Surely, at Jasper's age, a stroke or heart attack could have caused the ATV he was riding to veer off the rocky trail and plunge to the bottom of a desert wash. The sheriff and his young deputy, who'd checked out the scene, had agreed that there were no suspicious circumstances. Will, to whom Jasper had given power of attorney, had turned down the suggestion of an autopsy. It would only delay the funeral, he'd insisted, and it would be a needless violation of the old man's body.

Still, Jasper's death had left unanswered questions.

"I begged him not to go out alone in that damned ATV," Will said, "but I know he liked hunting birds, and he hated being told what he shouldn't do. The sheriff said he died sometime between six and eight last night. He would have been on his way home about then."

"When did you realize he was missing?" Erin had gone to a movie in town the previous night and hadn't come home until after her father was in bed.

"As I told the sheriff, he wasn't around at supper time, but that wasn't unusual. Sometimes he just warmed up leftovers and ate in his duplex. Later on I was busy making phone calls and didn't check on him." Will's voice roughened with emotion. "Lord, if I had, maybe we could've found him in time. This is on me."

"Don't talk that way, Dad. However Jasper died, chances are you couldn't have done anything." Erin reached across the space between their chairs and squeezed his hand. Without the truth, her father would always blame himself for the death of his old friend. Maybe finding that truth would be up to her. She would be busy until the funeral was over. But after that, she would take some time to look into the so-called accident.

"Were you able to reach Uncle Beau?" she asked, changing the subject. "Will he be here for the funeral?"

"He'll be flying into Lubbock on Friday with Natalie and their daughter. I offered to pick him up, but he said they'd rather rent a car." Will's jaw tightened. "I'm guessing he'll want to leave right after the funeral."

Will's younger brother had grown up on the ranch. He'd left to join the military, then moved back after their father's death. But ranch life, and being bossed by Will, had grated on him. Three years ago, after a final blowup between the brothers, Beau had left the Rimrock to take up his former job in Washington as a senior agent for the DEA. He and Will had never made peace. But that didn't keep Erin from missing Beau's charming, fun-loving ways.

A night breeze had sprung up, its hot breath stirring the parched grass and peppering Erin's face with fine dust. This summer's drought was as bad as any she could remember in her nineteen years. The water holes had gone dry, and, as the creaking windmill reminded her, even the wells were getting low. There'd been talk of cutting back the Rimrock's herd of white-faced Herefords, selling off the steers and older cows early to save water for the ranch's precious breeding stock. Selling before the animals reached prime weight in the fall would mean less money for the ranch. But it would be better than watching cattle die of thirst.

Only yesterday, over breakfast, she'd listened as Will and Jasper discussed what would be best to do. And now, like a candle blown out by a breath of wind, Jasper was gone.

"Someone else is coming for the funeral," Will said. "You've never met her, but she's an old friend. I called her tonight, and she said she'd be here. I hope you won't mind if I volunteered you to pick her up at the airport. She's in her sixties, and I could tell she was nervous about driving a rental car in city traffic."

"I'll be happy to pick her up," Erin said. "But who is she? Why haven't I heard anything about her before?"

Will took his time in answering. "Her name is Rose Landro McCade. I haven't seen her since I was a boy. But she's not the sort of person you'd forget. Toughest woman I've ever known, and probably the most stubborn, too."

"I can hardly wait to meet her," Erin said.

"Rose can tell you a lot about the old days. She and my father scrapped like a couple of wildcats, but they never lost their respect for each other. And

Jasper loved her like a daughter. They had a special bond, those two. When I spoke with her, even after all these years, I could tell how hard it hit her that he was gone."

"What happened to her? Where did she go?"

"She married a Wyoming rancher and never came back. I guess they had a good life, raised a couple of girls. He's passed on, and their daughters are grown now, so Rose is alone. I'm hoping she'll stick around for a while. She can stay in the empty side of the duplex. Maybe you can get it ready for her—something pretty on the bed, clean towels and soap in the bathroom, some snacks in the fridge . . . even some flowers, once she lets us know her arrival time."

"She must've been special."

"She was—is. She wasn't around here long, but she was like a big sister to Beau and me." Will paused, remembering. "I'll never forget the night Rose almost gave her life to save us. If it hadn't been for Bull, all three of us, and the man she ended up marrying, could have died."

"That sounds like quite a story. How come you've never told me about it?"

He exhaled, took a pack of Marlboros from his pocket, and tapped one into his hand. "Some stories are best saved for the right time. I'll leave the telling to Rose."

His lighter flared in the darkness. The tip of the cigarette glowed as he inhaled.

"I wish you wouldn't—" Erin stopped herself from lecturing him. This wasn't the time for it. Years ago, Will had given up smoking to please his wife, Tori. But when she'd died of cancer four months ago, he'd taken up the habit again, as if to say *So what if it kills me? What's the point in living?*

"I suppose you've called Kyle," he said.

"Yes. He offered to come over, but I told him I'd see him at the funeral. Until then, I won't be much company."

Kyle Cardwell, whose father managed the neighboring Prescott Ranch for the syndicate that had bought it from the family, had been dating Erin since she'd finished high school. Last night, after their weekly movie date, he'd pulled his SUV off the road, slipped a small velvet box out of his pocket, and asked her to marry him. The diamond was impressive—at least a full carat. But Erin couldn't imagine wearing it to muck out the stable or wash down a horse, which was how she spent most of her days.

Stunned, she'd mumbled a reply. "I'm only nineteen, Kyle. I need time to think about this."

"Take all the time you need." His Hollywood smile had flashed in the darkness as he dropped the ring box back into his pocket. "But I hope you won't keep me waiting too long. I love you, Erin, and I can't wait to make you mine. Now come here and kiss me."

After a few minutes of necking, she'd asked him to take her home. For the rest of the night she'd lain awake, weighing her choices. Maybe she should've said yes. Kyle was twenty-two, handsome, respectable, and well-mannered. Her father liked him and had hinted that he wouldn't mind having a grandchild or two. Why not do what everyone seemed to expect of her?

Why was she still unsure?

Was Kyle meant to be her husband, to love and honor and cherish? What if she were to refuse him? Would she live to regret it for the rest of her days?

And what about her own plans, her own dreams of breeding and training a stable of fine horses? Would she have to put those dreams aside when she became a wife?

Toward morning, she'd fallen into a fitful sleep—only to be awakened by Will with the news that Jasper was missing. An hour later his body had been found in a desert wash, under his wrecked ATV.

Kyle's proposal would have to wait.

Rising from his chair, Will crushed the cigarette with his boot and kicked it over the rail, onto the gravel below, then glanced at the luminous dial on his watch. He stood for a moment, peering out into the darkness.

"What is it, Dad?" Erin asked. "Is something wrong?"

"Can't say for sure." Will shook his head. "I was expecting the new man I hired last week. He said he'd be here by tonight, but it's getting late, and I haven't seen hide nor hair of him."

"A new man? And you didn't tell me?"

"Sorry. Slipped my mind, I guess." Will sank wearily back into the chair. "Sky knows he's coming. The man's a farrier."

"A farrier? Just to shoe horses? That's going to cost us, Dad. And with the drought on, there's no money to spare. We've been getting by for years with the cowboys shoeing their own horses, and Sky taking care of the rest."

"Sky doesn't have time. And neither do the cowboys, especially with the roundup coming up. Hear me out, Erin. I talked this over with Jasper, and he agrees—" Emotion stopped the words in his throat. He took a deep breath. "He *agreed* with me. We need a man who can keep our horses decently shod and in top condition. A good farrier's like a doctor, and he has to know almost as much. He looks at their gait, their alignment, the whole animal. Then he trims the hooves for the best weight distribution and chooses a shoe to fit the horse's needs."

"That's still going to cost money."

"True. But I had a couple of hands quit last month to go on the rodeo circuit, so that's two less to pay. And I figure that in the long run, having a farrier won't cost us any more than having the cowboys take time from work to slap shoes on their mounts, then having horses go lame because they didn't do the job right. We could get by with fewer horses if they were all in good shape. And if we had to sell off part of the remuda, we'd get a better price if they were well shod and in prime condition."

"I understand where you're coming from," Erin said. "But a farrier would have to be paid a lot more than a common ranch hand. Can we afford a full-time man just to shoe horses?"

"We've got more than sixty horses in the remuda, as well as the brood mares and stallions," Will said. "When roundup's on, those cow ponies go through a lot of shoes. There should be plenty of work for him, at least through fall. And we already agreed that if he runs out of work here, he can take outside clients."

"As I recall, the last stranger you hired didn't work out so well," Erin said. "He stole everything that wasn't tied down."

"Don't remind me." Will shook his head. "But it won't happen again. This man was recommended by a customer. I met him a couple of weeks ago, when I picked up a truckload of hay from that big outfit east of the Prescott place. He said he'd been on the road since spring, going from ranch to ranch. I think he liked the idea of a steady job with a roof over his head. Quiet sort. He struck me as the kind of fellow who'll do his work and never make trouble."

"We'll see." Erin had always trusted her father's business sense. But since his wife's death, Will's judgment seemed to be less acute. Was it the shock of grief, a passing distraction, or only her imagination? Whatever the cause, she found herself questioning the decisions he made.

Like this farrier Will had hired. He could turn out to be just fine. But the fact that he hadn't shown up as promised wasn't a good sign.

"Why don't you get some rest, Dad?" she suggested. "You've had a hellish day, and tomorrow won't be much better."

"At least I can try. What about you?" He stood and turned toward the door, then hesitated, as if reluctant to leave her outside alone.

"I'll be along later. If your man shows up, I'll introduce myself and point the way to the bunkhouse."

"You're sure?"

"I'm sure. I'm too strung out to sleep."

"All right, but don't stay up too late. His name's Maddox. He'll be driving a black Chevy truck with a shell on the back and a two-wheel trailer behind. You can tell him there's a couple of empty rooms and a bath on the second floor."

"Don't worry, I'll keep an eye out for him. If he pulls in after I've gone to bed, that'll be his problem."

As her father went inside, shutting the front door behind him, Erin settled back in the chair and closed her eyes. After the emotionally draining day, she felt as if the earth had dropped away under her feet. In her growing-up years, three strong people had always been there for her—her mother, her father, and Jasper.

Tori, her beautiful, golden-haired mother, had slipped away four months ago, just weeks after her cancer diagnosis. Now Jasper was gone, too, and she sensed that her father was sinking into despair. He was putting on a brave face, but she could see the shadows that ringed his eyes and the slump of his once-proud shoulders. Erin knew the signs. It was as if she were losing him, too.

How could she even think of getting married when Will needed her? Her losses were his losses, perhaps even more deeply felt. This was no time for him to lose his daughter, his only child, to another man.

She had her answer for Kyle. Any talk of marriage would have to wait.

Erin greeted the decision with a sigh of relief. Until now, she hadn't realized how much pressure Kyle's proposal had put on her, and how unprepared she'd been to say yes and let him put that stunning diamond ring on her finger. Maybe later, she thought. Maybe in a year or so. But not yet.

As moments passed, she could feel herself relaxing in the chair. The peaceful sounds of night crept around her—the *chirr* of crickets under the porch, the faint creak of the windmill, the murmur of horses in the paddock, and the far-off wail of a coyote. Little by little, she began to drift. . . .

The security light, mounted with a motion sensor on a leg of the windmill, flashed on, startling Erin awake. She jerked bolt upright in the chair, blinking in the brightness as she struggled to focus her sleep-dulled mind. What time was it?

A black pickup towing a small trailer was pulling into the ranch yard. That would be the farrier her father had hired, arriving late, without so much as a phone call to let anyone know when he'd be here.

What was his name? Matlock? No, Maddox, that was it. Pushing to her feet, she took a deep breath and strode down the steps to meet him.

Luke Maddox let the truck's engine idle a moment while he watched the Rimrock welcoming committee walk toward him. He'd expected Will Tyler to come lumbering out of the house, ready to rip a piece out of his hide for showing up after midnight. Instead, here was this woman—a pretty one at that. She was dressed like a boy, in jeans and a plaid shirt. But there was nothing boyish about her lithe, confident walk, her willowy figure, or the honey-colored hair that fluttered in the wind.

She looked young—too young for him, Luke reminded himself. So why did he find himself wishing he'd bought a pack of breath mints before leaving that poker game at the Blue Coyote in town? He would've been here sooner, but what the hell, he'd been winning. Tyler couldn't fault him for that—not as long as he showed up ready for work in the morning.

Mildly intrigued, he opened the door of the cab, swung his feet to the ground, and waited as she approached him. Close up she was even prettier than he'd expected. Maybe younger, too. Boss's daughter, he guessed from her confident manner. Strictly off limits if he didn't want to get butt-kicked off the ranch by her father. But glory be, he couldn't be fired for looking.